Great Japanese Stories

Jay Rubin is a translator and academic. He is the translator of several of Murakami Haruki's major works, including *Norwegian Wood* and *The Wind-Up Bird Chronicle*, Natsume Sōseki's *The Miner* and *Sanshirō* and Akutagawa Ryūnosuke's *Rashōmon and Seventeen Other Stories*. He is the author of *Making Sense of Japanese*, *Haruki Murakami and the Music of Words* and a novel, *The Sun Gods*.

Great Japanese Stories

Ten Parallel Texts

Edited by Jay Rubin

PENGUIN BOOKS

PENGUIN CLASSICS

UK | USA | Canada | Ireland | Australia
India | New Zealand | South Africa

Penguin Books is part of the Penguin Random House group of companies
whose addresses can be found at global.penguinrandomhouse.com

Penguin
Random House
UK

First published 2024
006

English texts first published in Penguin Classics in *The Penguin Book of Japanese Short Stories* 2019

The acknowledgements on pp. 259–260 constitute an extension of this copyright page

The moral right of the editor and of the translators has been asserted

Set in 10.4/14pt Dante MT Std and 10.8/17.08pt Shippori Mincho
Typeset by WorldAccent, London
Printed and bound in Great Britain by Clays Ltd, Elcograf S.p.A.

The authorized representative in the EEA is Penguin Random House
Ireland,
Morrison Chambers, 32 Nassau Street, Dublin D02 YH68

A CIP catalogue record for this book is available from the British Library

ISBN: 978–0–241–63447–9

www.greenpenguin.co.uk

MIX
Paper | Supporting
responsible forestry
FSC® C018179

Penguin Random House is committed to a
sustainable future for our business, our readers
and our planet. This book is made from Forest
Stewardship Council® certified paper.

Contents

Contents

Editor's Note

目次

Editor's Note

The works contained in *The Penguin Book of Japanese Short Stories*, from which this volume is a selection, were ones I chose because I had been unable to forget them, in some cases for decades, or I found them forming a knot in the solar plexus or inspiring a laugh or a pang of sorrow each time they came spontaneously to mind over the years. When choosing more nearly contemporary works, I asked my fellow translators to send me stories they felt compelled to translate because they found them reverberating in their own lives. In his Introduction to the original volume, Murakami Haruki* likened the book's contents to a traditional Japanese *'fukubukuro'*, or 'lucky grab bag', offering the same kind of mysterious and unpredictably rewarding experience. I hope that sampling the works in the original Japanese will only heighten the reader's sense of freshness and surprise.

Finally, I would like to add a word of thanks to Angus Turvill and Okahisa Etsuko for their indispensable help in assembling this parallel-text edition.

* Throughout this book, all Japanese names appear with the surname first, as is Japanese convention.

編者まえがき

本書の母体となった『ペンギン・ブックスの日本短篇小説集』に収録された作品は、私にとって忘れがたい――ときには何十年も忘れられない――ものや、あるいは、ふと思い出したとき胸が苦しくなったり、笑いや悲しみが込み上げてきたりするものです。近年の作品を選ぶ際には、翻訳仲間たちにも、心の琴線に触れ、訳さずにはいられなかった物語を寄稿してくれるよう依頼しました。序文を寄せてくれた村上春樹氏は、本の中身を日本に昔からある福袋にたとえて、ここにはミステリアスな、そして射幸的な楽しみがあると言っています。その いくつかを原文の日本語で味わってみることで、本書を読む皆さんも、さらなる新鮮さと驚きを感じてくれるよう願っています。

最後に、この対訳版を形にするにあたって、欠くことのできない手助けをしてくれたアンガス・ターヴィル、岡久悦子の両氏に一言感謝の意を表したいと思います。

Great Japanese Stories

日本_{にほん}の名_{めい}短_{たん}篇_{ぺん}

MURAKAMI HARUKI

The 1963/1982 Girl from Ipanema

Translated by Jay Rubin

> Tall and tan and young and lovely,
> The girl from Ipanema goes walking.
> When she walks, it's like a samba
> That swings so cool and sways so gently.
> How can I tell her I love her?
> Yes, I would give my heart gladly.
> But each day when she walks to the sea,
> She looks straight ahead, not at me.

This was how the girl from Ipanema looked at the sea back then, in 1963. And that's how she keeps looking at the sea now, in 1982. She hasn't aged. Sealed in her image, she drifts through the ocean of

村上春樹

1963/1982年のイパネマ娘

すらりとして、日に焼けた
若くて綺麗なイパネマ娘が
歩いていく。
歩き方はサンバのリズム
クールに揺れて
やさしく振れる。
好きだと言いたいんだけれど
僕のハートをあげたいんだけれど
彼女は僕に気づきもしない。
ただ、海を見ているだけ。

1963年、イパネマの娘はこんな具合に海を見つめていた。そしていま、1982年の
イパネマ娘もやはり同じように海を見つめている。彼女はあれから年をとらないのだ。彼女

time. If she had continued to age, she'd probably be close to forty by now. Or maybe not. But at least she wouldn't have her slim figure any more, and she wouldn't be so tan. She might retain some of her old loveliness, but she'd have three children, and too much sun would damage her skin.

Inside my record, of course, she hasn't grown any older. Wrapped in the velvet of Stan Getz's tenor sax, she's as cool as ever, the gently swaying girl from Ipanema. I put the record on the turntable, set the needle in the groove, and there she is.

How can I tell her I love her?

Yes, I would give my heart gladly.

The tune always brings back memories of the corridor in my high school – a dark, damp high-school corridor. Whenever you walked along the concrete floor, your footsteps would echo off the high ceiling. It had a few windows on the north side, but these were pressed against the mountain, which is why the corridor was always dark. And it was almost always silent. In my memory, at least.

I'm not exactly sure why 'The Girl from Ipanema' reminds me of the corridor in my high school. The two have absolutely nothing

はイメージの中に封じ込められたまま、時の海の中をひっそりと漂っている。もし年をとっていたとしたら、彼女はもうかれこれ四十に近いはずだ。もちろんそうじゃないということもあり得るだろうけれど、彼女はもはやすらりとしてもいないだろうし、それほど日焼けもしてはいないだろう。彼女にはもう三人も子供がいるし、日焼けは肌を傷めるのだ。まだそこそこに綺麗かもしれないけれど、二十年前ほど若くはない——ということだ。

しかしレコードの中では彼女はもちろん年をとらない。スタン・ゲッツのヴェルヴェットのごときテナー・サクソフォンの上では、彼女はいつも十八で、クールでやさしいイパネマ娘だ。僕がターン・テーブルにレコードを載せ、針を落とせば彼女はすぐに姿を現わす。

僕のハートをあげたいんだけれど……

好きだと言いたいんだけれど、

この曲を聴くたびに僕は高校の廊下を思い出す。暗くて、少し湿った、高校の廊下だ。天井は高く、コンクリートの床を歩いていくとコツコツと音が反響する。北側にはいくつか窓があるのだが、すぐそばまで山がせまっているものだから、廊下はいつも暗い。そして大抵いつもしんとしている。少なくとも僕の記憶の中では廊下は大抵いつもしんとしている。

なぜ「イパネマの娘」を耳にするたびに高校の廊下を思い出すことになるのか、僕にはよ

to do with each other. I wonder what kind of pebbles the 1963 girl from Ipanema threw into the well of my consciousness.

When I think of the corridor in my high school, I think of mixed salads: lettuce, tomatoes, cucumbers, green peppers, asparagus, onion rings and pink Thousand Island dressing. Not that there was a salad shop at the end of the corridor. No, there was just a door, and beyond the door a drab twenty-five-metre pool.

So why does that corridor in my old high school remind me of mixed salads? These two don't have anything to do with each other, either. They just happened to come together, like an unlucky lady who finds herself sitting on a freshly painted bench.

Mixed salads remind me of a girl I sort of knew back then. Now, this connection is a logical one, because all this girl ever ate was salads.

'How about that (munch munch) English assignment (munch munch)? Finished it yet?'

'Not quite (munch munch). Still got to (munch munch) do some reading.'

I was pretty fond of salads myself, so whenever I was with her, we had these salad-filled conversations. She was a girl of strong convictions, one of which was that if you ate a well-balanced diet, with plenty of vegetables, everything would be all right. As long as

くわからない。脈絡なんてまるでないのだ。いったい1963年のイパネマ娘は、僕の意識の井戸にどんな小石を放り込んでいったのだろう？

高校の廊下といえば、僕はコンビネーション・サラダを思い出す。レタスとトマトとキュウリとピーマンとアスパラガス、輪切りたまねぎ、そしてピンク色のサザン・アイランド・ドレッシング。もちろん高校の廊下のつきあたりにサラダ専門店があるわけじゃない。高校の廊下のつきあたりにはドアがあって、ドアの外にはあまりぱっとしない25メートル・プールがあるだけだ。

どうして高校の廊下が僕にコンビネーション・サラダを思い出させるのだろう？　ここにもやはり脈絡なんてない。そのふたつはたまたま何かの加減で結びついてしまったのだ。ペンキ塗りたてのベンチに知らずに腰をおろしてしまった不運な御婦人のように。

コンビネーション・サラダが僕に思い出させるのは昔ちょっと知っていた女の子である。この連想はとても筋がとおっている。なぜなら彼女はいつも野菜サラダばかり食べていたからだ。

「もう、バリバリ、英語のレポート、バリバリ、済ませた？」
「バリバリ、いやまだ、バリバリ、少し、バリバリバリ、残ってるな」

僕も野菜はけっこう好きな方だったから、彼女と顔を合わせればそんな風に野菜ばかり食べていた。彼女はいわゆる信念の人で、野菜をバランスよく食べてさえいれば全てはうまく

everyone ate vegetables, the world would be a place of beauty and peace, filled to overflowing with love and good health. Kind of like *The Strawberry Statement*.

'Long, long ago,' wrote a certain philosopher, 'there was a time when matter and memory were separated by a metaphysical abyss.'

The 1963/1982 girl from Ipanema continues to walk silently along the hot sands of a metaphysical beach. It's a very long beach, lapped by gentle white waves. There's no wind, nothing to be seen on the horizon. Just the smell of the sea. And the sun is burning hot.

Sprawled under a beach umbrella, I take a can of beer from the cooler and pull the tab. She's still walking by, a primary-coloured bikini clinging to her tall, tanned body.

I give it a try: 'Hi, how's it goin'?'

'Oh, hello,' she says.

'How 'bout a beer?'

She hesitates. But after all, she's tired of walking, and she's thirsty. 'I'd like that,' she says.

And together we drink beer beneath my beach umbrella.

いくものと信じ切っていた。人々が野菜を食べつづける限り世界は美しく平和であり、健康で愛に満ちあふれているであろう、と。なんだか「いちご白書」みたいな話だ。

「昔むかし」とある哲学者が書いている。「物質と記憶とが形而上学的深淵によって分かたれていた時代があった」

1963／1982年のイパネマ娘は形而上学的な熱い砂浜を音もなく歩きつづけている。とても長い砂浜で、そこには穏やかな白い波が打ちよせている。風はまるでない。水平線の上には何も見えない。潮の匂いがする。太陽はひどく暑い。

僕はビーチ・パラソルの下に寝転んでクーラー・ボックスから缶ビールを取り出し、ふたをあける。彼女はまだ歩きつづけている。彼女の日焼けした長身には原色のビキニがぴたりとはりついている。

「やあ」と僕は思い切って声をかけてみる。

「こんにちは」と彼女は言う。

「ビールでも飲まない？」と僕は誘ってみる。

彼女は少し迷う。でも彼女だって歩き疲れている。喉だって乾いている。「いいわね」と彼女は言う。

そして、我々はビーチ・パラソルの下で一緒にビールを飲む。

'By the way,' I venture, 'I'm sure we met in 1963. Same time. Same place.'

'That must have been a *long* time ago,' she says, cocking her head just a bit.

'Yeah,' I say. 'It was.'

She empties half the beer can in one gulp, then stares at the hole in the top. It's just an ordinary can of beer with an ordinary hole, but the way she stares at the opening, it seems to take on a special significance – as if the entire world were going to slip inside.

'Maybe we did meet – 1963, was it? Hmmm . . . 1963. Maybe we did meet.'

'You haven't aged at all.'

'Of course not. I'm a metaphysical girl.'

I nod. 'Back then, you didn't know I existed. You looked at the ocean, never at me.'

'Could be,' she says. Then she smiles. A wonderful smile, but a little sad. 'Maybe I did keep looking at the ocean. Maybe I didn't see anything else.'

I open another beer for myself and offer her one. She just shakes

「ところで」と僕は言う。「たしか1963年にも君をみかけたよ。同じ場所で、同じ時間にね」

「ずいぶん古い話じゃないこと?」と言って彼女は少し首をかしげる。

「そうだね」と僕は言う。「たしかにずいぶん古い話だ」

彼女は一息でビールを半分飲み、缶にぽっかりと開いた穴を眺める。それはごく普通の缶ビールの穴だ。でも彼女がじっと見ていると、それはすごく意味のあるもののように思える。世界じゅうがすっぽりとそこに入ってしまいそうに思える。

「でも会ったかもしれないわね。1963年でしょ? えーと、1963年……うん、会ったかもしれない」

「会ったかもしれないね」

「君は年をとらないんだね?」

「だって私は形而上学的な女の子なんだもの」

僕は肯く。「あの頃の君は僕の存在になんて気づきもしなかったよ。君はいつもいつも海ばかり見てた」

「あり得るわね」と彼女は言った。そして笑った。素敵な笑顔だった。でも彼女はたしかに少し悲しげに見えた。「たしかに海ばっかり見ていたかもしれない。その他には何も見ていなかったかもしれない」

僕は自分のためにビールを開け、彼女にも勧めてみた。でも彼女は首を振った。それほど

her head. 'I can't drink so much beer,' she says. 'I have to keep walking and walking. But thanks.'

'Don't the soles of your feet get hot?' I ask.

'Not at all,' she says. 'They're completely metaphysical. Want to see?'

'Okay.'

She stretches a long, slim leg towards me and shows me the sole of her foot. She's right: it's a wonderfully metaphysical sole. I touch it with my finger. Not hot, not cold. There's a faint sound of waves when my finger touches her sole. A metaphysical sound.

I close my eyes for a moment, and then I open them and slug down a whole can of cold beer. The sun hasn't shifted at all. Time itself has stopped, as if it has been sucked into a mirror.

'Whenever I think of you, I think of the corridor in my high school,' I decide to tell her. 'I wonder why.'

'The human essence lies in complexity,' she replies. 'The objects of scientific investigation lie not in the object, you know, but in the subject contained within the human body.'

'Yeah?'

たくさんビールは飲めないのだと彼女は言った。「ありがとう。でもこれからまだずっと歩いていなくちゃならないから」と彼女は言った。

「そんなにずっと歩いていて、足の裏が熱くならないの?」と僕は訊いた。

「大丈夫よ。私の足の裏はとても形而上学的にできているから。見てみる?」

「うん」

彼女はすらりとした足を伸ばして、足の裏を僕に見せてくれた。それはたしかに素晴しく形而上学的な足の裏だった。僕はそこにそっと指を触れてみた。熱くもないし、冷たくもない。彼女の足の裏に指を触れると、微かな波の音がした。波の音までもが、とても形而上学的だ。

僕はしばらく目を閉じていた。それから目を開けて、冷えたビールをひとくち飲んだ。太陽はぴくりとも動かなかった。時間さえもが止まっていた。まるで鏡の中に吸いこまれてしまったようだ。

「君のことを考えるたびに、僕は高校の廊下を思い出すんだ」と僕は思い切って言う。「どうしてだろうね?」

「人間の本質は複合性にあるのよ」と彼女は言う。「人間科学の対象は客体にではなく、身体のうちにとりこまれた主体にあるのよ」

「ふうん」と僕は言う。

'In any case, you must live. Live! Live! Live! That's all. The most important thing is to go on living. That's all I can say. Really, that's all. I'm just a girl with metaphysical soles.'

The 1963/1982 girl from Ipanema brushes the sand from her thighs and stands up. 'Thank you for the beer.'

'Don't mention it.'

Every once in a while – every long once in a while – I see her on the subway. I recognize her and she recognizes me. She always sends me a little 'Thanks for the beer' smile. We haven't spoken since that day on the beach, but I can tell there is some sort of connection linking our hearts. I'm not sure just what the connection is. The link is probably in a strange place in a far-off world.

I try to imagine that link – a link in my consciousness spread out in silence across a dark hallway down which no one comes. When I think about it like this, all kinds of happenings, all kinds of things, begin to fill me with nostalgia, bit by bit. Somewhere in there, I'm sure, is the link joining me with myself. Some day, too, I'm sure, I'll meet myself in a strange place in a far-off world. And if I have

「とにかく生きなさい。生きる、生きる、生きる。それだけ。生きつづけるのが大事なことなのよ。私にはそれだけしか言えない。本当にそれだけしか言えないの。私はただの──形而上学的な足の裏を持った女の子なの」

そして1963／1982年のイパネマ娘はももについた砂を払い、立ちあがる。「ビールをどうもありがとう」

「どういたしまして」

時々、ほんのたまにだけれど、地下鉄の車両の中で彼女の姿をみかけることがある。僕は彼女を知っているし、彼女は僕を知っている。そのたびに彼女は〈あの時はビールをどうもありがとう〉式の微笑を僕に送ってくれる。あれ以来我々はもうことばは交わさないけれど、それでも僕らの心はどこかでつながっているんだという気はする。どこでつながっているのかは僕にはわからない。きっとどこか遠い世界にある奇妙な場所にその結び目はあるのだろう。

僕はその結び目を想像してみる。誰も通らない暗い廊下にひっそりと横たわっている僕の意識の結び目。そんな風に考えていると、いろんなことが、いろんなものが少しずつ懐かしく思えてくる。どこかにきっと僕と僕自身をつなぐ結び目だってあるはずなのだ。きっといつか、僕は遠い世界にある奇妙な場所で僕自身に出会うだろう、という気がする。そしてそ

anything to say about it, I'd like that place to be a warm one. And if I've got a few cold beers there as well, who could ask for anything more? In that place, I am myself and myself is me. Subject is object and object is subject. All gaps gone. A perfect union. There must be a strange place like this somewhere in the world.

*

The 1963/1982 girl from Ipanema continues to walk along the hot beach. And she'll continue to walk without resting until the last record wears out.

れはできることなら暖かい場所であってほしいと思う。もしそこに冷えたビールが何本かあるなら、もう言うことはない。そこでは僕は僕自身であり、僕自身は僕である。主体は客体であり、客体は主体である。そのふたつのあいだにはどのような種類のすきまもない。ぴたっと見事にくっついている。そういう奇妙な場所がきっと世界のどこかにあるはずなのだ。

＊

1963／1982年のイパネマ娘は今も熱い砂浜を歩きつづける。レコードの最後の一枚が擦り切れるまで、彼女は休むことなく歩きつづける。

HOSHI SHIN'ICHI
Shoulder-Top Secretary

Translated by Jay Rubin

Gliding down the plastic-paved street on his automatic rollerskates, Zame glances at his watch.

4.30. Hmm, maybe I'll try one more place before I go back to the office. Zame slows his skates and stops in front of a house.

Zame is a salesman. In his left hand he carries a big case full of merchandise. Perched on his right shoulder is a parrot with beautiful wings. Such parrots ride atop the shoulders of everyone in this era.

He presses the doorbell and waits. Eventually the door opens and the woman of the house appears.

'Hi,' Zame mumbles, and immediately the parrot on his shoulder begins to declaim: 'Madam, please be so kind as to forgive me for intruding on you at this busy time.'

星新一
肩の上の秘書

　プラスチックで舗装した道路の上を、自動ローラースケートで走りながら、ゼーム氏は腕時計に目をやった。

　四時半。会社にもどる前に、このへんでもう一軒よってみるとするか。ゼーム氏はこう考えて、ローラースケートの速力を落し、一軒の家の前でとまった。

　ゼーム氏はセールスマン。左手に大きなカバンを下げている。このなかには、商品がつまっているのだ。そして、右の肩の上には、美しい翼を持ったインコがとまっている。もっとも、このようなインコは、この時代のすべての人の肩にとまっている。

　彼は玄関のベルを押し、しばらく待った。やがてドアが開き、この家の主婦が姿をあらわした。

「こんにちは」

　と、ゼーム氏は、口のなかで小さくつぶやいた。すると、つづいて肩の上のインコがはっきりした口調でしゃべりはじめた。

「おいそがしいところを、突然おじゃまして申し訳ございません。お許しいただきたいと思

The parrot is a robot. It is equipped with a precise electronic brain, a vocal apparatus and a speaker, and is designed to elaborate on the mutterings of its owner in conversations.

After a brief pause, the parrot on the woman's shoulder replies, 'Oh, thank you very much for coming today. Please forgive me, though. My memory is so bad, I can't quite recall your name . . .'

Zame's parrot leans close to his ear and whispers, ' "Who're you?" she's asking.'

These robotic parrots also function to summarize and report the speech of the other person.

'I'm from the New Electro Company,' Zame mutters. 'Buy this electric spider.'

The parrot then interprets with the utmost politeness: 'Actually, madam, I am a sales representative of the New Electro Company. I believe you probably know that we as a company pride ourselves on our long tradition and reliability. I am here today to show you a new product that our research division has finally managed to perfect after many years of experimentation. It is none other than this magnificent electric spider . . .'

いる。

このインコはロボットなのだ。なかには精巧な電子装置と、発声器と、スピーカーをそなえている。そして、持ち主のつぶやいたことを、さらにくわしくして相手に伝える働きを持っ

「います」

しばらくすると、主婦の肩にとまっているロボット・インコが答えてきた。

「よくいらっしゃいました。だけど、失礼ですけど、あたくし、もの覚えがよくございませんので、お名前を思いだせなくて……」

ゼーム氏の肩のインコは首をかしげ、彼の耳にこうささやいた。

「だれか、と聞いているよ」

このロボット・インコは、相手の話を要約して報告する働きもするのだ。

「ニュー・エレクトロ会社のものだ。電気グモを買え」

彼のつぶやきに応じて、インコは礼儀正しく話した。

「じつは、わたしはニュー・エレクトロ会社の販売員でございます。もちろん、ご存知のこととぞんじますが、長い伝統と信用を誇りにしている会社でございます。ところで、きょうお伺いしたのは、ほかでもございません。このたび、当社の研究部が、やっと完成いたしました新製品をお目にかけようと思ったわけでございます。それは、この電気グモでございます……」

At this point, Zame opens his case and pulls out a small metal device that looks like a shiny golden spider. His parrot continues: 'And here it is. When, for example, your back becomes itchy, you slip this under your clothes. Then the spider automatically finds its way to the itchy spot and gives it a delightful scratching with these little legs. I'm sure you will agree that it is a marvellously convenient invention. I have made a special point of bringing it with me today because I am sure that an elegant household such as yours should be equipped with one.'

When Zame's parrot stops speaking, the parrot on the housewife's shoulder whispers into her ear too quietly for Zame to hear: 'He says, "Buy this automatic backscratcher."'

She mutters back to her parrot, 'Don't wannit,' which her parrot expands for her as follows: 'Oh, how marvellous! Your company makes one new product after another! Unfortunately, however, we simply do not have the means to outfit our home with such a superb mechanism.'

Zame's parrot reports to him, 'She says, "Don't wannit."'

Zame mutters, 'Aw, c'mon!' His parrot proclaims with increased warmth: 'But you see, madam, what a marvellously convenient product this is. It enables you to scratch where your hand is unable to reach, and it can be used in the presence of guests without their ever suspecting. Not to mention the drudgery it saves! And we have outdone ourselves in setting the price as low as possible.'

　ここでゼーム氏はカバンをあけ、なかから金色に光る昆虫のクモのような、小さな金属の機械をとりだした。肩のインコは、しゃべりつづけた。

「……これでございます。背中などかゆくなった時に、下着のなかにそっとしのばせましょう。かゆい部分にひとりでたどりつき、この手で快くかいてくれます。便利なものでございましょう。おたくのような上品なご家庭には、ぜひ一個おそなえになられたらよろしいとぞんじまして、とくにお持ちいたしたわけでございます」

　ゼーム氏のインコの話が終ると、主婦の肩のインコが、ゼーム氏に聞こえない小声で彼女の耳にささやいた。

「自動式の孫の手を買え、と言っています」

　主婦が「いらないわ」とつぶやいたので、インコはそれをくわしくしゃべった。

「すばらしいわ。おたくの社は、つぎつぎと新製品をお作りになられるのね。だけどうちでは、とてもそんな高級品をそなえるほどの余裕がございませんもの」

　ゼーム氏のインコは「いらないそうだ」と要約し報告したが「そこをなんとか」という彼のつぶやきで、インコの声は一段と熱をおびた。

「でもございましょうが、こんな便利な品はございません。手のとどかない背中もかけますし、お客さまの前でも気づかれません。それに、つまらない労力がはぶけます。お値段もぐっとお安くいたしてあります」

'He says, *"Please* buy it."'

'What a pain.'

After this exchange with its owner, the woman's parrot answers, 'To tell you the truth, I never buy anything without consulting my husband. Unfortunately, he hasn't come home from work yet, and so I can't possibly make such an important decision. Perhaps I can discuss it with him tonight, and then, possibly the next time you're in the area, you might be so good as to stop by again. I would love to buy it, but it really is out of the question. I'm terribly sorry.'

Zame's parrot summarizes this for him: 'She says, "Get lost."'

Zame resigns himself, and as he is returning the electric spider to his case, he mutters, 'So long, babe.'

The parrot on his shoulder announces his departure with the utmost politeness. 'Oh, well, it truly is a shame. All right, then, if you don't mind, I will call on you again at some point in the near future. I am sorry for having taken up so much of your valuable time. Please give my regards to your husband.'

Zame steps outside. With the parrot still clinging to his shoulder, he revs up his roller skates again and goes back to the office.

「ぜひ買え、と言っていますよ」

「うるさいわね」

主婦の肩のインコは、彼女とささやきあってから、こう答えた。

「でも、あたくしは、品物を買う時には、すべてと主人と相談しておりますの。あいにく、主人がまだ帰ってまいりませんので、いまはちょっと、きめかねるんですの。今晩でも、よく話してみますから、そのうち、おついでの時にでも、お寄りになっていただけませんか。あたくしは欲しいんですけれど、それがだめなのよ。本当に残念ですわ」

ゼーム氏のインコは、それを彼に要約した。

「帰れとさ」

ゼーム氏はあきらめ、電気グモをカバンにしまいながら、つぶやいた。

「あばよ」

肩のインコは別れのあいさつを、ていねいにつげた。

「さようでございますか。ほんとに残念でございます。では、近いうちに、またお伺いさせていただくことにいたしましょう。どうもおじゃまいたしました。どうか、ご主人さまにも、くれぐれもよろしく」

玄関を出たゼーム氏は、インコを肩にとまらせたまま、ふたたびローラースケートのエンジンを強め、会社にもどった。

He is seated at his desk, adding up the day's receipts on his calculator, when the parrot on the department chief's shoulder calls out to him: 'Hey, Zame!'

'Oh, great, another lecture,' Zame mutters to himself, whereupon his parrot responds: 'Right away, sir! Just let me finish straightening up here . . .'

Soon Zame is standing before the chief's desk. The parrot on the chief's shoulder says with authority, 'Now see here, Zame, these are critical times for the company. We are being called upon to make a great leap forward. I believe you know this as well as anyone. And yet, when I look at your results, I can't help feeling that you could do better. This is a deplorable situation. I want you to understand what I'm saying here. You need to buckle down.'

Zame's parrot whispers to him: 'He says, "Sell more." '

'Yeah,' Zame mutters back, 'like it's so easy.' His parrot meekly responds, 'Yes, sir, I understand completely, and I am determined to increase my sales volume yet again. Our competitors, however, are using all kinds of new techniques. Selling is not as easy as it used to be. I will of course increase my efforts, but I would be most grateful,

机にむかって、電子計算機のボタンを押し、きょうの売上げの集計をしていると、

「おーい、ゼーム君」

と、部長の肩のインコが呼んだ。

「やれやれ、また、お説教か」

ゼーム氏がつぶやくと、肩のインコは部長に答えた。

「はい。すぐにまいります。ちょっと、机の上の整理をすませまして……」

やがて、ゼーム氏は部長の机の前に立った。部長の肩のインコが、もっともらしくしゃべった。

「いいかね、ゼーム君。わが社の現状は、いまや一大飛躍をせねばならない重大な時だ。それは、きみもよく知っていることと思う。しかるにだ、このところ君の成績を見るに、もう少し上昇してもいいのではないか、と考えたくなる。はなはだ遺憾なことと言わざるをえない。ぜひ、この点を認識して、大いに活動してもらいたい」

ゼーム氏のインコは「もっと売れとさ」とささやき「そう簡単に行くものか」とゼーム氏はささやきかえした。肩のインコは、神妙な口調で部長に言った。

「よくわかっております。わたくしもさらに売上げを増進いたす決心でございます。しかしこのごろは他社も手をかえ、品をかえ、新しいことをやっております。販売も以前ほど楽ではございません。もちろん、わたくしもさらに努力いたしますが、部長からも、研究生産

sir, if you would ask Research and Development to create more and more new products.'

The bell sounds the end of the workday at New Electro. *Over at last! It's exhausting to run around all day like that. Gotta have a drink.*

Zame pushes open the door of the Galaxy, a bar he often visits on his way home. Spotting him, the landlady's parrot calls out to him in a sexy voice: 'Oh, it's you, Mr Zame! Please come in. It's been ages since I last saw you. Without a handsome man like you here, this place can be *so* depressing . . .'

For Zame, this is the most enjoyable part of the day.

部門に、もっとぞくぞく新製品を作るよう、お伝えいただけると、さらにありがたいとぞんじます」

ベルが鳴り、退社の時刻となった。やれやれ、やっときょうの仕事がすんだ。だが、一日じゅう売りあるくと、まったく疲れる。帰りにバーにでも寄らなくては、気分が晴れない。

ゼーム氏は、ときどき寄るバー・ギャラクシーのドアを押した。それをみつけたマダムの肩のインコが、なまめかしい声でむかえた。

「あら、ゼームさん。いらっしゃいませ。このところ、お見えになりませんでしたのね。ゼームさんのような、すてきなかたがいらっしゃらないと、お店のムードがなんとなくさびしくて……」

ゼーム氏にとっては、このひとときが、いちばんたのしい。

ABE AKIRA

Peaches

Translated by Jay Rubin

I know all too well that memory cannot be trusted, and I have surely
heard this said by others. But I am constantly being shocked anew at
how wildly deceptive memory can be. It beguiles us at every turn. I
was taken by surprise again not too long ago.

Winter. Night. The moon.

I am a young boy and with my mother. We push a pram filled
with peaches.

The single road connecting our town with the town on the
west runs through open farmland, then rises and falls as it slopes
gently downwards beyond an elevated stretch of sand dunes. It was
a narrow, rock-strewn country road back then. On the slope there
were no houses, only thick pine woods lining either side.

My mother and I make our way slowly down the hill. Soon we
will come to the river at the bottom. The river runs to the sea. Beyond
the river's wooden bridge, paddy fields stretch into the distance. The
air throbs with the bull-frogs' heavy cries, the wet smacking of the

阿部昭

桃

人間の記憶があてにならぬものだとは、つねづね痛感してもいるし、聞かされてもいるはずだ。ところが、その当てにならなさ加減が、いかに度外れなものか、あらためて愕然とさせられる瞬間が絶えないところをみると、われわれはまだまだ記憶なんていうものにいくらでもたぶらかされているのであろう。つい最近も、そんな驚きの一つを経験したばかりなのだ。

冬。真夜中。月が照っている。

子供の自分が、母と桃の実を満載した乳母車を押している。

この町から西隣の町に通ずる畑中の一本道は、なにがし台と呼ばれる小高い砂山の岡をこえて、ゆるやかな坂道で登り降りする。これは、当時も現在も同じだ。ただ、その頃は、道もせまく、舗装されていず、石ころだらけの山道で、両側は深い松林、人家もしばらくはとぎれた。

その坂道を、いま、母と静かに下ってくるところだ。やがて、この坂を降りきれば、川にさしかかり、川のゆくては海、木橋のむこうは一面の田圃で、食用蛙の牛のような啼き声や、

mud snails. We are almost home.

I doubt if there has been a year in the thirty or more that have gone by since then when I did not recall that night scene. The image in my mind is always the same – if not so fixed as a painting, then perhaps more like some frames of underexposed film flickering on the screen. Especially on cold winter nights when I walk alone through the darkness with my coat collar turned up, the fragmentary memory of that night on the road comes back to me.

And each time, I have said to myself: *Oh yes, I remember that – odd how well I do remember that night.* The very words of this monologue, too, are the same, repeated year after year with all the intensity a second-rate actor would give them. And while I am busy congratulating myself on my stagecraft, the memory always slips away, its veracity untested.

But the scene needs more commentary.

My mother had taken me along to the neighbouring town that night to lay in a stock of peaches at an orchard or some such place. She could get better ones than at the local greengrocer's, and they would be fresh picked. It was probably worth making a special trip and buying enough to fill the pram.

Peaches. Fruit like pure, sweet nectar – nothing else. Easily

ふつふつ言う田螺のつぶやきがあたりの空気をふるわせている。もうすぐ、家に着く。すっかり仕

三十何年後の今日まで、わたしは毎年のようにその晩のことを思い出した。露出の足りないムーヴィ・フィルムの

上った一枚の絵のように、とまでは行かなくとも、わたしが脳裡にえがく影像は、いつもきまり

何コマ分かのちらつく画面かなにかのように、大人になってからも、ことに寒い冬の夜ふけなど、オーバーの襟を立て

きったものだった。三十年以上も昔の、その夜道の記憶の断片がよみが

て一人暗がりを歩いている時などに、

えった。

すると、わたしは自分にいったものだ。——ああ、あんなことがあったな、あの晩のこと

はふしぎによく覚えているもんだな、などと。そのつぶやきまでもが、毎年毎年、同じセリ

フのくりかえしだ。下手な役者の思い入れそっくりなのだ。そして、自分の演技にいささか

の満足をおぼえると、記憶そのものの真偽に関しては、べつに何の疑念も抱かずに、また忘

れてしまうということをくりかえしてきた。

それはともかく、この描写には、もう少し注釈が必要だろう。母は、その晩、子供のわた

しをつれて、隣の町のどこかへ桃の買い出しに行ったのである。そこに大きな桃の栽培場か

果樹園があったのだろう。この辺の八百屋で買うよりも新鮮な上質の桃が手に入るので、わ

ざわざ出向き、出向いたついでに乳母車一杯も買い込んだというわけなので、

桃の実。とりわけ水蜜桃というのは、全部が甘い汁で出来ているようなものだ。それは、

bruised, quick to spoil. And each one heavy, almost unnervingly so. Filled with several dozen of these heavy peaches, the pram must have been more difficult to push than if it had held a live baby. And like the downy skin of a newborn, each could be scuffed and bruised in an instant if my mother did not push the pram slowly and carefully.

The darkness must have exaggerated the distance, long as it was. The night was cold and, up well past my bedtime, I must have been very sleepy. Partway down the hill, my mother stopped and wrapped her beige shawl around me.

More than the cold, it was my fear of the dark shapes arising one after another along the moonlit road that prompted her to do this. She probably had to cover my eyes with the shawl and walk along holding me against her.

Perhaps she had been careless enough to tease me about foxes along the way, and this was what aroused my fears, dark shadows or no. She had told me several stories of the foxes she had encountered as a little girl. My mother was born in Osaka at the turn of the century and she spent her childhood in the city, but on walks to the deserted countryside she would always hear the foxes crying, and people would say that they could cast a spell on passers-by.

Her stories must have come back to me one after another, the shawl around my head powerless to calm my fears. Why did she have

傷つきやすく、いたみやすい。そして、――何よりも、不気味なくらいずっしりと重たいものである。その重い実を数十個も積んだ乳母車は、きっと人間の赤ん坊をのせた以上に押してのあるものであったろう。そしてまた、一個一個が、金色の産毛のはえた赤ん坊の肌のように擦れて傷つきやすいので、乳母車はあくまでそろそろと押さなくてはならないのだ。

夜道にしても、長い道のりだった。なにしろ、寒い晩のことだった。子供のわたしは、ふだんの就寝時刻をとうに過ぎて、ずいぶん眠くもあったにちがいない。母は、坂の途中で立ちどまって、自分の肩からラクダの毛のショールを外すと、わたしの首に巻きつけた。

しかし、それは寒さのせいばかりでもなかったにちがいないのだ。母は、幼いわたしが、月光に染まった夜道に入れかわり立ちかわり現われるさまざまな物体の影におびえるので、ショールで目かくしをして、脇に抱きかかえるようにして歩かなくてはならなかったのだろう。

しかしまた、わたしが、そうでなくても怯えやすくなっていたのは、母が最初は冗談のつもりでうっかり狐のことを口にしたからかもしれないのである。わたしは、母から昔の狐の話を聞かされたことが何度かあったから。母は、明治の三十年代に大阪の街なかで生まれ育った女だったが、それでも、娘時代にちょっと人家のない所へ行くと、狐が出た。啼く声を聞いた。通りかかる人に悪さをするという噂もよく立った。

わたしは、そんな母の昔話がつぎつぎと思い出されて、ショールで頭をくるまれても、ま

to start talking about foxes *here*? I'm sure I wanted to get down the hill and among houses again as soon as possible.

But to walk any faster would have been out of the question. The pram would have bounced along the rocky road, damaging the peaches. I had been the baby in this pram until not long ago. Now it was only good for carting things. Most of the time, it stayed in the storage shed in the corner of the yard.

And so the young mother and her little boy, pressing close and sharing whispers, slowly pushed the old, little-used pram down the hill of the deserted country road. Bathed in moonlight, the one added the clip-clop of her wooden sandals, the other the soft padding of his tennis shoes to the creak of the pram's rusting wheels.

This, then, was the scene that had lived in the fondest part of my memory for so many years. In none of its details had I found anything to wonder at.

And then one day – in fact, just two or three days ago – as I was gazing blankly at the view from my window, it struck me with such force that, for a moment, I was unable to breathe. Peaches in the winter? Frogs and mud snails in the winter? How could I have failed

だ気もそぞろだったにちがいない。母が、よりによってこんな場所で狐のことなんか持ち出さないでくれればよかったのにと悔み、一刻も早くこの坂道をくぐり抜けて、人家のある通りへ出たいと思っていたにちがいない。

だが、これ以上早く歩くわけには行かない。急げば、乳母車が石ころ道をはねて、積んである桃が駄目になってしまう……。その乳母車は、ついこないだまで、このわたしが乗せられていたものだ。いまはもう荷車の役にしか立たないので、ふだんは庭の隅の物置小屋にしまってあった。

そんなふうに、久しぶりに出した古い乳母車を押しながら、若い母親と小さな男の子が、昼間でもあまり人通りのないこの田舎道の、ちょうど坂の中腹あたりを、ぼそぼそと言葉をかわしながら、寄りそうようにしてゆっくり降りてくる。月の光をあびて、一人は下駄の、もう一人は運動靴の足音をさせて、さびかかった乳母車の車輪を軋らせて。

わたしが長いこと慣れしたしんでいた記憶の中の光景は、ざっとこのようなものだ。わたしは、この夜の情景のデテイルに何のおかしなところも、一度だって発見したことはなかった。

ある日、といってもほんの二、三日前のことだが、わたしは、部屋の窓からぼんやり外の景色を眺めているうちに、あっ！　という声にならない驚きにつかまえられた。息をのんだようになった。冬の桃とは一体なにごとか！　冬啼く蛙とは！　田螺とは！　なんとい

to notice *that* until now? And, stranger still, what had inspired me – possessed me – at this one moment to seize upon the vital clue? For it was this that lay bare the hoax that memory had played on me year after year. Now, for the first time, I saw the wildly impossible connection that memory had made: carting a load of peaches on a cold winter night! Nowadays, perhaps. But back then? Unthinkable.

One after another, doubts began to overtake me. I would have to think it through from beginning to end. All right, then, exactly when was it? Why, in fact, were my mother and I walking down that hill so late at night? Were those really peaches in the pram? And if not, what were we bringing from the other town?

When it came to this, all I could be sure of was that one year, on one particular night, my mother and I had come down the hill on the road that linked our town with the next one. These unsubstantial facts were all that remained. Had it been peach season or shawl season? I did not know. I was far too young to have been alone – of that I was certain. But of that and nothing else.

We still had the pram that night, which meant I could not have gone past the first few years of primary school – or 'People's School', as it was called during the war. The one photograph that shows me in the pram – wearing a little white robe, my face a white mask of baby powder – was taken a month before my second birthday. If we

うことだろう？　なぜまた、わたしは、そのことにいまのいままで気がつかなかったのだろう？　それにまた、もっと奇怪なことには、なぜいまこの瞬間に、魔がさすようにして、永の年月自分をたぶらかしてきた記憶のペテンを突きとめる手がかりが摑めたのだろう？——現代ならともかく——当時として

わたしは、冬の寒い晩に大量の桃の実を運ぶという——現代ならともかく——当時としてはおよそあり得ないような奇妙な記憶の結びつきに、はじめて気がついたのだ。

すると、わたしは、つぎからつぎへと別の疑念にとりつかれはじめた。一から考え直さなければならなくなった。では、あれは一体いつのことだ？　それにまた、乳母車に積んでいたのが桃のためにそんな夜ふけにその坂道を通ったのか？　母と子供のわたしは、一体何のないとしたら、何を隣の町から運んできたのだ？

そうなると、確実なのは、わたしが、ある年のある晩に、隣の町とこの町とをむすぶあのなにがし台の坂道を、母と二人で降りてきたことがある、という漠然たる事実に尽きそうだった。それが桃の季節だったのか、ショールの季節だったのかが判らない。いずれにしろ、子供のわたしが一人で、ということはあり得ない。はっきりしているのは、それだけだということになる。

乳母車は、とにかくそれがまだ家にあったということから、少くともわたしの国民学校低学年までのことにはちがいない。同じ乳母車に、顔に真っ白にシッカロールを塗り、ゆかたを着せられたわたしが乗っている唯一の写真は、満一年と十一ヵ月の時のものだ。それが荷

were using the pram to cart things, it must have been falling apart, the hood broken, the waterproof cloth of the body peeling. Had I been so rough on it as all that? Had we thrown it in the storage shed because it was a wreck? And how about my age? I think I walked both to and from the other town, a goodly distance for me even now. My mother didn't have to carry me. Surely I had left kindergarten by then and was going to primary school.

This was probably true, because I seemed to recall that when we got home late that evening, my brother, who was at middle school, was very put out with my mother and me. By then the war was on, and my father, a navy man, was no longer at home. Even assuming there was a moon that night, the road should have been dark because of the blackout. Still, the war was in its early stages; the air raids had not really started. It was probably the summer or the winter of 1942. My brother, so annoyed with us then, had left home by the following year. That night, he was probably hard at work preparing for the Naval Academy entrance examination. He must have been angry at my mother for being so late with his dinner.

But even as I go on making one reasonable-sounding guess after another, I realize that my 'evidence' has no more validity than any other tricks of memory. Not a thing I have mentioned here is certain.

車として使われているところを見ると、もう幌の部分もこわれ、本体の防水布で出来た袋なども、表面が剥げて、やぶれかかっていただろう。わたしがさんざん乗ったためにそうなったのか、こわれたから物置きに放りこんだのか。わたしの年齢も、いま大人の足で歩いても相当の道のりがある隣町との往復の距離を、そんなふうに、母に負ぶわれてでもなく、せっせと歩き通したらしいということから、まず幼稚園ではなく学校にあがってからだろう、と思われる程度のことだ。

それはまた、その晩、母とわたしが帰宅すると、中学生の兄が二人の帰りが遅すぎるので、ふくれっ面をしていた（ような気がする）ことからも察しがつく。つまり、すでに戦争がはじまっていて、もう軍人の父は家にいなかった。その晩、仮りに月が出ていたとしても、道が暗かったのは、だから、灯火管制のせいでもあったにちがいないのだ。

だが、その戦争もまだごく初期で、むろん空襲も本格的にははじまっていなかった。たぶん、昭和十七年の夏か、冬なのだ。なぜなら、その晩、母と弟のわたしを不機嫌な様子で迎えた兄は、つぎの年にはもう家にいないからだった。その頃、兄はたぶん兵学校の受験勉強の真っ最中だった。母の帰りが遅いので、空腹にもかかわらず夜食にありつけなくて不機嫌になっていたのだろう。

しかし、こんなふうにもっともらしく推測を並べながら、わたしは、その裏づけたるや例の記憶のペテン同様にあやふやきわまるものであることに気がついている。いま並べたよう

Indeed, I can refute every item without even trying.

First, there is the old pram. How long did we actually have it around the house? When did we get rid of it? And how? By leaving it in a nearby field? Sending it to the junk shop? I have no definite answers. It could just as well have stayed in the storage shed during the war and even for a time thereafter. Then the hoax would have been so easy to play: I might simply have confused that night scene with a post-war episode of stocking up on something.

Far from my mother's leading me by the hand, it seems more likely that I was there to protect her, that the road was unsafe for a woman alone at night. By then I would have been in my sixth year of primary school or my first year of middle school. And we were wheeling not a pram-load of peaches, but of black-market rice or potatoes or sweet potatoes or – if I'm going to insist on a cold winter night – perhaps some New Year's rice cakes. Then again, fuel being as hard to come by as food, it might have been kindling or charcoal or scraps of coal with which to stoke our old-fashioned bathtub.

Under this kind of scrutiny, the lovely image of a mother and child slowly pushing a pram downhill on a moonlit night is suddenly transformed into something less charming – a suspicious-looking couple transporting black-market goods. We would then have had our reasons for moving about under cover of night.

But where does my scowling brother fit in? He should not have

な事柄は、少しも確実でないどころか、一つ一つあっさりと否定できもするようなものばかりだからだ。

第一、その古い乳母車がいつごろまで家にあったのか、いつどう処分したのか——例えば、近所の原っぱに棄てるとか、屑屋に持って行かせるとか——わたしにはもう確かなことは言えない。戦争中はずっと物置きにあり、戦後もまだしばらくはそのままになっていたかもしれないではないか？　そうだとすると、ペテンのからくりはまことに簡単で、その晩の光景は、おそらく戦後の買い出しの記憶の一コマと区別がつかなくなっているだけなのだ。

わたしは、母に手を引かれてついて行くどころか、母が女一人では夜道が不用心なので、わたしをお供に連れて行ったのだ、といったほうがよさそうだ。わたしは、もう小学校の六年か、中学一年だった。そして、乳母車の中身は、水密どころか、闇米か、サツマイモか、ジャガイモか、——なお冬の寒い晩という記憶にこだわるとしても——せいぜい正月の餅ぐらいだったのであろう。ひょっとして、それは食糧と同じく入手困難だった燃料、薪や木炭や屑石炭のたぐいだったのではあるまいか？　わたしの家は、五右衛門風呂だったから。

そうして眺め直すと、月夜の晩にそろそろと乳母車を押して坂道を降りてくる母と子のうるわしい影絵は、たちまち闇物資運搬のあやしげな二人連れということになるのだ。夜陰に乗じて行動したのには、われわれにもそれ相応の事情があったのだということになる。

だが、もしそうだったとすれば、さて家に着いてみると、仏頂面をした兄貴が待ちかまえ

been there waiting for us. Following his demobilization after the war, he was almost never at home. And if it so happened that he was in the house on that particular day, he would have had no reason to be angry with us. If anything, he would have been grateful. And so it was not my brother, probably, but my father who was waiting for us. It was always my father who stayed at home. Or rather, as a former officer, waiting at home was the only job there was for him to do.

But no, this has to be wrong. Those were peaches, I'm sure of it. All I have to do to make the memory consistent is change the cold winter evening to a summer night. This casts doubt, of course, on my mother's wrapping her shawl around me and the feeling I have that she told me tales of foxes as we walked along. But literary tradition aside, there is nothing wrong with the subject of foxes in summer. Only the shawl is out of place.

As far as literary hoaxes go, the most obvious one is the moonlight that comes flooding into my so-called memory. I could easily have been led from an old story of the fox's cry on a cold winter night into yet another story that my mother probably told me around the same time.

It was a story about a distant relative of hers, a young girl, something that happened when my mother was herself a girl. Born with a bad leg, the girl was sent to a convent when the other girls her age were marrying. She was suspected of having stolen something from

ていたという場面はおかしいのだ。戦後、復員した兄は、ほとんど家を明けていることが多かったし、その日たまたま家にいたとしても、食糧の買い出しに行ってきた母とわたしに不機嫌な顔を見せる理由はない。感謝こそすれ、だ。家で待っていたのは、だから、兄ではなくて父のほうだったのだろう。というより、元軍人の父には留守番をするぐらいしか仕事がなかった。留守番をするのは、いつも父だった。

だがしかし、やはりそれはそうではなかったにちがいない。あれは、やっぱり桃を運んできたのだ。あの冬の寒い晩というのを、夏の夜というふうに訂正するだけで、わたしの記憶の辻褄は合うのだ。ただ、そうなると、母がわたしの首に自分のショールを巻いてくれたこと、歩きながら昔の狐の話をしたような気がすることだけが、あやしくなるのだ。いや、夏だからといって狐の話題がふさわしくないとは言いきれないのだから、ショールのことだけが誤りということになるのだ。

そして、その種の文学的ペテンの最たるものは、わたしの記憶と称するものの中に射しこんでいる月光というやつではないだろうか？　冬の寒い晩にコンコンと啼いたという古狐の話から、たぶん同じ頃母がしてくれたもう一つの物語にみちびかれるのは、わたしとしては造作もないことだったろう。

母の娘時代に、遠い親戚に一人の娘がいた。その娘は、生まれつき足が悪くて、同じ年頃の少女たちが嫁に行く頃、尼寺へやられた。ところが、その寺で、他の尼さんの持ち物を盗

one of the other nuns, however, and the older nuns beat her cruelly. That day, or perhaps it was the next day, or a short time thereafter, the girl drowned herself in a pond. It happened on a moonlit winter night, my mother said, unfolding the bright scene of death before me.

Within the grounds of the convent – somewhere in Kyoto, or possibly Nara – there was a large pond, on the banks of which grew a giant plum tree. Its heavy, gnarled branches stretched out low over the water to the middle of the pond. It looked just like a bridge, my mother said, as though she had seen the tree herself. Dragging her bad leg, the poor young nun crawled quietly along the branch in her white robes as the moonlight flooded down. Then she fell and disappeared beneath the surface. The thing she had supposedly stolen was found some days later among another nun's belongings.

I suspect my mother embroidered rather freely on the story of the young girl's suicide but, child that I was, it moved me very deeply. More than the horror of her fate itself, however, what struck me was the fact that such a dark drama of an ill-fated life should be concealed somewhere out on the furthest branches of the bloodlines that connected me to others. Its ancient stage settings, like something out of the Nara or Heian past; the indistinct backdrop, like the ones in the shadow plays: these were what left an impression on me.

Is the image in my mind, then, of the same tradition as my mother's eerie tale? Did I create it for myself, as one often hears is done, by unconsciously fusing two wholly distinct memories into a single

んだ嫌疑をかけられて、年長の尼たちにひどい折檻をうけた。その日か、そのつぎの日だったか、それともしばらく経ってからだったか、その娘は池に身を投げて死んでしまった。月の明るい冬の晩に、と母はいって、投身の場面の月光の描写を幼いわたしの前にくりひろげてみせた。

その尼寺——京都のほうだったか、奈良のほうだったか——には、大きな池があり、そのほとりに一本の梅の巨樹があった。その曲りくねった太い枝が、水面すれすれに低く伸びて、池の中ほどにまで達しているさまは、まるで橋を架けたようであった、というのが、母の見てきたような描写だった。その梅の枝の上を、白い衣をまとった不幸な若い尼が、不自由な足をひきずって、月の光に照らされながら、静かに這って行って、落ちて、水面から消える。彼女が盗んだといわれた品物は、後日、別の尼のところから発見された。

たぶんかなりの程度まで母が潤色したにちがいないその自殺した娘の話は、それでも子供のわたしの心を打った。彼女の運命のむごたらしさがというより、自分のはるか遠い血縁の末端に、そんな冬の夜ばなしめいた数奇な挿話がかくされていたという事実が。まるで奈良か平安の昔のことのような、なんとも古めかしい道具立てと、影絵でも見るようなぼんやりした書割りのゆえに。

では、母の夜ばなしと同じ伝で、わたしのあのイメージも、よくあるといわれるように、あたかもわたしが頭の中で一つの記憶と別のもう一つの記憶とをいつのまにか癒着させて、

night's occurrence? Was this one of those 'beautiful recollections', a pack of lies put through a sentimental tinting job until it comes out 'like a little story'? It might well have been.

The memory I have (or seem to have) of pushing the pram down the hill with my mother is unique: it happened that once and never again. Her wrapping her shawl around me when we were out together was a common enough occurrence, however, and her storytelling was by no means confined to night-time walks. It could and did happen anywhere – at the dinner table, in my room, and probably most often while she was sewing.

At that age – be it summer or winter – I would most often walk with my mother at night on the way back from my aunt's house, which lay in precisely the opposite direction from the hill, in the town to the east. There was a river in that direction as well, but it was a river we followed for a while rather than crossed. The water's dark surface used to frighten me badly. My cousins had told me of a boy my own age who had fallen in when hunting crabs on the bank and had sunk into the mud and died. The story had an eerie epilogue, which the girls had eagerly supplied: on windy nights, you could hear the dead boy's sobbing from the riverbank.

I would hide my face in my mother's sleeve, trying not to see the faint glow of the river as we passed by in the dark. Here, too, there were few dwellings, and the road was lonely and hemmed in by

一夜の出来事のごとくに創作していたにすぎないのか？　つまり、あの「ちょっとした小説のようなもの」、感傷の気分で染めあげた嘘八百の「美しい追憶」というやつなのか？　それは十分あり得ることだ。

なにがし台の坂道を、母と乳母車を押して下ってきた（ような）記憶は、たしかに、わたしにはまたとない記憶ではあるが、母が外出先でわたしの首に自分のショールを巻いてくれたようなことは、日常茶飯の光景だったし、昔話なら、なにも夜道をとぼとぼ歩きながらではなく、食卓でも子供部屋でもした。むしろ、裁縫でもしながらのほうが多かったはずだ。

それに、その年齢のわたしが、夏といわず冬といわず、母に連れられて夜道を歩くことが多かったのは、むしろ、なにがし台とは正反対の方角、つまり東隣の町にある伯母の家へ行った帰りだった。そっちのほうには、もう一本別の川が流れていたが、これは渡るのではなしに、それに沿ってしばらく歩くのだった。そして、わたしは、この川の暗い水面をひどくおそれた。というのも、いつか、その川のふちで、ちょうどわたしぐらいの男の子がカニを取ろうとして水に落ち、泥に埋まって死んだ、という話をいとこたちに聞かされていたからである。彼女たちの話には、風のつよい夜など、その川のふちから死んだ子の泣きじゃくる声がするという怪談じみたオマケまでついていたものだ。

川のそばを通りかかるとき、わたしは闇にほのかに光る水面を見まいとして、母の袂に顔をかくしたりした。道は、やはり松林にかこまれた、人家の少ない、さびしい道だったが、

pine woods, but once we left the river behind I felt safe. Sometimes my mother would stop to gather a few pine cones and put them in her basket. One night, she stopped walking quite unexpectedly and, instructing me to stay put, waded cautiously into the deep grass by the roadside. I watched until she squatted down, then waited, praying that no one would come from either direction.

Thus, while I was familiar with the road to the east from an early age, I passed the hill in the other direction late at night only that once. If I am right in recalling that those were peaches we carted, it could have been no later than shortly after the war broke out. While my father was away, my mother had part of the lawn dug up and four peach trees planted, three yellow and one white. They were mature trees and bore fruit the following year – in such numbers that my mother had to spend many evenings tearing up old copies of her ladies' magazines and pasting the pages together to make covers for the still-green peaches. Every summer through the war years and after, we had more peaches than we could eat, and she was kept busy giving them away to relatives and neighbours. We never had to buy any.

All of which leads me to believe that the night in question had to have been in 1942. The trip she made to buy that load of peaches may have given my mother the idea to plant her own trees. Or, possibly, having decided to grow peaches, she went to the orchard in the next town to see how it was done. But, in fact, where these questions are concerned, my memory tells me nothing at all.

川から遠ざかると、わたしは安心した。母は、ときどき足をとめて、大きなマツボックリをいくつか拾い、買物籠に入れた。ある晩、母は不意に立ちどまると、わたしにその場で待っているようにといって、おそるおそる草むらに入った。わたしは、母がしゃがむのを見届けてから、道のどちらからも人が来ないようにと祈りながら、待った。

そんなふうにわたしには早くからなじみ深かった東隣の町への道にくらべて、あのなにがし台の坂道を深夜に通行したこととは、あとにも先にもその一回きりだった。そして、もしも桃を運んだという記憶が正しければ、それはやはり戦争がはじまってまもなくの時期までのことだった。なぜなら、母は、父の留守に、庭の芝生の一部分を削って、そこに水蜜桃を三本と、白桃を一本、植えさせたからである。それらは、苗木というより、もうかなり成熟した立木で、つぎの年にはちゃんと実がなった。その数は何百という数で、母は、青い実にかぶせる袋を用意するために、古い婦人雑誌のたぐいを何冊もつぶして、夜なべに糊で貼り合わせた。

以後、戦中戦後の何年間か、母は毎夏たべきれぬほどの桃を親戚や隣近所にくばるのに忙しく、よそで買う必要は全然なかったのだから。

してみると、あれはどうしても昭和十七年のこととしか思えない。母は、あのたくさんの桃を買って帰ったのがきっかけで、自分でも桃の木を植えようという気になったのかもしれない。あるいは、もうそのつもりで、隣町の果樹園を見学に行ったのかもしれない。しかし、その辺の記憶は、わたしにはまるで残っていないのだ。

What I do remember, however, as inseparably associated with the peach trees, are the face and voice of a man. It was he who had encouraged her to plant them, who actually brought the young trees and put them into the ground. And every year he would come with fertilizer, inspect and prune the trees, and have a long chat with my mother before he left. He was the son of a local landowner whose family had built and rented many houses here for several generations and who also farmed the land. He was 'the son', but he was of my mother's generation and by then was head of the household. He had often visited us before the war, too. My father bought our land from his father. Apparently, it had once been their watermelon patch.

My mother never invited the man in, but whenever he dropped over to say hello, bringing a bundle of vegetables at the peak of the season, she would serve him tea on the open veranda outside the dining room and sit nearby to talk. She left the care of the peach trees entirely to him, and the time would come when she would ask him to dig a bomb shelter as well. He could be asked to scoop the night soil, do any job. A round, ruddy man, he wore a cloth cap and a workman's waistcoat with a large pocket on the front. He had a loud, ringing laugh that he would suppress for no one.

The dining-room veranda was my 'territory'. On the cement floor underneath were kept bundles of firewood, bales of charcoal, dried tulip and hyacinth bulbs, cobwebbed flowerpots and a watering can. It was a sunny spot, and cats from other houses would come to stretch out there. I once saw a sick-looking cat eating weeds that had sprouted from cracks in the cement. They were long, slender

わたしの記憶にあるのは、それらの桃の木と切り離せない一人の男の顔と、声だ。母にそれを植えることを熱心にすすめ、実際に苗木を持ってきて植えた男。毎年、施肥や剪定にやってきては、木のぐあいを調べ、母と話し込んで行った。その男は、この土地に代々たくさんの家作を持ち、自分でも百姓をやっている、地主のせがれだった。せがれといっても、ほぼわたしの母と同年輩で、いまは家督も彼の代になっていた。男は、戦前からわたしの家に出入りしていたが、そもそもは父が彼のおやじから現在の土地を買ったという因縁だった。わたしの家の敷地は、もともと男の家のスイカ畑だったようだ。

母は、その男をけっして家に上げることはなかったが、彼がシュンの野菜でもさげてご機嫌伺いにぶらっとたずねてくると、食堂の濡れ縁のところでお茶を出し、自分もそばに坐って相手になっていた。桃のことは男にまかせっきりだし、いずれは防空壕も掘ってもらうことになるだろう。男は、たのめば、便所の汲みとりも引きうけるし、何でも引きうけた。鳥打帽に、ドンブリのついた腹掛けをした、赭ら顔の、でっぷり太った男だった。笑うときは、野ぶとい声で、からからとあたりはばからずに笑った。

その濡れ縁は、いわば、わたしの領分だった。下のたたきには、薪の束や炭俵がしまってあり、干からびたチューリップやヒアシンスの球根や、蜘蛛の巣のまつわりついた植木鉢やジョウロが置いてあった。日あたりがよいので、よくよその猫が来て、ねそべっていた。病気らしい猫が、コンクリートの割れ目から生えた草をたべるのも見られた。金平糖みたいな

plants with seed clusters like bonbons. I used to lie on the veranda, looking at all these things through the spaces in the planks.

One day, as the afternoon sun was fading from the veranda, the man and my mother sat there engrossed in conversation. It was just then that I came home from school.

Their talk was more light banter than anything serious.

'I know *your* type. You've done it all. With all sorts of women . . .' I heard my mother saying.

'No, not me, no . . .'

To hide his embarrassment, he laughed his ringing laugh, but he did not look at my mother. His eyes stayed fixed on the peach trees he had planted.

I was having my afternoon snack close by, and all at once I found myself listening to their every word. The banter continued for a time, but then my mother caught her breath.

'What? Would a woman dare to do such a thing?' I heard her say.

I knew nothing about sex at that age, of course, but I had some vague idea of what they were talking about, enough to know that

実をつけた、すんなりした草。——これらのものを、子供のわたしは、濡れ縁に寝そべって、桟と桟のすきまから眺めたのである。

ある日、午後の日ざしがかげりだしたその濡れ縁に、男が腰を下ろして、母と話しこんでいた。ちょうど、わたしは国民学校から退けて帰った時刻だったのだろう。

母と男は、大した要件もないらしく、冗談をかわしていた。

「……あなたなんか、もうさんざんしたい放題のことをしたんでしょう？　いろんな女のひとと……。」

そんなことを母がいったのが聞えた。

「いや、いや、とても……。」

男は、てれかくしに例の野ぶとい声でからからと笑ったが、母のほうは見ないで、自分が植えた桃の木のほうにじっと視線をやっていた。

すぐ近くでおやつをたべていたわたしの耳を、ふっと二人の会話がとらえたようだった。

二人はしばらくそのつづきで冗談をいい合っていたが、やがて、母がふっと息をひそめて、

「まあ、女のほうからそんなことをしたりするんですの？……」

といったのを、わたしは聞いた。

わたしは、勿論房事のことが分る年齢ではなかった。しかし、二人がおおよそ何のことを話しているのかは察しがついた。二人の会話のあやうさを感じとるには、おおよそのところ

it was a dangerous topic.

Not long afterwards, on a day when the smell of the peaches was stifling in the summer heat, I was in my room with my mother, listening to the broadcast announcing the end of the war. My father did not come back until September, too late for him to be served peaches. But the fruit that lay rotting on the ground continued to fill the garden and the house with its heavy, sweet perfume, and my father must have been aware of it long before he reached the doorway.

Still, what had my mother been talking about with the man that day? As I thought about it years later, their strangely forced repartee began to flare up, incandescent, a point of peculiar brilliance in my memory. Here was the landlord, a man with a reputation for debauchery, trying to laugh off indecencies that he had broached with reluctance, while on the other hand, there was my mother, increasingly serious to the point of catching her breath. Indeed, it was she, a woman in her prime left alone to guard the chastity of her marriage bed, who sought to draw out this kind of talk. The sharp contrast between the two of them struck my heart again and again: the man grown weary of women; the woman separated from her husband by years of war. As far as I could tell, her life had undergone no change, and it was precisely because of this that I recalled the scene as though witnessing a dangerous tightrope act.

I had been a child then, but surely I had said to myself: *My mother is a soldier's wife, not the kind of woman to enjoy such vulgar talk with another man.* But my skin, no doubt, had been feeling something a little different. I still liked to sleep with my mother in those days.

でも十分だったのだ。

やがて桃の匂いが暑気にむせ返るような夏の日に、わたしは、子供部屋で母と終戦のラジオ放送を聞いた。父が帰ってきたのは、九月になってからで、もう桃はたべさせられなかったはずだ。しかし、熟れて落ちた桃が、地上で蒸れて腐りながら放つ甘ったるい芳香は、まだ庭にも家の中にも充満していて、父にも遠くからでもわかったにちがいない。

それにしても、あの時、母はあの男と何を話していたのだろう？　二人のどこか不自然なやりとりが、ずっと後年わたしの記憶の中で白く燃え上がって、その一点だけが輝くばかりに感じられだした。放蕩者だという評判の地主の男のほうは、なにかみだらな話を出し惜しみするように、へらへらと笑いながらしかけるのに、母はますます気まじめに応じて、息をのんだようにさえなった。しかも、そんな話を積極的に聞き出そうとしていたのは、孤閨を守っている女ざかりの母のほうだったのだ。二人の態度のきわだった対照が、何度もわたしの心を打った。女に飽きたような男と、戦争で何年も夫から遠ざけられている女と。母の身の上になにごとも起こったとは見えなかっただけに、わたしは、危険な綱渡りのシーンでも見るように、その日の場面を思いかえした。

わたしは、たぶん子供ながらに思っていた――自分の母は軍人の妻だ、父以外の男とそんなはしたない話題をもてあそぶような女ではない、というふうに。だが、わたしは自分の肌では、もう少し別のことも感じていたにちがいない。わたしは、その頃、まだ夜は母の寝

And in the winter, especially, there were many opportunities to do so. At bedtime, of course, I would get into my own bed, but I would snuggle into hers after going to the toilet in the middle of the night. Too sleepy to chase me out, she would have to make room for me. Then, drifting on the edge of sleep, she would clasp me to her breast, entwine her naked legs with mine. Where the nightgown had slipped open, the flesh was hot, as if with fever.

Before long, this had become my nightly pleasure, until finally I myself no longer knew whether I was waking up because I needed to go to the toilet, or going to the toilet was an excuse to be held by my mother. Surely, when she held me, the feeling that came through my skin was not just my own pleasure, but the jagged restlessness of my mother's flesh, and the sinful awareness that I had thrust myself into the void left by my father and was enjoying her greedily.

Yes, a third person not actually present could well have been part of that night scene on the hill. And was it not my father? Some unusual circumstance must have been responsible for my mother's being there at that strange time and having me with her.

They had quarrelled, perhaps, and the repercussions had come to me. I do seem to remember something that happened between them just before the war.

床に入りたがった。ことに冬には、そのチャンスがいくらもあった。寝る時は自分の蒲団に入るのだが、夜中に、オシッコに起きたのをしおに母の蒲団にもぐりこんだ。母も、ねむいので、叱る気力もなく、仕方なしに躰をずらして、わたしのスペースをこしらえた。そして、夢うつつでか、わたしを胸に抱きすくめたり、寝巻からはだけた脚をわたしの脚にからませてきたりした。その裸の部分は、どこも熱病にでもかかったように熱かった。

こんなことが、いつのまにか、わたしの毎夜の快楽になっていたのだ。そして、しまいには、本当にオシッコがしたくて目をさますのか、母に抱かれる口実を作るために、オシッコに行くのか、自分でもわからなくなっていたにちがいない。抱かれながら、わたしが肌で感じていたのは、自分の快楽ばかりでなく、母の肉体のいらだちや、父の不在につけこんでいつまでもそんなふうに母をむさぼっている罪障感のようなものでもあっただろう。

そうだ。もしかすると、あの冬の夜の坂道のシーンには、その場にいない第三者が介在していたのではないだろうか？　とすると、それはやはり、父なのだろうか？　母があんな時刻に、あんな場所を、わたしをつれて通りかかったというのには、よほど特別な事情があったのにちがいない。

ひょっとすると、わたしは、父と母の不和のとばっちりを受けただけだったかもしれない。わたしが覚えているのは、戦争直前の二人のこんな場面だ。

「行ってこい！」

My father was warming one hand over the charcoal brazier and commanding my mother, sitting on the matted floor opposite him, to 'Go, I said! Go now!'

The ringing of the copper kettle made the silence that followed seem horribly long and suffocating.

'I'm telling you, go and settle it properly, once and for all,' he said, his authority overwhelming. My mother hung her head in silence. He turned away.

'But it's so late . . .' she murmured in desperation.

'I don't give a damn. You go,' he said and looked away again.

'Please, not tonight. I'll go in the morning. I swear I will.'

'I said tonight and I meant it.'

Their confrontation went on, and eventually my mother seemed to be crying.

'Oh, please forgive me,' she sobbed. 'Forgive your wife!'

She reached for the hand he held over the brazier, but he swept her hand away as if it were something vile, knocking the fire tongs into the ashes. As they fell, she crumpled before him, clinging to his knees.

父が、茶の間で、火鉢に片手をかざしながら、母に強要していたような気がする。

銅壺で沸いている湯がチンチンと鳴る音が、父と母との無言の対座を、おそろしく長く、息苦しいものに感じさせた。

「どうしても行ってこい！　行って、ちゃんとそのように話をつけてこい！」

黙って下を向いている母に、父はおっかぶせるようにまた言って、横を向いた。

「こんな夜中に……。」

母が困りはてたようにつぶやくのを、父は、

「構わん。行け。」

といって、またむこうを向いてしまう。

「でも、今夜はもう遅いですから、明朝まいります。きっと、まいります。」

「いや、ならぬ。」

二人の押し問答がつづいた。

それから、とうとう母が泣きだしたようだった。

「堪忍して、あなた！」

そういって、母が火鉢にかざした父の手にすがろうとすると、父は母のその手をけがらわしいもののように振りはらった。立てかけてあった火箸が灰の中に倒れ、母の姿勢も崩れて、父の着物の腰にしがみつくような恰好になった。

Perhaps he had only been trying to avoid her touch, but his hand had struck hers, and this filled me with terror. Now it was my turn to burst into tears, I suspect, and my mother, resigned to what she must do, probably led me out into the night.

The failing for which my mother was being blamed that night may have amounted to nothing at all. Obstinate military man that he was, my father often tormented her this way, and she submitted meekly.

That scene, too, ends abruptly, and I have no idea where it leads, no way of knowing what came of it. But even now I can hear my mother in tears at my father's knee: 'Oh, please forgive me. Forgive your wife!' Her cry rings through the darkness, caressing, seductive. I do not doubt that my father heard the almost unseemly erotic appeal in her voice, the soft, clinging tones of the Osaka woman. And he did not succumb to her sexual onslaught because I was there, watching.

Was not *this* my cold winter night? And if it was, then my mother had taken me to the neighbouring town not to buy anything, but to accomplish something far more important – or at least, something far more painful. But the further I pursue this line of reasoning, the more confused I become, for another part of me clings stubbornly to the memory of pushing the old pram down the hill with my mother through the winter moonlight, our breath white in the cold.

父が、たとえよけた拍子にせよ、母の手を打ったので、子供のわたしは恐怖におそわれた。今度は、わたしが、火がついたように泣きだしたのではないか？　そして、母はあきらめて、泣きじゃくるわたしの手を引いて、暗い戸外へ出たのではないか？

その時、母が責められていたあやまちは、べつに大したことではなかったのかもしれない。頑迷な軍人の父は、よくそんなふうに振舞って、忍従している母を苦しめた。

その場面も、そこでぷっつり切れて、どこへつづくのかわからない。結果がどうなったのかも知るよしがない。わたしがいまも闇に聞く思いがするのは、「堪忍して、あなた！」といって父の膝もとに泣き伏した母の、どこかしなだれかかるような、媚びを含んだ、澄んだ悲鳴だけだ。上方育ちの母の言葉は、まつわりつくような柔かい発声と抑揚のために、よけい場違いなほどエロチックに父の耳にもひびいたにちがいない。父が、この母の性的な奇襲にも折れようとしなかったのは、きっと子供のわたしが見ている前だったからだ。

その晩こそ、あの冬の寒い晩ではなかったのか？　だとしたら、母は隣の町へ何を買いに行ったのでもなく、なにかもっと重大な、とまではいわなくても、もっと心苦しい用向きのために、幼いわたしを連れて出かけたのであったろう。こんなふうに考えてきて、わたしはいよいよ判らなくなる一方なのだ。そして、もう一人のわたしは、依然として、吐く息も白い冬の月あかりの中を、母と二人、古い乳母車を押して、あのなにがし台の坂を下ってきた記憶に固執する。

After wandering thus in endless circles, I feel as though I have been hurled once again on to the hill on the road that – today as then – links our town with the next.

I know that my mother and I passed that place wheeling a pram – but does all certainty end there?

Having retreated fifty paces, let me fall back a hundred: perhaps I was merely *riding* in that pram? Or, yielding another hundred paces: perhaps the dark hill – the one place that seemed more eerily unknown than any other to my boyhood imagination – perhaps this setting could be an image that stayed with me from a time when I passed there alone several years later? And through some weird manipulation of memory, I may have been arbitrarily throwing into this setting an image of myself in the pram wrapped in my mother's shawl, or an image of myself on another road on another night that I passed asleep and only heard about later, or yet a wholly different scene of my mother and me pushing something in the pram.

What emerges from this is the arcane spectacle of me as a boy, wheeling a pram that holds my infant self.

長い堂々めぐりのあとで、わたしは、ふたたび隣町とこの町をむすぶ──結ぶことにおい

ていまでも変らないあの坂道の中腹にほうり出されるように感ずる。

では、はっきりしているのは、いつかそこを母とわたしが乳母車を押して通ったことがあ

る、ということに尽きるのだろうか?

百歩をゆずって、もしやわたしは、その乳母車に乗っていただけではないのだろうか?

あるいは、さらにもう百歩をゆずって、わたしは、その後何年も経ってから自分一人で通り

かかったなにがし台の闇に、──たぶん子供の自分にとって他のどの場所よりも気疎く想像

されていたその坂道の一角に、──奇怪な回想の操作によって、乳母車の中で母のショー

ルにすっぽり包まれた自分を、あるいはどこか別の夜道を、その時は眠っていて、あとで通っ

てきたと教えられた自分を、あるいはまた、乳母車を押して何かを運ぶ母とわたしの別のあ

る情景を、気ままに投げこんで眺めているのにすぎないのだろうか?

それはまるで、少年のわたしが、ずっと年下の幼児のわたし自身を、乳母車に乗せて押し

ているような、不可解な光景だ。

BETSUYAKU MINORU

Factory Town

Translated by Royall Tyler

One day, just like that, a small factory appeared on the outskirts of the town. Its chimney began puffing out great billows of black smoke.

'Goodness!' some townsfolk exclaimed when they happened by. 'What's going on here?'

'Looks like a factory to me, with all that smoke coming out of the chimney.'

'Fine, but what's it *making*?'

'I wonder.'

So they stole up to the factory and one man peeked in through a knothole in the fence.

'What's that going thunka-thunka-thunka?'

'Must be the machine. There's a huge, black machine in there going round and round. But what can it be making?'

'Come on, now, give me a look! Yes, it's the machine, all right. A *big* one! Oh – I see some men working!'

別役実

工場のある街

その街のはずれに、いつの間にか小さな工場がひとつ出来て、煙突から黒い煙をモクモクと吐き出しはじめました。

「おや、変なものが出来ましたね?」

通りかかった街の人が気づいてそう言いました。

「どうやら工場みたいですよ、煙突からあんなに煙が出ています」

「でも何を作っているんでしょう?」

「さあ……」

そこで街の人たちは、コッソリ工場に近づいて節穴から中の様子をのぞきこみました。

「何かゴトゴト音がしますね?」

「きっとそれは機械ですよ、黒い大きな機械がゆっくり動いています。でも、いったいあれは何を作る機械でしょうね?」

「どれどれ、私にも見せて下さい。ははあ、確かに機械ですね、大きなものですなあ、おや、誰か働いています」

'What are they like?'

'There are three of them. The older one must be the father and the two younger ones his sons.'

'So – a family.'

'They're covered with grease, and they're certainly going at it!'

'Can you tell what they're making?'

'I wish I could.'

Anyway, the news about the factory spread that day by word of mouth through the whole town. Mothers back from shopping, fathers strolling in the park, gals and guys sipping tea in the coffee shop – everyone was talking about it.

'Pots and pans, that's what they're making, if you ask me. Our town has a serious shortage of both, you know.'

'I'll go for sickles and hoes. Tools like that wear out right away. You keep needing new ones.'

'I'd say they're baking bread. We do have a baker, but he's always so slow getting the bread out.'

The baker thought otherwise.

「どんな人です？」

「三人いますね。年をとったのはお父さんでしょう。若い二人は息子たちです、きっと」

「親子でやっているんですね」

「三人とも、油だらけになって、良く働いています」

「何を作っているか、わかりますか？」

「さあ……」

でも、その街に工場が出来たという話は、人から人に伝わってその日のうちに街中に知れわたってしまいました。買物帰りのお母さんたちも、公園をお散歩するお父さんたちも、喫茶店でお茶を飲むお姉さんやお兄さんたちもみんなその話をしました。

「いったい何を作っているんでしょうね」

「私は、オナベかオカマだと思うわ、この街では、オナベもオカマもひどく品不足ですからね」

「私はクワかカマだと思うよ。ああしたものは、すぐ駄目になるし、次から次に必要になるものだからね」

「もしかしたら、パンじゃないかしら、この街にもパン屋さんはいるけど、焼き上りがいつも遅いし……」

しかし、パン屋さんはそうは思わないのでした。

'No, it's not bread. Must be charcoal briquettes. That black smoke isn't from baking. It's from making briquettes.

The briquette-maker disagreed, of course.

'No, not briquettes. The smell's wrong. That's a brick factory. They're making bricks.

'Bricks? Not a chance!' the brick-maker roared, red in the face. 'I'm damned if I'll have them coming around here, making bricks! No, no, it's something else. Must be glass. They're making bottles and glasses.'

Day after day the talk went on, but there was still no sign of the product. Not that the men at the factory were slacking off. Black smoke billowed daily from the chimney, and through the knothole you could see the two sons and the father, black with grease, working away like mad. You had only to stroll past the place to hear the machine's endless thunka-thunka-thunka.

'When do those people *rest*?' the townspeople wondered whenever they peeked through the knothole.

'What incredible workers!'

'I've never seen anyone work like that!

'I want my son to see this!'

「私はパンではなく、タドンだと思うよ。パンを焼く時にはあんな黒い煙は出さない。あれはタドンを作る煙さ」

もちろん、タドン屋さんはそうは思っていません。

「タドンじゃないさ。匂いでわかる。あれはね、レンガ工場だよ。レンガを作っているのさ」

「レンガだって？　とんでもない」

今度はレンガ屋さんが顔を真赤にして怒鳴りました。

「レンガなんか作られてたまるもんか。あれはね、何か別のものさ。きっとガラスだね、コップだとかビンを作ってるに違いないよ」

人々のうわさは毎日続きましたが、工場の製品はなかなか出来上ってきません。もちろん、工場がさぼってるわけではないのです。煙突は毎日、真黒い煙をモクモクと吐いておりましたし、節穴からのぞくとお父さんも二人の息子も、真黒になって忙しそうに働いているのです。工場のそばを通っただけで、機械の動くゴトゴトという音が、休みなく聞こえてきます。

「あの人たち、いったいいつ休むのかしら？」

節穴からのぞく度に、街の人々はいつもそう考えました。

「本当によく働くわね」

「あんなに勤勉な人たち、私、見たことないわ」

「うちの息子に今度、見せてやりましょう」

'I'm going to tell my husband he needs to do better!'

All the people in this town much preferred relaxing to working. And why not? The crops in the fields grew by themselves, the sea yielded more fish than they could eat, and you could work hard and save all the money you liked, but there was still nothing to spend it on.

Once the factory turned up, though, people's ideas began to change. That black smoke billowing up so bravely from the little factory stirred everyone deeply. From the hilltop you could see the whole town, sleepily nestled in green. The factory alone looked sturdy, like a steam locomotive chugging through the fields.

'That's what I call *bold*!' the boys looking down from up there exclaimed to one another.

'That's what I call *macho*!'

Meanwhile, their mothers and big sisters kept egging them on.

'The factory starts work at 7 a.m., you know.'

'They take only ten-minute breaks.'

'They work with the lights on after dark.'

The boys pulled themselves together and tried getting up early and going to bed late. They still had no work to do, though. They could only wander around town looking busy and

「私、主人に話して聞かせるわ」

街の人たちは、どちらかというとのんびりしている方が好きな人ばかりでした。

それというのも、畑の作物は放っておいても育ちましたし、海のお魚は食べきれないほどとれましたし、一所懸命働いてお金をためても、使いみちがなかったからです。

しかしその工場が出来てからは、人々の考えも少し変りました。誰でも、その小さな工場の煙突から真黒い煙がモクモクと勇ましく出てくるのを見ると、ひどく感激してしまうのです。丘の上から見ると、緑に囲まれたのんびりした街の中で、工場だけが田んぼの中を走る蒸気機関車のように力強く見えます。

「何て勇ましいんだろう」

「何て男らしいんだろう」

若い男の子たちは、丘の上から工場を見下して、そう言いかわしました。その上お母さんたちや、お姉さんたちがしきりにそそのかします。

「工場の人たちはね、朝の七時から仕事を始めてるわよ」

「工場の人たちはね、お昼休みも十分しか休まないの」

「工場の人たちはね、暗くなるまで電気をつけて働いているわ」

そこで若い男の子たちも、決心して朝早く起きてみたり、夜遅くまで起きていたりして、街中を何となく忙しそうにウロウロ歩きまわって、みましたが、肝心の仕事がありません、

end up at the factory fence. They took turns at the knothole, sighing with envy.

'Their eyes are so bright!'

'Look at that sweat! He doesn't even wipe it off!'

'And those arms! He picked up that heavy hammer like nothing!'

The factory kept at it, but there was still no sign of a product.

'They're really working, though. It'll be fantastic, whatever they're making.'

'Absolutely! Look what a big machine they have!'

The townspeople kept picturing this product or that, and they could hardly wait for it to come on sale.

'Still, don't you think there's a little too much smoke coming from that chimney?'

'Actually, yes, I suppose there is. The sky always seems kind of cloudy.'

The black smoke kept boiling up from the factory chimney. Day after day the sky over the town, once blue, stayed grey.

'They can't help it, though. It's such a big machine!'

'I just know they're racing to get the product out as soon as they can.'

結局工場のまわりにみんな集まってしまうのでした。節穴から代りばんこに中の様子をうかがって、うらやましそうにため息をつくのです。

「目がいきいきとしているね」

「あの汗を見ろよ、ふこうともしないんだぜ」

「たくましい腕だなあ、あの重そうなハンマーを片手で持ち上げたよ」

ところで、工場は相変らず忙しそうに活動しておりましたが、その製品はまだいっこうに出来上ってこないのでした。

「あれだけ一所懸命作っているんだもの、きっと凄いものが出来るよ」

「そうね、そうに違いないわ。あんなに大きな機械があるんですものね」

街の人たちは、出来上ってくる製品をあれこれ想像しながら、それが市場で売り出される日を楽しみに、そんな話をしておりました。

「でも、どうなんでしょう。あの煙突の煙はちょっと、物凄すぎますわねえ」

「そういえば、そうです。空が何となくいつも曇っているような感じがしますね」

「とにかく、毎日毎日、真黒い煙があとからあとから吹き上げてくるのです。青く澄んでいたその街の空も、どんよりと曇っているような日が続きました。

「あれだけ大きな機械を動かしているんだから、しようがないでしょう」

「きっと、一日も早く新製品を作りたいと思って、がんばっているんですわ」

'It's got to be something good.'

'Yes, indeed.'

One of the boys who got up early one morning let out a great shout in front of his house.

'Hey! Look! The factory's got *two* chimneys!'

Everyone within earshot came out to see, rubbing their sleepy eyes. The sight was impressive. Two great smokestacks now towered over the little factory, spewing two thick columns of black smoke into the dawn sky. The smoke drifted heavily, lazily towards the town. You could just make out tiny black specks glittering down from it.

'That's awesome!'

'That smoke makes me feel a sort of power rising up inside me.'

'They must've reached the last stage. That's why they've added another stack. They know how much we look forward to what they're making, and they're rushing to get it done.'

'What's it going to be?'

'Something amazing, something we can really use.'

'I'm sure you're right.'

Every day after that the twin stacks belched out twin columns of smoke. What with the soot, the people could no longer walk about

「いいものが出来るんでしょうね」

「出来ますとも……」

或る日の事です。　朝早く起きた若い男の子の一人が、家の前でビックリして大声を出しました。

「おい、見ろよ。　工場の煙突が二本になったぞ」

聞いた街の人々が起きたばかりの目をこすりながら出てみますと、何という勇ましさでしょう。小さな工場に、のしかかるような大きな煙突が二本立ち、夜が明けたばかりの空に、もう太い真黒な煙を、モクモクと吐いているのです。煙は、重々しくゆっくりと街の方へ流れ、よく見ると、黒い小さなものが、チラチラと舞い落ちてきております。

「勇ましいもんですね」

「あの煙を見ていると、何か腹の底から、力が湧いてくるような気がします」

「きっと、最後の仕上げにはいったのでしょう。　だから煙突を二本にしたんです。　私たちが待ちこがれているのを知って、工場の人たちも急いで作ろうとしているのですよ」

「何が出来るのでしょう?」

「きっと素晴しいものですよ、そして私たちの役に立つものです」

「そうですね」

二本の煙突は、それから毎日二本の煙を吐き出しました。　街の人たちは、落ちてくるスス

with their eyes open. Their throats were so sore that they coughed every minute or two. Laundry hanging on the line, their clothing, even their faces turned black. Still, they put up with it all patiently, sure that the product would be something truly special.

At last one day, though, they couldn't take it any more. They went to talk things over with the mayor.

'We're wondering what to do. The smoke is so bad now. We hate to complain to such hard workers, but couldn't we at least get them to tell us when they'll have their product ready and what it'll be?'

'I see what you mean. We can hold out a little longer if they're making something really good. All right, let's go and hear what they have to say.'

The mayor and the townspeople trooped out to the factory, coughing and brushing off the soot as they went.

'Hello, gentlemen of the factory!'

Out came the hard-working factory chief, his blackened face beaming.

'Hello! So it's you, Mr Mayor! And everyone else, too? What's up?'

'You see, the people of the town would like to know when your product will be out.'

'Oh, is *that* it? Then, I have good news. It's finally ready.'

'Really? It *is*?'

'Yes. Come right in. I'll show you. You will all be very pleased.'

で目を開けて歩けないほどでしたし、喉はガラガラで一分おきにゴホンゴホンとセキをしましたし、洗濯物も着ているものも顔も真黒になりましたが、それでもきっと素晴しいものが出来るのだろうと考えて、じっと我慢しました。

でもとうとう或る日、街の人々はやり切れなくなって市長さんに相談しました。

「どうでしょう。煙がかなりひどくなりましたし、一所懸命働いている工場の人たちには悪いのですが、せめて、いつどんなものが出来るのかだけでも教えてもらったら……？」

「そうだね、もし本当にいいものが出来るのなら、私たちも、もう少し我慢してもいい、とにかく、行って聞いてみよう」

市長さんと街の人たちは、すすをはらいながら、ゴホンゴホンとセキをしながら、ゾロゾロと工場までやってきました。

「こんにちは、工場のみなさん」

「やあ、市長さんですか。それにみなさんおそろいで、どうなさいました？」

働きものの工場長さんが、真黒い顔をニコニコさせながら出てきました。

「実はね、街の人たちがみんな、お宅の製品がいつ出来るのか聞きたいと言うんだよ」

「ああ、そのことですか、それなら喜んで下さい。とうとう出来上りました」

「何、出来上った？」

「ええ、まあどうぞ。お入り下さい。これからお見せしましょう。みなさんに、きっとよろ

Cheering, the townsfolk followed the chief inside. He and his sons welcomed them with smiles.

'Now, have a look at this!'

He pointed to a shiny little machine next to the great big one they'd seen through the knothole. Pearl-like beads were popping out one end and dropping into a hopper.

The chief handed the mayor a bead. The mayor stared at it in his hand.

'Umm, what is this?'

'Put it in your mouth! It's a cough drop.'

'A cough drop?'

The people cheered loudly again. Just then, you see, they were coughing so much that they could hardly breathe.

'Yes, indeed. Ladies and gentlemen, our product is cough drops. They are a little expensive, but they really work!'

'So you *have* been making something wonderful!'

'It's exactly what we need right now!'

'I'll take one this minute!'

街の人々は、ワッと歓声をあげながら、案内されて工場の中に入りました。工場長も二人の息子さんも、ニコニコしながら、みんなをむかえます。

「さあ、これを見て下さい」

工場長の指さす方を見ると、節穴から見えた大きな機械の隣に、キラキラ光る小さな機械があって、その先の方から真珠のようなものが、ポトリポトリと落ちております。

「何ですか、これは?」

市長さんは、渡されたその真珠のようなものを手にとって眺めながら言いました。

「飲んでみて下さい。それはつまり、セキ止めの薬なんです」

「セキ止めの薬ですって?」

街の人々は、もう一度大きな歓声をあげました。何故って街の人々はその時、息がつけないほどゴホンゴホンやっていたからです。

「そうです。みなさん、私たちはセキ止めの薬を作っていたんです。これは少し高価いものですが、とても良く効きます」

「何ていいものを作ってくれたんだろう」

「私たち、ちょうど今、それが欲しかったんですの」

「早速、いただきますわ」

They bought the drops straight from the hands of the smiling chief and his sons and began taking them, right there in the factory. Meanwhile the mayor asked his burning question.

'Excuse me, Mr Factory Chief, I understand that the little machine makes cough drops. But what does the big one make?' He gestured towards the big machine that the townsfolk had seen through the knothole. 'It has two smokestacks, after all. It must make something even better.'

'Oh, that one?' the chief asked, still beaming. 'That one doesn't make anything.'

'It doesn't make *anything*?'

'No. Just smoke. We had quite a time, you know, putting up that second stack. Still, when you get right down to it, two stacks put out a lot more smoke than one.'

ニコニコした工場長と二人の息子さんの手から、人々が薬を買ってその工場で飲み始める

と、市長さんはどうしても聞いてみたかったことを聞いてみました。

「ねえ、工場長さん。その小さい方の機械は薬を作るためのものだったんでしょうけど、こ

の大きな機械は何を作ってるんです?」

そう言って街の人々が節穴から眺めた大きな機械を指さしました。

「煙突が二本もついているんですから、きっと、もっと素晴しいものを作っているんでしょ

うね」

「あ、それですか」

工場長さんは相変らずニコニコしながら答えました。

「それは、何も作りません」

「何も作らないんですって?」

「ええ、それは煙を出すだけです。これに煙突を二本つける仕事には苦心しましたよ。でも、

何といっても、一本より二本の方が煙を沢山出しますからね」

KŌNO TAEKO

In the Box

Translated by Jay Rubin

It wasn't as if I'd had an unpleasant experience while I was out that day. I wasn't especially tired, either; in fact, I came back in a good mood. I stepped into the lift and pressed 'Door Close' and '3', but when I saw another woman rushing towards the closing door, I pressed 'Door Open'.

Hugging a large paper-wrapped package, she stepped through the reopened door to join me in the lift, but she spoke not a word of thanks. Even so, once I had pressed 'Door Close' again, I might have asked this woman with her arms full 'What floor?' and pressed the button for her, but before I could do so, she said:

'Ninth floor, please.'

Without a word, I pressed '9', but I felt sorry I hadn't simply ignored her. It was her problem she had chosen to have her arms wrapped around such a big package: she shouldn't be imposing on other people that way.

I fumed over the woman's rudeness in the few breaths it took the box containing the two of us to rise to the third floor. When it stopped and the door opened, on an impulse I ran my hand over the

河野多恵子

箱の中

その日、私は外出先で不快な出来事に出会ったわけではない。さして疲れてもおらず、穏やかな気分で帰ってきたのである。私はエレベーターに踏み入って釦板の「閉」と「3」のところを押したが、締まりかけた扉へ駆けてくる女の姿を認めると、「開」の釦を押えて乗せてやった。

開き直した扉から、女は大きな紙包みを両手で抱いて同乗してきた。が、ありがとうとも、すみませんとも、言わなかった。それでも、私はもう一度「閉」の釦を押すついでに、両手の塞がっている女に、「何階で?」と訊いて釦を押してやったかもしれなかった。ところが、それより早く、女は言った。

「九階、お願いします」

私は黙って、「9」の釦を押してやった。が、無視しなかったことを後悔した。大きな包みを抱えているのは彼女の勝手である。当然のように人手を煩わすことはないのである。二人を入れた箱が三階へ突きあがってゆく数呼吸の間に、私は女の無礼に心の中でそう息まき、箱が停って扉が開くと、咄嗟の思いつきで、釦板に手を走らせた。「4」の釦から既

rest of the buttons – from the '4' past her damned '9' with its light already glowing.

'There you go,' I said. 'I've pressed them all for you.'

Leaving her with these words and a panel full of glowing buttons, I stepped out of the lift.

'Of all the –' I heard behind me and turned to find the woman struggling to pull her keys from her handbag without losing her grip on the big package.

Usually if there were still people in the lift when I got off at the third floor, I would press 'Door Close' for them on my way out. People exiting at the second floor would often perform the same kindness for me. The door would eventually close on its own, but it took a very long time – so long you sometimes wondered if the door were broken.

If you pressed 'Door Close', the door would close right away. No one remaining in the lift would ever wait for the door to close automatically, and so it was a nice gesture for people getting off to not simply walk away but to press the button on their way out. 'Thank you', 'Thanks', 'I appreciate it': such phrases would naturally be exchanged in the process.

In taking my revenge on the woman by illuminating all the buttons, however, the one button I naturally chose *not* to press was the 'Door Close' button. I hurried away while the door remained open with the woman in full view. Now that she not only had her arms wrapped around that big package but also had her keys pulled halfway out, she would have to struggle to push the 'Door Close' button; otherwise, the door would seem as if it were never going to close and let her continue to the next floor. Even if the person getting out before her had not been me but someone else who failed to do her the kindness of pressing 'Door Close', she would have had no way

にランプの点いている忌々しい「9」の釦の次まで、素早く触れて、

「皆、押しておきましたわ」

ランプだらけにした釦板とその言葉を残して、外へ出る。「まあ！」と言うのが聞こえ、振り返ると、女は大きな紙包みを抱えた手で、扱いにくそうにハンドバッグから鍵を取り出しかけていた。

日頃、三階でエレベーターを降りる私は、箱の中に残っている人があると、外へ踏み出すついでに、大抵は「閉」の釦を押しておいた。二階で降りる人たちから、そういう心遣いを受けることもある。放っておいても締まる扉だが、締まるまでにはえらく間がある。

「閉」の釦を押すと、早速締まる。内の人は自動的に締まるのを待っているようなことは誰もしないから、降りっ放しにしないで釦を押して往く心遣いは感じがいい。「すみません」「どうも」「ありがとう」などと、つい言い、言われる。

しかし、女に対する意趣返しで、釦板をランプだらけにした私は、勿論「閉」の釦を押すことは逆に省略した。私はまだ扉が開いていて女の姿が丸見えになっているうちに、早々とそこを立ち去ったけれども、両手で大きな紙包みを抱えていたうえに鍵まで取りだしかけていた女は、難儀をしながら「閉」の釦を押すか、そうでなければ故障でもしたのかと思うほど待たされなければ扉は締まらず、運びあげられてはゆかないのだ。しかも、最初の一回だけは、先に降りたのが私でなくても、そうした場合の心遣いをしない人であれば仕方はない

around this struggle, but now she would face the same dilemma on every floor. Fourth floor, fifth, sixth, seventh, eighth: every time, the car would stop and the door would open for nothing. And the way the lift worked, even if you kept the 'Door Close' button pressed, when a number of buttons had been pushed the car would not bypass a floor. By the time she reached her destination, the woman would have had to repeatedly struggle to make the open door close or be kept waiting on every floor until the door closed automatically. 'There you go, I've pressed them all for you' – what a marvellous line!

The memory of that day would often come to me after that when I boarded the lift and pressed the buttons. Perhaps because I used the lift at irregular times and some days didn't take it at all, I never rode with the woman again. I had the impression that I had never encountered her before that day, but judging from the way she went straight for her keys while holding her big package, she was almost certainly a resident of the building. Apparently, although we both lived there, we always missed each other. These occasional thoughts about the woman made me more considerate than before whenever people boarded the lift after me – perhaps because I was ashamed of myself for having taken rather excessive revenge that day. And perhaps I wanted to believe that I was not usually like that: I had done what I did because the woman had been so ill-mannered. If people thanked me for letting them on, I would often ask them 'What floor?' even if they were not carrying anything.

That day, too, I asked 'What floor?' in a show of thoughtfulness.

にしても、女はそのあと各階ごとにそんな目を見なくてはならない。四階、五階、六階、七階、八階——そのたびに、箱は停止し、無駄に扉が開く。それぞれの釦が押してあれば、「閉」の釦を押し続けていても、箱は通過しない仕組みになっている。女は九階に着くまで、各階で一々開く扉の後始末に手古摺るか、自動的に締まるまで一々待たされなくてはならない。

「皆、押しておきましたわ」とは、何と小気味のよい科白だろう。

以後、私はエレベーターに乗って釦を押しながら、ふとその日のことを思いだすことがあった。

私がエレベーターを使う時刻が不規則で、全く乗らない日もあるせいか、その後は一度も女と乗り合わせたことがなかった。以前に会った印象もない女だった。が、大きな荷物を抱えながら、エレベーターの中で早々と鍵を取りだしていた様子からすると、やはり住人にちがいないと思われた。互いに住人でありながら、いつも擦れちがっているらしかった。私はふとそんなことを思う一方、あとから同乗者があると、以前よりも又少し心遣いを見せがちになっていた。あの日の度の過ぎた意趣返しを恥じたからかもしれない。あるいは、自分が自分があんなことをしたのも相手が不躾な女だからであって、普通はそうではないと、自分を認めたかったからかもしれない。「すみません」とあとから乗り込んできた人が荷物を持っていなくても、「何階で？」と私は親切に釦を押すことがあるのだった。

その日も、私はやはり箱の中で心遣いを見せて言った。

'Ninth, please.'

Automatically, I pressed '9', but the person continued almost as if she had been waiting for this moment, 'Or if you like, press them all.'

I realized that I had not had a good look at the woman's face either that first day or now. Still, I couldn't let her get away with taking her revenge for that day by exploiting my act of kindness. Perhaps she realized that I would end up the loser either way – whether I pushed all the buttons from 4 to 8 again in compliance with her challenge or she managed to reach the ninth floor without incident.

'Fine, I'll do that.'

As I said this, I ran my hand up the button panel, which instantly lit up. That same moment, the lift came to a stop. I stared hard at the red button with its white-engraved 'Emergency'. Had the doors opened, I was planning to press the 'Door Close' button, announce 'I'll press this for you, too', hit the red button and slip out through the closing doors.

But the doors did not open. Normally, the doors opened right away even without the aid of the 'Door Open' button . . . I pressed 'Door Open', but still they did not open.

「何階で?」

「九階ですの」

私は何気なく、「9」の釦を押した。すると、それを待っていたかのように、相手はこうつけ加えたのである。

「——およろしかったら、全部でも」

私は、あの日もその日も、ろくに女の顔を見なかったことに気がついた。それにしても、ひとの好意に乗じて、今度は逆にあの日の意趣返しをしようとする女が許せなかった。女は私に「4」から「8」までの釦を更に押させるか、それが厭ならば事もなく自分に九階まで行かせるか、どちらをとっても私がしてやられた恰好になることを承知しているのかもしれなかった。

「ええ、押しましょう」

言うなり、私は釦板に手を走らせた。忽ち、ランプだらけになる。折柄、箱が停った。私はこれまで一度も触れたことのない赤に白で「非常ベル」と彫ってある釦を見定めた。扉が開いたならば、「閉」の釦を押し、「これも、押しておきますわ」と赤い釦を押しざま、締まりかかる扉の外へ身を転じるつもりだったのである。

ところが、扉は開かなかった。開く時には、放っておいても早速に開く扉なのだが……。

私は「開」の釦を押してみた。が、やはり開かない。

'We haven't reached the third floor yet,' the woman said behind me. 'The light is still on.'

Of course, she was right.

'Still,' the woman continued, 'it has definitely stopped, hasn't it? It must be broken.'

Perhaps I had thrown it off-kilter by hitting all those buttons at once so roughly.

'You can always use this if you're in a hurry,' I said, pointing to the emergency button and moving away from the panel to let her see it.

'No, I'm in no hurry,' she said with a wave of the hand, leaning against the back wall of the lift.

I, too, leaned back, giving her a view of my profile.

「まだ、三階じゃありませんわね」

と背後で女が言った。

なるほど、その通りなのだった。「ランプが消えていませんもの」

「でも、停まってはいますわね。故障したのでしょう」

女がまた言う。故障したのは、あまりに手早く、激しく、沢山の釦を押したからかもしれ

なかった。

「お急ぎでしたら、こういうものもありますから、どうぞ」

私は非常ベルを指して女に言い、釦板のまえを退いてみせた。

「急ぎませんの」

と女は手を振って、背後の板にもたれかかった。

私も彼女に横顔を見せる位置で、背後にもたれかかった。

KAWAKAMI MIEKO

Dreams of Love, Etc.

Translated by Yoshio Hitomi

I don't know what these particular roses are called – there are hundreds of different species in the world, after all. But roses they are, for certain. Under the cloudy June sky, I see the buds on the new green stems that stretch out left and right, some still small and tight and some about to bloom, and I sometimes wonder what it is that makes them so obviously roses. Is it the thorns, the petals, or something else? Somewhere in the world, there must be roses that have shapes and colours and clusters that I could never imagine, and if I were to encounter them unexpectedly, perhaps on a journey – in Edinburgh or maybe Macedonia – what then? Yet, even if I had never laid eyes on them before, I would know . . . right. As I water my flowers with an insanely long hose that leaks at the nozzle – it must be torn or rotten or something – I let my thoughts wander this morning, the way they do every morning.

There is one decent flower shop in the arcade near the train station. By decent, I mean you can pop in, give them a price and count

川上未映子

愛の夢とか

ばらの花には何百という種類があるから、このばらの、ほんとうの名前はわからない。でもこれが、ばらだということはわかる。六月の曇り空の下で、左右に伸び広がっていく新しいみどりの茎のさきざきについた、固いのやすぐにでも咲こうとしているつぼみを見ていると、どこをみて、これがばらだとわかるのだろうと、ときどき不思議な気持ちになる。刺がみえるし、花びらも、やっぱりどこかしらがばらだから、見るだけでそれはばらということがわかってしまう。でもきっと、世界には、あたりまえだけどわたしの想像もつかないかたちと色とふさをもったばらの花というのは存在していて、たとえば思いがけない旅先で──エジンバラとかマケドニアとか？──それらに遭遇したら、どうなんだろう。でも、それがどんなにはじめてみるばらであっても、それがばらであるなら、それはばらであることを、わたしはただちに知るだろう──なんちって。持ち手のところが破れているのか腐っているのかわからないけど、とにかく水が漏れつづけていていやになる馬鹿みたいにくるくると長いホースで水をやりながら、今朝もぼーっとそんなことを考えた。まともっていうのは、ぱっと入って値段をいっ駅前にはひとつだけまともな花屋がある。

on them to make a nice bouquet. That day, I saw they had some with white flowers and tiny dark green leaves, and, wanting to, in a way, celebrate the beautiful weather, I said to the shopkeeper, Could I have three of those rose bushes please?

As I was paying, I added, I've never bought flowers that weren't pre-cut, and the overly plump girl said with an overly large smile, This one here, it'll bloom all year long if you take good care of it. Buoyed by her swelling presence, I returned the girl's smile and said with a wave, I'll take good care of it.

The big earthquake hit two months after we bought a house near the river, and for a while I felt depressed and out of sorts. My husband has always maintained that there's nothing to worry about in Tokyo – who knows if he really believes that or if he's just fooling himself? A month after the earthquake, though, my tension and anxiety were starting to wear off, and then before I knew it spring had passed by in a daze. That's how I ended up buying the roses. I recall the flower shop that day was crowded with local housewives and mothers. One practically shoved her face into the bushy pots of ivy and olive, pointed to the colourful flowers in the back of the cool glass case and said, Could I have more of those? Others said things like, You'll call me when new ones come in, won't you? or, Actually, I'll have some of these too. They bustled back and forth in the narrow shop with armloads of plants as if in some kind of competition. I remember thinking how tasteless one woman's oversized purse was with its pimply grey ostrich leather.

て花束をまかせられそうかどうかが基準。深いみどりの小さな葉に白い花を咲かせているのが目に留まって、その日はわりにすばらしいような天気だったからそのことを何となく記念して、このばら、みっつください。なといってみた。代金を払うとき、切り花じゃないのを買うのははじめてなんですよとつけくわえると、この子、丁寧に世話をすると一年中咲いてくれますよ、なんてものすごい笑顔ですごく太った店の女の子が笑うので、わたしもそのヴォリュームの余韻をかりて笑顔をつくって、大事にしますと手をふった。

川の近くに家を買って、二ヶ月したらとても大きな地震がきて、しばらくはゆうっつでぐったりしていた。夫はわざとそう思いこんでいるのか、ほんとうにそういう感想なのか、東京は何の心配もないと最初から今まで一貫してそういうスタンス。そして地震の日から一ヶ月もたてば、緊張も心配もゆうつもたしかにどんどん薄まりはじめて、気がつけばぼんやりした春を通過していて、ばらなんかを買ってみたというわけだ。そういえば、あの日の花屋はそのあたりの主婦というか母親というかそういった人たちでなんだかずいぶん混みあっていて、アイビーとかオリーブとかふさふさしたのに顔をうんと近づけて、それから冷えたガラス戸の奥にある色つきの花を指さして、これもっといただける、おなじのが入ったら連絡して、やっぱりこれもいただくわ、なんて口々に言ってまるで競いあうように植物を抱えて狭いところをいったりきたりしているんだった。わたしは、そのとき目に入った財布の色なんかを覚えてる。灰色のぶつぶつのオーストリッチの長財布なんて、すごく趣味がわるいな

That evening, I asked my husband when he came home from work, Do you think people buy flowers and things because it makes them feel safer to pretend that everything is back to normal?

Yeah, there's probably something to that.

So much for that topic.

Oh, that reminds me of a story I heard – or maybe read somewhere. You know some mixed couples, they apparently fight over whether to leave Japan or not. They get caught between the Japanese partner saying they shouldn't leave no matter what and the foreign partner saying they'd be crazy not to leave in such an emergency. They have so much trouble putting those feelings into words, a lot of them have ended up divorcing. That's what I read.

Hmm, well it's true that people are dealing with a lot these days, my husband said before slipping from my sight as usual.

But I had been hoping to say more. At the very least we're both Japanese, you and me – I don't know, who knows what will happen, maybe there'll be a big explosion and we'll all die – but still don't you think we're better off than they are? Because we're inherently the same, even if that means we're just resigned to our fate. And maybe that's not such a bad thing? That was what I wanted to say.

My husband comes home late. Usually I try not to think about how I fill my days when I'm alone, and when I do, it depresses

と思ったことも覚えてる。

それでその夜、帰ってきた夫にちょっと話してみたんだった。みんな花でも買って、なんか日常っぽい感じを演出して安心とかしたいのかな。そういうのはあるだろうね。話はそこで終わってしまった。そうだ、そういえばさ、こんな話きいたよ。っていうか、読んだよ。外国人同士の夫婦とかでさ、日本を離れるか離れないかですごくもめるらしいんだよ。なにがあっても逃げたくないっていう日本人の倫理と、こんな非常時に出国しないなんて信じられないっていう外国人の考えがあって、そのお互いの気持ちをうまく言葉にすることができなくって、けっきょく別れた人たちけっこういるってそういう話、読んだ。まあ、いろんなことが試されてるのは間違いないねと夫は言って、いつものようにそそくさとわたしからは見えない場所へ行ってしまった。でもわたしの話にはつづきがあって、わたしたちは最低でもおなじ日本人だから、なんていうのかな、どうなるかはわからないけど、もしかしたら何かが爆発して死んでしまうかもしれないけれど、むずかしいことはよくわからないけど、彼らよりはまだましなんじゃないのかな。なんていうか、先天的な一致の部分で。あきらめっていうか、そういう部分で。そしてそれはちょっといいことなんじゃないのかなって、そういう話だったんだけど。

夫の帰りはおそい。わたしはひとりで過ごす一日をいったい何で埋めているのか、ふだん考えることはないけれど、だからときどき考えてみようとすると気がめいるから、ほとんど

me. I don't work. I'm not pregnant. Housework for two, washing and cleaning, takes two hours at most, even now that we live in a proper house. I don't watch TV. I don't read books. Come to think of it, I don't do anything. I don't take lessons, and I don't have the skills or the patience to cook a fancy meal. I really don't do anything at all. Stretched out on the sofa, I would hear a piano trilling away somewhere every day. It sounded so good I thought it was a recording at first, but sometimes it would break off or repeat a passage so I knew it was someone practising. Or maybe that was part of the interpretation? In any case, it would start at random hours. Sometimes at nine in the morning, sometimes in the evening, sometimes as late as ten o'clock at night. So someone is playing a piano somewhere, but that someone is not me. Whenever I start thinking about how I do absolutely nothing at all, these pairs of white doors slide open behind my forehead, one after another, and once I dozed off and had a really pointless dream. I want to avoid things like that. But I can't help thinking about it sometimes, so the other day I sat down at the dining table and wrote the Chinese character for *what*. It felt like a totally useless exercise, until I discovered that the character for *what* looks exactly like my face when you examine it closely.

So that's how I go about my days, doing nothing, but since buying the roses I started picking up some potted plants when I was in the mood, and now I have quite a collection. We don't have a garden,

しない。仕事もしていないし、妊娠しているわけでもないし、ふたりぶんの家事なんて洗濯とか掃除とか、まあ一軒家になって多少広くなったとはいっても、そんなの二時間あれば済んでしまうし、テレビもみないし本も読まない。考えてみれば何もしていないし、凝った料理をつくる根気も技もないし、ほんとうに何もしていない。ソファで横になってると、毎日どこかからぼーんぼーんっていうピアノの音が聴こえてくる。けっこう上手くてはじめは録音した曲なのかと思ったけれど、途中で切れたりやりなおしたりしてるから誰かの練習だってことがわかった。あるいは表現？　いずれにせよ時間はばらばら。朝九時に聴こえてくることもあれば、夕方のときもあるし、最高におそくて夜の十時のときもある。そんなふうに誰かはピアノを弾いているけど、わたしはピアノを弾いていない。わたしの何もしていなさについて考えはじめると、どういうわけか、おでこのうらに真っ白なふすみたいなのがぱたんぱたんと広がっていくのがみえて、いつだったかそのまま昼寝をしたときにとても無駄な夢をみたから、ああいうの、かかわりたくないなって思ってしまう。だけどやっぱりときどきは考えてしまうときもあるから、このあいだはダイニングテーブルにむかってとりあえず、何って字を書いてみた。まったく意味のない時間だったけど、それはそれで発見したこともあって、よくよくみると何って字はわたしの顔にそっくりなのだ。そんなふうに何もしていないわたしだけれど、ばらの花をきっかけに、気がむいたら植物の鉢植えなんかをぽつぽつ買うようになっていって、今ではけっこうな数になった。庭はな

so they're all laid out around the edge of the front porch. I set a pot of ivy on top of the lamp post attached to the mailbox and let the leaves dangle like hair. I put a potted olive tree next to it, and underneath a row of maidenhair ferns, violets, eucalyptus and those robust little blue flowers that I can never remember the name of. And some chocolate cosmos too, so they looked just so, like the entrance of a café. I transplanted those first roses into larger pots, and to my surprise, they expanded so shamelessly that their size almost doubled. The buds kept multiplying like rabbits. I visited online forums to learn how to plant different varieties in a single pot, and while I was there bought all sorts of things, like a shovel, fertilizer and those little pebbles that you line the bottom of pots with. I bought special scissors and started snipping off the yellow and black leaves that were no longer healthy. That made me feel good, like I was giving someone a haircut.

The more I got into it, the more I started to wonder about other people's gardens and flower beds, and so I began going for walks every morning. You could easily tell which plants were being well taken care of and which were not. Seeing neglected flowers or trees always reminded me of my childhood. I saw countless camellias – one of the few flowers I could identify – growing straight and sober. They seemed to be popular around here. Their thick, oily petals had always struck me as artificial, and I wondered why so many people

いから玄関のポーチみたいなところ。郵便受けといっしょになってる外灯のてっぺんにはアイビーの鉢をおいて髪の毛みたいにだらりと垂らして、わきにはオリーブの鉢植え、その下にはアジアンタム、すみれ、ユーカリ、あと何度きいても覚えられない小さな青い花のこちょこちょした、でもすごく丈夫なやつに、それからチョコレートコスモスをそれっぽく並べたりなんかした。それっぽくっていうのは、カフェの入り口みたいなああいう感じ。最初のばらは大きな鉢に植えかえてやると、恥ずかしいくらいに盛りあがって、気がつけば倍ぐらいにひろがってるから驚いた。うさぎみたいにあとからあとからつぼみがふえる。ほかには寄せ植えのやりかたもネットの掲示板でおしえてもらって、スコップとか肥料とか、鉢の底にしく小さい石ころとか、そういうのもネットでそろえた。あと、専用のはさみなんかも買って、黄色くなったり黒くなったりしてだめになった葉っぱとかをざくざく切って、それこそ散髪するような感じがあってそれはすこし気分がよかった。

そんなふうにやりはじめると、よそのうちの庭というか花壇事情も気になりだして、朝はそのためにかかさず散歩にでかけるようになった。手入れをしている植物とそうでない植物は一目瞭然。放っておかれてだんだんだめになっていく花とか木とかを見つけると子どものころを思いだす。それから、花のことなんか何も知らないわたしがかろうじて知っている花のひとつ、つばきはこのあたりじゃとても人気があるみたいで、すごく実直な感じで生えているのを数えきれないくらいみた。油っぽい壁みたいなつばきをみると、いつも無理矢理っ

planted these walls of camellias around their houses. Well, apparently camellias prevent fire, and come to think of it they really do look impervious to flames, so I guess it's a good thing.

I sometimes fantasize about our house being broken into. Of course it wouldn't be an ordinary burglary. It would be really gory and ghoulish – I'd be torn to shreds and whatnot – and then reporters with nothing better to do would swarm like flies to our house from all over and interview the neighbours, pointing mics at them and asking the usual, What was the victim like? And they would probably answer, Well, yes, we never talked or anything, but I got the impression that she was very fond of gardening. I'd see her taking really good care of her plants in the morning and afternoon, and even at night. These thoughts made me feel a little better as I unravelled the ever-expanding ivy tangles.

One afternoon, I was trimming the overgrown roots of my wild strawberries when I heard the garage door rumble up lazily next door and a Mercedes stuck its nose out. A big car, round and dull. A woman with her arms crossed came out to see the car speed off, though the driver remained in the shadows from where I stood.

ていう言葉がうかんだ。どの家もどの家も、どうしてつばきで建物をくるんでるんだろうって思っていたらそれは火をふせぐ効果があるからで、たしかに簡単には燃えてくれないような顔してる、とそれはそれで感心したりもするんだった。

もし強盗かなにかに入られたら、とわたしはときどき夢想する。もちろん盗まれるだけじゃすまなくて、けっこう派手に――ずたずたに切り裂かれたり、そのほかの手口でわかりやすく惨殺なんかされたりしたら、きっと暇なやつらがわらわらと家のまわりにやってきて近所の人にマイクをむけて、殺されたかたはどんな人だったんですかっていうあのお決まりのコメントを求めるはずだった。そのときわたしはきっと「ええ、お話をしたことはないんですけど、とにかく土いじりのだいすきなかたという感じでしたね。朝も昼も、それから夜もとても熱心に、いつもお手入れされていて。ええ」みたいな感じで語られることになるんだろう。うねりながらまって、どんどんふえようとするアイビーを指先でほぐしながらこれもすこし気分がよかった。

ある日の昼すぎに、根っこが伸びすぎたワイルドストロベリーをじゃきじゃきやってると隣の家の車庫のシャッターのまきあがる気だるい音がして、そこからベンツが鼻をだした。大きな車。まるい鈍さ。見送りにでてきた女の人は胸のあたりで腕を組んで、運転席は陰に なっててよくみえなかったけれど、車はすぐにいきおいよく走り去った。彼女はわたしに気

Noticing me, the woman gave me a very friendly smile and said, Hello there, your flowers always look so lovely, then smiled again.

Oh, not at all, I just buy them and stick them here. I smiled back, just as friendly.

Her face suggested that she was in her early sixties, but the rest of her said seventy. Her hair was almost entirely white, as if the thought of dyeing it had never occurred to her. Her face was no longer firm; devoid of make-up, it had an eerily transparent quality. It reminded me of an old woman I once saw in a sauna or at a hot-springs resort, whose nipples had completely lost their pigment and looked like a child's.

When we first moved here, I had paid courtesy calls around the neighbourhood with boxes of sweets. Since her house had remained silent no matter how many times I rang the doorbell, this was the first time I had had a chance to speak to her.

You have such an eye for flowers. I always enjoy looking at them.

Thank you for saying that. By the way, is there someone who plays the piano in your home? Someone who plays extremely well?

Oh my! That's me – I'm the one playing.

Really! How wonderful. I enjoy listening to it so much. You're a terrific pianist.

がつくと、こんにちは、とすごく感じよく笑っていつもきれいにされてますね、とさらににっこり笑ってみせた。

買ってきたのを並べているだけで、ぜんぜんなんです。

わたしもおなじくらいににっこり笑ってみせた。彼女の年齢は、顔は六十歳前半、そのほかの部分は七十歳前後って感じだった。なにしろ髪のほとんどが白くなっていて染めるとか、そういうことは考えたこともない感じだった。化粧っけのない肌はもちろんもう張りはないけど妙な透明感があって、それはいつだったかサウナか温泉かどこかで見た色素がもう抜けきって子どもみたいになってるおばあちゃんの乳首なんかを思いださせた。

ここに越してきたときに、いちおうの挨拶として菓子折りなんかを持って近所の何軒かの呼び鈴を鳴らしたけれど、彼女の家は何度行っても誰も出てこなかったから、けっきょくともに口をきくのはこれがはじめてだった。

すごくお花のセンスがよくて、いつも楽しませてもらってるの。

うれしいです。ひょっとして、おうちのどなたか、ピアノを弾かれていませんか？　すごく上手なピアノ。

えっ、上手だなんて。あれ、わたしなんです。わたしが弾いてるのよ。

そうだったんですか。なんか感激。わたしこそいつも楽しませてもらってます。とってもお上手なんですね。

Not at all. I played for about ten years when I was growing up, then stopped. I'm embarrassed to say that I only started fooling around with it again in my old age.

That's so nice. I don't know . . . I really envy that you can play for yourself. I think it's wonderful.

The car that left just now, he's the piano tuner. I asked him to sit down and listen to me play, but oh my, I couldn't play at all. When I'm all alone, I somehow manage to play a piece through till the end, but with someone listening I always make mistakes.

But I really thought it was a CD at first.

I wonder which piece that was?

I couldn't say, but I'm sure it's famous since even I recognized it. It goes duum, da, dum in the beginning and then repeats the same notes.

Oh, that's Liszt. Liszt's *Liebestraum*. Dream of Love.

Yes, that sounds right. The melody does sound like it might have a title like that. It's such a pretty piece.

Why don't you come over one of these days? My piano is nothing to listen to, but I could offer you a cup of tea at the very least.

ぐらい飲みにいらしてね。

じゃあ今度、ぜひ遊びにいらして。ピアノは聴かせられるようなものじゃないけど、お茶

きですよね。

そうなんですか、ああ、そうかもしれない。いわれてみればそんな感じのメロディ。すて

リストね、リスト。愛の夢だわ。

思います。たーん、たん、たんっておなじ音が最初のほうで鳴って。

わたしぜんぜん知らないんですけど、わたしでも聴いたことあるからきっと有名な曲だと

何の曲かしら？

でもわたし、最初、CDかと思っちゃいましたよ。

弾けるのに、誰かの耳があると必ず間違えちゃうのよ。

もらったの。じゃあもうだめね、ぜんぜん弾けないの。ひとりのときならいちおう最後まで

さっきの車、調律のかたなんだけど、ちょっと聴いてみてって座ってもらってね、聴いて

らしいですよね。そういうのって。

いいですね。なんていうか、自分自身のために演奏できるなんてうらやましいです。すば

かったの。それでこの歳になってまたゆるゆる弾くようになってしまって。

ぜんぜんなのよ。子どものころ、十年くらいやってたんだけど、もううまったく弾いていな

So the day after the day after next, I bought a pile of colourful macarons at the macaron shop in the arcade, stopped at the Takashimaya department store nearby to pick up the second most expensive box of cherries, and rang her doorbell. It was two o'clock in the afternoon – that most vacant time of the day when the laundry is done and the vacuum put away, but it's still too early to go food shopping. The time when you feel most keenly that you are useless and the world is silently laughing at you from afar. No matter how hard you try to inflate your fantasies, mobilizing all the memories, imaginings and gossip you can muster, you just can't seem to fill up the space. It was right then, when one is stupidly waiting for anything to happen, that I rang the doorbell and soon heard her voice over the intercom. Why hello!

Hello, a friend gave me a big box of cherries – I thought you might like some.

Hold on just a moment, I'll open the door.

Her house seemed much more spacious than mine. It was spotlessly clean and the furniture went together perfectly. Every single piece seemed expensive, every curve had its own particular sheen. There was that distinctive smell that always lingers in other people's homes, which I found pleasing. The large, superbly soft leather couch felt cold on my thighs, but after a few seconds it warmed up. I placed the boxes of macarons and cherries on the coffee table with a polite bow. Thanking me with a smile, she took the two boxes to the kitchen and soon returned with some coffee and the macarons neatly arranged on a plate. I had half expected to see a maid walk

つぎのつぎの、そのまたつぎの日、わたしは駅前のマカロン専門店でカラフルなマカロンをどっさり買って、それから並びの高島屋の地下に二番目に高い値段のついたさくらんぼの箱を買って、呼び鈴を鳴らした。午後の二時。洗濯物をとりこんで掃除機のコードをぬいて買い物にでるまでのみんながいちばん暇な時間。あんたにだけは用がないと離れたところからひそひそと笑われているようなそんな時間。思い出とか想像とかうわさ話とかありとあらゆる手持ちの材料を総動員して妄想をふくらましても、それがうまくふくらんでいるのかどうかもわからないそんな時間。あほみたいな出来事待ちのそんな時間に呼び鈴を一度鳴らして、しばらくすると彼女の声がした。こんにちは。こんにちは。さくらんぼ、たくさんいただいちゃって。もしよかったら。今あけるわ、ちょっと待って。

彼女の家はわたしの家よりずいぶん広いように感じた。きれいに掃除がゆきとどいていて、家具には統一感がばっちりあって、ぜんぶのカーブには重そうな艶がのっていて何もかもがいちいち高そうだった。人の家に独特の、きらいじゃないあの匂いがふわんとしていた。リビングにとおされて革なのにやけにふかふかした大きなソファは太もものうらに触れたとき冷たかったけど、数秒後には体温としっとりなじんで、わたしはテーブルのうえにさくらんぼの箱とマカロンの包を置いてどうぞと言った。彼女はありがとうとにっこり笑ってそのふたつをもってキッチンへゆき、しばらくしてコーヒーとマカロンを感じよく盛った皿と一緒にもどってきた。お手伝いさんが出てきてもおかしくない雰囲気だったけどさすがにそれ

in. I sipped the coffee and took a tiny bite of a macaron. It's such a peculiar feeling, buying macarons. You feel like a complete idiot, and yet that very absurdity makes it somehow satisfying. They're unbearably sweet, and the outer shell never fails to stick to the roof of your mouth, and besides the name is so silly. It's infuriating how overpriced they are, only because people think they're something special. They only remind you that you've never once thought they tasted good.

I'll have the pink one, if you don't mind.

Please. This yellow one is quite exquisite too.

After a while, she began to tell me the history of her relationship with the piano. Her first teacher, her first recital. Bach's Inventions and the effects of age on one's hands and one's ear, etc., etc. I was more curious about what her husband did for a living, or her family members, or about so-and-so in the neighbourhood, or whether property values had really fallen in our area because of the earthquake, or anything that would pass the time – frivolous topics perfect for occasions such as this – but she seemed uninterested in small talk and never asked me about such things either. As I listened to her, remembering to nod from time to time, I began to recognize

はないみたいで、わたしはコーヒーを一口飲んでマカロンをつまんで前歯でちいさく齧った。

ところでマカロンを買うときのあの気分っていったい何だろうといつも思う。自分が掛け値なしの馬鹿になったみたいな気持ちになっていっそ清々しいような気持ちになるあの感じ。ただ甘いだけで蓋みたいなのも上顎にべったりくっついてうっとうしいし、そもそも名前がすごく間抜けだし、中身がないのにそれっぽいってだけで重宝されてみんなほいほい買っていくから値段が高いのもむかつくし、第一おいしいと思ったことなんてこれまでただの一度もないことを思いださせるあの感じ。

じゃあわたし、ピンクのをいただくわ。

どうぞ、この黄色のもおいしいですよ。

しばらくすると彼女は自分とピアノのこと。バッハのインベンションなんとかのこととか、はじめてついた先生のこと。はじめての発表会のこと。そのほかいろいろ。わたしはもっと、たとえば彼女の旦那が何をして稼いでるのかとか、家族構成はどうなってるのかとか、近所の誰それがどうだとか、地震のせいでこのへんの土地が値下がったってきいたけどじっさいのところはどうなのかとか、どうでもいいけどこういう場合にはお誂えむきの軽い話題で時間をつぶしたかったんだけど、彼女はそういう話にはまったく興味がないみたいでわたしにもいっさいそういう感じの質問をしなかった。仕方がないのでうんうんと肯いて彼女の話に耳を傾けていたけれど、

something familiar hidden in the tone of her voice, or maybe in her way of speaking. I didn't know what it was exactly. It felt as if a piece of fabric was fluttering at the edge of my vision. I couldn't tell its colour or size. All I could catch was the fluttering movement. And as I sat listening to this unfamiliar woman tell unfamiliar stories while sitting on an unfamiliar sofa in an unfamiliar house, I felt something loosen up somewhere between my throat and my belly button. It was a kind of aimless, gentle feeling, like someone holding my hand and tracing my palm with their fingers, reminding me of the unsurprising fact that I too was a complete stranger to someone else. But it wasn't the sort of gentle feeling that I could simply surrender myself to. It also reminded me of all the anxieties, jealousies, impulses and passions that had once made me, and those around me, suffer so irrationally – stupid as it sounds as I write about it now – and of the fact that those things have left without a trace, and that what I see now, what I can touch and smell from here onwards, are only remnants of all that once was.

Having talked and nodded and let a certain amount of time go by, we both realized we had nothing more to offer one another, and probably had nothing to begin with. I should be going soon, I said, I had such a wonderful time. As I smiled and gestured to leave, she

そのうち、彼女のしゃべりかたなのか声のトーンなのか、どこかに見覚えのあるものがなんとなくひそんでいることに気がついた。でもそれが何なのかはもちろんわからなかった。布のはしっこが視界のはしっこでちょっと揺れてみせるようなそんな感じ。色もおおきさもわからない。ただ揺れてたってことだけが目に残るようなそんな感じ。それに知らない家の知らない女の人のまえに座って知らないソファにもたれて知らない話をきいていると、喉からへそにかけての何かがゆるやかになっていく感じもした。それは誰かにとっては自分だってただの知らない人なのだというそんなあたりまえのことを、手のひらをやさしくにぎってそこを指でなぞってそっと教えてくれるような、そんなあてのないゆるやかさだった。

でもそれは安心して身をゆだねられる種類のゆるやかさではぜんぜんなかった。それはかつて、わたしやわたしにかかわった数人の人たちをほとんど理不尽にくるしめた不安とか嫉妬とか衝動とか情熱とか――こうして書いてみると馬鹿みたいだけど、そういったものはすでにあとかたもなくわたしを去ってしまって、いま見えているもの、これから触れることができるもの、かぐことのできるものはすべてそれらの残りかすにすぎないんだってことをどうじに教えてくれるからだった。

ひととおりのことを話して、ひととおりのあいづちを打って、それからひととおりの時間がすぎてしまうと、お互いにもう――というか最初から、何も渡しあうものがないことに気がついた。そろそろおいとましますね。

とにっこり笑って腰をあげ

asked, hesitantly, if I wouldn't mind listening to her play just one piece on the piano. Of course, I replied with a reassuring smile, following her into the room with the piano.

The piano was in her bedroom, a spacious room of about fifteen tatami mats; here too, expensive furniture lined the walls with the heavy forthrightness of a coffin for a bear that had lived an admirably ascetic life. Sitting down on the ottoman, I said, What a lovely bedroom. Tell me, Ms . . . I realized that I couldn't remember her name. What was it? What was the name of this woman standing before me? No matter how many times I wiped my imaginary mind with an imaginary cloth, nothing revealed itself. I could have just let it go, but, flustered by the fact that I had completely blanked on her name, I blurted out the question, What should I call you?

Terry, if you will.

Looking me straight in the eye, she said once again: Terry, if you will.

Terry?

Yes, I'd like to be called Terry.

ようとしたときに、彼女がすこし言いにくそうにして、ピアノを一曲だけ聴いていってくれ
ないかとたのんできた。わたしはもちろん、と答えてさらににっこり笑ってみせて、彼女の
あとについてピアノのある部屋に入っていった。

そこは十五畳ぐらいある彼女の寝室で、ここにもまた高級家具が並んでいて、その重く
てまっすぐな感じは禁欲的な一生を送ることに成功した立派な熊のための棺桶を思わせた。
オットマンに腰をおろして、すごくすてきな寝室ですねと言った。あなたの趣味って、とい
いかけて、あなた、というのは何となく面倒な距離を感じさせてよくないと思いなおし、そ
れからわたしは彼女の苗字が思いだせないことに気がついた。なんだったっけ。目のまえの
この女の人って、いったい何さんだったっけ？　どれだけ架空の布で架空の頭の中をぬぐっ
てみてもその架空の布には何のあともつかなかった。べつに家を出るまで名前を呼ばないで
いれば済む話だったんだけれど、苗字をど忘れしてしまったことに動揺していたせいか、わ
たしは思わず、何とお呼びしたらいいですか、と口走ってしまった。

テリーって呼んで。
彼女はわたしの目をまっすぐに見つめてからもう一度言った。
テリーって呼んで。
テリー、ですか。
そう。テリーって呼ばれたいの。

I wondered for a moment whether her real name was Teruko or Teruyo, but I refrained from asking. I should call you Terry, just like that? Yes, I'd like that. Okay. I managed to answer with a smile, but an awkward silence ensued. It occurred to me that I should follow this exchange by saying with a straight face, So Terry, play me something – but I obviously lacked the nerve to do so. All I could muster was an awkward smile, gesturing with my hands to urge her to go ahead.

She looked at me intently and asked, with a smile, What should I call you?

Me? All I had to do was remember my own name, but for some reason, I couldn't answer right away. She waited for me patiently, while I sat silent. I began to feel desperate, trying to grasp any name that came to mind, but naturally, I hesitated choosing a name that wasn't mine. It didn't matter what I chose, yet it did matter somehow. Every name that popped into my head sounded wrong. Not that there was right or wrong in any of this.

Please call me Bianca.

Bianca. What a beautiful name.

ほんとうの名前が照子とか照代とかなのかと一瞬思ったけれど、それはきかないでおいた。

テリーって、それは呼び捨てでいいんですか。いいのよ。わかりました。笑顔のまま何とかわたしは答えたけれど、そのあとちょっとだけ気まずい空気が流れた。こういうときは、なんというのか流れ的に、じゃあテリー、何か弾いてみせて、とかさらりと言ってみせるべきなのかなと迷ったけれど、当然ながらそんなことをうまく言える自信がなかった。わたしはかろうじて笑顔を顔にのせたまま彼女に両方の手のひらをみせてそれをすこしあげてから、どうぞ、という仕草をしてみせた。すると彼女は、わたしをじっと見たまま、あなたのことは何て呼べばいい？　とにっこり笑ってきいてくるのだった。わたしですか。わたしは自分の名前を思いだして、それをただ言えば済む話だったのだけれど、なぜだかすぐに答えることができなかった。彼女は黙ったままのわたしをしんぼう強く待った。わたしは焦りはじめ、ええと、ええと、と頭の中にあるこれまで見聞きした名前を適当につかまえてそれを言ってしまおうとしたけれど、当然のことながらそれはわたしの名前ではないので、それを口にする決定に、なんだかいまいち欠けるのだった。どれでもいいけど、どれでもよくない。頭にうかぶどの名前も、何かがどこかが、嘘のような気がする。もちろんそれは嘘に違いないんだし、嘘でまったくかまわないはずなんだけれど。

ビアンカ、でお願いします。

ビアンカ。すてきね。

I felt my face turn bright red. Bianca? I had no idea why that name of all names popped out of my mouth. Where did it come from? It was probably a character from some comic book I had read as a child, nothing more. But Bianca! As I called myself that in my mind, one part of me felt strangely liberated, while another part began to melt into a deep slumber.

Bianca, will you listen to me play?

Yes, of course.

Realizing she was waiting for me to say more, I quickly added, Terry. Terry smiled contentedly and began playing her usual duum, da, dum piece. But she stumbled almost right away, and kept stumbling over the same spot. Starting over again and again, Terry eventually shook her head and turned towards me, sighing deeply.

See, Bianca, I told you. I can't play when I know someone is listening.

But it's so beautiful. I'm completely drawn in by the sound – it's as if the whole landscape changes with a single note. Isn't it just a matter of getting used to? I mean . . . oh, I'm sorry, I really don't know what I'm talking about.

わたしは自分の顔がものすごい勢いで赤くなるのを感じていた。なぜビアンカ。よくわからないけれど、口から出た名前はビアンカだった。どこの国の名前だろう。たぶん子どものころに読んだ漫画か何かの主人公の名前とか、きっとそういうことなんだろうけど。それでもビアンカ、と頭の中でもう一度、自分のことを呼んでみると、おかしなことにどこかが妙な解放感めいたものに包まれて、またどこかがしっかりとしたまどろみにむかって漏れだしていく感触がするのだった。

ビアンカ、聴いてくれる?

もちろんです。

わたしが返事をしてもピアノのほうをみようとしないので、あわててテリー、とつけくわえた。するとテリーは満足そうに微笑んでみせて、聴き覚えのあるあのたーん、たん、たんの曲を弾きはじめた。しかし出だしですぐにつまずいて、そのあとも何度もおなじところでつまずいた。それを何度も繰りかえして、しばらくするとテリーは首を左右に動かして深い深いため息をついてから、わたしのほうをふりかえった。

ビアンカ。ね、言ったでしょう。わたし、誰かに聴かれているとだめなのよ。

でも、すごくいい音ですよ。音にまず引きこまれちゃうっていうか、一瞬で景色が変わっちゃうっていうか。それにこういうのって慣れだと思いますよ。ってすみません、よくわからないのに適当なこといって。

No, you're right. It's probably just that. You know, it really made me happy the other day, Bianca, when you told me that you liked listening to me play the piano. It made me so happy to hear that you were touched. And today, you kindly came to my house. I have such bad memories attached to playing the piano, so for me, this is like a fresh new start. Liszt's *Liebestraum* brings back such bittersweet . . . no . . . truly awful memories. So if I can play it all the way through without making a mistake in front of you, Bianca, I feel very strongly that . . . that I could be a whole new person.

I think I understand how you feel.

I had a sense, you know, when I talked to you the other day – a kind of intuition.

I know exactly what you mean.

Terry continued to play the *Liebestraum* for two hours straight – I know because I kept looking at the antique clock on the wall. I sat still and erect on the backless ottoman, letting my attention wander from Terry's back to the shiny furniture, then to jumbled landscapes in my memory and to words exchanged with a certain someone somewhere. Whenever I remembered to focus on the melody, I would hear Terry stumbling. After playing for a full two

うん。そういうことだと思う。でもね、わたしすごくうれしかったの。ビアンカがこのあいだ、わたしのピアノをとてもいいって言ってくれて、それから感激だなんて言ってくれて、わたしそれがすごくうれしかったの。そして今日、ほんとうにこんなふうに来てくれて。

わたし、ピアノにはすごくいやな思いがあるから、そういう思いだけが残ってるから、それとさよならするための、再開でもあったの。リストの愛の夢はわたしにとってちょっとした苦い……というのでもないわね、かなりつらいメモリーとともにある曲なの。これをビアンカのまえで失敗せずに、つまずかずに弾ききることができたら、わたしすごく、なんていうのか、すごく変われるような気がするの。

そういうのって、わかります。

このあいだ話してみて、直感したの。

直感の感じ、わかります。

テリーはそのあと、たっぷり二時間――壁にかかったアンティークのぼんぼん時計を見ていたから間違いないけど、休憩も何もなしでその愛の夢っていう曲をひたすら弾きつづけた。

わたしは背もたれのないオットマンにずうっとおなじ姿勢で座ったまま、テリーの後ろ姿とぴかぴかに磨きあげられた家具と、ときおり甦ってくる記憶のなかのごちゃごちゃした風景や誰かと交わした言葉なんかを行き来し、そしてときどきはっとしてピアノの旋律に耳をやると決まってテリーはつまずいているのだった。二時間をやるだけやったテリーは、今日は

hours, Terry finally got up, saying, That's enough for today. I gave an enormous mental sigh of relief, larger than anything I'd ever seen or touched, and stood up, nodding vigorously. My hips were as stiff as if a metal plate had been inserted into them, and my eyes felt stuffed with cotton wool. We descended the stairs in silence, but as I put on my shoes in the entranceway, Terry said:

Bianca, won't you come twice a week, whenever you're free? Until I complete my Dream of Love?

How about Tuesdays and Thursdays?

And so it was decided that every Tuesday and Thursday, I would spend the afternoon listening to Terry play the piano.

Is it possible to be utterly unable to play a piece that one used to play smoothly, however many years ago? And after practising every single day? It must be. Maybe that's how difficult and profound and complex playing an instrument is, but still it was bewildering how slowly Terry progressed. She would unfailingly stumble at the beginning, and just when I thought she had finally got into the flow, she would stop again at a familiar spot. It made me wonder if she was doing it on purpose. This piece, with its sugary title that made me want to squirm in my seat, Dream of Love, could not be much more than four minutes long, and yet Terry could never play those four minutes

もうこれくらいにするわと言って立ちあがった。わたしもこれまで見たことも触ったこともないぐらいの巨大な息を胸の中で心ゆくまで吐いてから立ちあがり、ちからをこめて肯いた。腰は鉄板を横から挿しこまれたみたいにこわばって、目の奥には古い綿をいっぱいにつめられたようなだるさがあった。ふたりとも黙ったまま階段を降りて、玄関で靴を履いているわたしにテリーが言った。

週に二度、ビアンカの都合のいいときにきてくれないかしら。わたしの愛の夢が完成するまで。

火曜日と木曜日に、しましょうか。

そうしてわたしは火曜日と木曜日の午後をテリーのピアノを聴いて過ごすことになった。

毎日かならず練習して、しかもかつてはべらべらと弾くことのできた曲を、いくらブランクがあるといってもこんなにまで弾けないってことってあるんだろうか。あるんだろう。それぐらい楽器を演奏するということはむずかしくて奥深くて繊細なことなんだろうけれど、でもテリーの上達のしなさっぷりといったらちょっとなかった。わざとなのかと思うくらい、テリーはかならず出だしでつまずき、間違え、そのあとちょっとうまく流れにのったように思えても、またすぐによく似たところで止まってしまう。愛の夢という、なんだかおしりの割れ目がむずむずするようなタイトルのこの曲はとどこおりなく弾いてしまうと四分ちょっ

straight through. Whether the piece was for beginners or for really advanced players, who knows, but its overdramatic progression – the way it built up to a climax felt so over the top, going up or coming down or both – always made me queasy. Just when you thought the piece was ending, a series of hysterically high notes would soar up, only to trail off as if to excuse itself, *Dear me, did that come off as hysterical? It's just that I'm so terribly pleased with myself.* Then the lower notes would follow with an oh-so-convincing air, pulling the listener back into the piece only to end abruptly, as if everything that had taken place had suddenly been abandoned. What was that about?

Terry, however, seemed to be emotionally attached to the music and continued to play it on Tuesdays and Thursdays for two hours straight without a break. Glancing at her in profile one time, I noticed that she was so consumed by her Dream of Love that sweat appeared to be dripping from every pore. It was all I could do to keep a straight face. When the time came for me to leave, Terry would always apologize. *Bianca, I'm so sorry. Next time, next time for sure, I'll knock it out of the park.* It made me smile to hear the phrase 'knock it out of the park' from someone like Terry, whose body was inhabited by a sixty-year-old and a seventy-year-old.

との長さなのに、その四分をテリーは弾き抜くことができなかった。初心者向けの曲なのか、そうでないのか、もしかしたらすっごく上級者のための曲なのかわからなかったけど、途中の盛りあがりのところとかにとにかくすごく大げさで、駆けあがっていくのか駆けおりてゆくのかその両方なのかわからないけど、過剰に劇的な雰囲気がちょっとこそばゆくって大変だった。もう終わりと見せかけて無駄にヒステリックな高い音でつながって、そしたらあらヒステリックに聴こえたかしら？　わたしただ気位が高いだけなんだけどみたいな言い訳まででが聴こえる始末、そのあとすかさず低音で説得力を響かせて、まだまだつづくと思わせておいてぷつんと切れてこれまでかかわったいろいろをいっさいがっさい、置き去りにすることの感じってなんだかいったいどうなんだろう。

それでもテリーはこの曲にたっぷりの思い入れがあるみたいだから、火曜日と木曜日はやっぱりたっぷり二時間を休憩もなしに弾きつづけた。ちらっと横顔をみてみると、いつだったかあるときなんて粒の汗をよだれみたいにいっぱい垂らしてみていて思わず笑ってしまうくらいに愛の夢にのめりこんでいるんだった。帰るとき、テリーはいつも謝った。ビアンカごめんなさい。今度こそ、次回こそ、一発で決めてみせるから。わたしは六十歳と七十歳が同居しているテリーの口から一発で決める、なんて言葉が出るといつもちょっとだけ愉快な気持ちになった。

I thought meeting regularly like that would lead to an exchange of personal stories or gossip, but no such thing occurred. Terry had no idea what my husband did for a living, and I had no idea what her husband did either. What's your family like? Where were you born? How old are you? What do you do every day? How long have you lived here? Do you even *have* a husband? Do you have children? Do I have any intention of having children? What kind of life do you lead? Those questions never passed our lips.

Terry would just play, saying nothing. During our brief teatime before each session, she would reflect on her mistakes from the last session and lay out her goals for that day, all sober and serious. I couldn't tell whether Terry was an unhappy woman. I have a habit of imagining how unhappy a woman is every time I see one. Of course, nothing comes of it since I can't ask a woman flat out, So are you unhappy or not? Terry was earnestness itself. But her eyes were timid when she looked at me. I would say every time, You're going to be great today, I have a feeling . . . Terry, I would hastily add.

Really, Bianca? It makes me so happy to hear you say that.

And yet, Terry still couldn't play the piece to the end without

何度か顔をあわせるうちに、そうはいっても個人的な話とか世間話とか、そういう話題も

いつかはでるだろうと思っていたけどテリーとわたしのあいだにそういう話はいっさいな

かった。テリーはわたしの夫が何をしてるのかを知らないままだったし、わたしもテリーの

夫が何をしているのか知らないままだった。家族はどんなのか、生まれはどこなのか。何

歳なのか。毎日、何をして過ごしてるのか。テリーに子どもはいるのか。ここにどれぐらい住んでいるのか。そもそも夫

はいるのかどうか。テリーに子どもはいるのかどうか。わたしに子どもをつくる気はあるの

かどうか。いったいどういう暮らしをしているのか。わたしたちはお互いのことについて、

何も話さなかった。

テリーはただ黙ってピアノを弾き、弾きはじめるまえのお茶のひとときには前回の反省を

とうとうと述べて、それから今日の抱負めいたものを真面目な顔でつぶやくのだった。わた

しからみて、テリーは不幸な女性なのか、そうでないのか、わからなかった。わたしは女の

人をみるたびに、かならずその人がどれくらい不幸かどうかを想像してみる癖がある。それ

であなたは不幸なんですか、どうなんですか、とちょくせつ本人に聞くわけにもいかないか

ら、その想像はそれきりで何の役にも立たないのだけど。テリーは真剣そのものだった。け

れどおなじくらい、いつも自信のない顔をしてわたしをみた。わたしはそのたびに、今日は

きっとだいじょうぶですよと言い、なんだかそんな気がするんです、そしてあわてて、テリー、

とつけくわえた。そう、ビアンカ。そう言ってくれるのが、なにより。それでもテリーはな

stumbling. Two weeks passed, then three weeks, like slowly walking down a long, empty corridor.

Sitting at home doing nothing, I could hear Terry practising her usual *Liebestraum*. I hummed along to the now utterly familiar melody, tracing the notes as I brought in the laundry and wiped the dishes. My husband, who happened to be at home, seemed surprised to hear me humming and asked me what the matter was. He seemed oblivious to the sound of Terry's piano.

It's nothing . . . hey, what do you think of the name Bianca?

Bianca? What's that about?

Don't you think Bianca is a great name?

I don't know . . . is it Italian? I guess it's not bad. But then, I don't know what makes a name great either.

Sometimes, when I heard the faint sound of a piano – while watching a news item about the nuclear meltdown, for example – I would turn off the TV and softly approach the wall. If I noticed it while vacuuming, I would flip the switch and open the window. And sometimes I would sit at the dining table very straight and take a deep breath. Then I would place my hands on the table and move them at random along with Terry's music. Even though I was just tapping away haphazardly – the last time I touched a piano was probably during a music lesson at primary school – when the music ended and my fingers stopped moving, an unfamiliar elation would

をゆっくり歩くみたいにすぎていった。

家でぼうっとしていると、テリーがあいかわらず愛の夢を練習しているのが聴こえてきた。わたしはもうほとんど覚えてしまったメロディを鼻で追いかけ、なぞりながら洗濯物をとりこみ、食器をふいた。たまたま家にいた夫が鼻歌なんてきいたことない、どうしたのかときいてきたけど、夫にはテリーのピアノの音は聴こえないみたいだった。ねえ、それより、ビアンカって名前、どう思う？　ビアンカ？　何だ、それ。ビアンカって、いい名前だと思わない。そうかな。イタリア語？　いいんじゃない。まあいい名前っていうのが、どういうのかわからないけど。

たまに原発関連のニュースなんかをみているときにかすかにピアノの音が聴こえると、わたしはすぐにテレビを消して壁にそっとちかづいた。掃除機をかけているときに気がつけば、すぐにスイッチをきって窓をあけた。それからときどき、ダイニングテーブルにむかって深呼吸をひとつして背筋をぴんと伸ばし、それから両手をそっと置き、テリーの鳴らす音にあわせてでたらめに指を動かしてみることもあった。それはまるっきりのでたらめで、ただ指をテーブルのうえでぱたぱたさせているだけなのに、ピアノにさわったのなんて小学校の音楽室が最後なのに、曲が終わって指が止まると、これまで経験したことのない高揚感が喉の

fall upon me like golden rain, maybe from the back of my throat or somewhere high in the air. It would be so intense that my heart would ache. And I felt, vaguely, how wonderful it must be to be able to do something like that with one's fingers and eyes and body. Then, a feeling of anxiety would rush over me. What exactly is 'something like that'? Touching a piano? Reading, memorizing and managing to play a piece through? What is it? Or, is it related to all that, but something else entirely? The more I thought about it, the more confused I became. All I knew was that it wasn't just about the satisfaction I gained by moving my fingers randomly to the sound of music that someone else had spent ages practising.

On my thirteenth visit, Terry finally succeeded in playing the entire *Liebestraum* without making a single mistake. It happened quite suddenly. By that time, I had given up wondering whether she would ever get through the piece. Terry's performance was simply magnificent. With tremendous concentration, she played as if marking something unrepeatable on something irretrievable, tenderly drawing the keyboard down to some soft place buried within her heart, then abruptly pulling it upwards. Each breath enveloped her fingers, her arms – enveloped Terry herself. The notes were tied together by

奥とか頭のずっとうえのほうから光のまじった雨みたいに降ってきて、それには胸がすこし痛いくらいだった。そして、こんなふうに自分の指と目とからだを使って、こんなふうなことができるということは、いいことなんだなとそんなことをぼんやり思った。それからふと不安になった。こんなふうなことというのは、何だろう。ただピアノにさわることなんだろうか。それとも音符を読んで、あるいはそらんじて、ほんとうのピアノで一曲を満足に弾いてみることなんだろうか。どうなんだろうか。それとも、そのことが連れてくる、それ以外のことなんだろうか。考えてもよくわからなかったけど、誰かが時間をかけて自分のものにしたピアノの音にあわせてでたらめに指をうごかしていい気分になってみることではないということだけは、何となくわかるのだった。

わたしが通いだして十三度目に、テリーはやっと愛の夢を間違えずに弾き切ることができた。それはとつぜんやってきた。どうせ今日もだめだろうと、それすらとくに思うこともなくなっていたわたしが言うのもなんだけど、テリーのその演奏は、すばらしいものだった。ものすごい集中力で、一度きりの何かを一度きりの何かにかけがえのないしるしをつけてゆくように、すべての鍵盤をふだんはふれることのできないこころのやわらかい場所にやさしく沈め、ときには激しくひっぱりあげ、すべての呼吸はテリーの指と腕と、それからテリー自身に寄りそった。音のひとつひとつは見えない糸でしっかりとつながれ、しかしそ

an invisible string, and yet they were so free. The glimmering trem-
olo in the middle of the piece made it feel as if the world itself was
quivering under its inconceivable brilliance. I pressed my hand over
my heart. Please never end – I almost spoke the words out loud.

When the echoes of the last note disappeared from the room,
Terry turned to me quietly and whispered, I did it. Then, she said in
a slightly louder voice, Bianca, I did it, Bianca. Were you listening?

Yes, Terry, I was listening. You did it, I said.

Terry flared her nostrils in excitement, her mouth closed. I stood
up, raised my hands up to my face and clapped as hard as I could.
I even raised my hands above my head and clapped. I clapped until
my hands grew numb. Terry clapped too, as if competing with me.
The room filled with our clapping, which made the two of us happy
all over again. We kept on clapping for one another. To a stranger,
we were nothing more than a white-haired old lady and a scrawny
pale-faced woman in her forties – but at that moment, I was Bianca
and she was Terry. And – I don't know how it happened – we pressed
our lips together, quite naturally. It was just that, a pressing of the
lips, but we did it with all our heart.

I stopped going to Terry's house after that. I stopped seeing her

れらはあまりに自由で、真ん中あたりの、あのまるで世界そのものがまぶしさをこらえきれ
ずに瞬きをしているようなあのきらきらしい連打に、思わずわたしは胸をおさえた。終わら
ないで、とわたしは思った。もうすこしで、声にしてしまいそうだった。

最後の一音の余韻が部屋からうしなわれてしまうと、テリーはしずかにこっちをむいて、
小さな声でやったわ、と言った。それからすこし、おおきな声で、ビアンカ、やった、ビア
ンカ、ちゃんと聴いていてくれた？　聴いてたテリー、やったわ、とわたしは言った。テ
リーは口をとじたまま、ふうふうと鼻の穴をふくらませて興奮しているようだった。わたし
は立ちあがって、顔の高さまで手をあげて思いきり拍手した。頭のうえでも拍手をした。手
の感覚がなくなるまで拍手をした。テリーも負けじと拍手をした。部屋はふたりの手をうつ
音でいっぱいになり、そのことがまたふたりをしあわせな気持ちにさせた。ふたりともずっ
と拍手を送りあっていた。わたしたちは、はたからみれば老人に近い白髪女と顔色の悪い痩
せぎすの四十女だったけど、そのときわたしはビアンカで、テリーはテリーだった。それか
ら——わたしたちはどうしてそんなことになったのか、いまもまったく思いだせないのだけ
れど、どちらからともなく、くちづけをした。ただくちびるをあわせるだけのそれはくちづ
けだったけど、わたしたちはとてもこころのこもったくちづけをした。

それからわたしはもうテリーの家へいくことはなかった。これまでもそうだったように、

altogether, just as it had been before. That's how it is, even among neighbours. I would sometimes hear the garage door open and watch from my kitchen window upstairs as a car left, but I could never see who was inside. I spent my days as aimlessly as before, watering the ivy pots, chocolate cosmos and violets that bordered the front porch, clipping the overgrown leaves, spraying insect repellent and adding fertilizer to the soil. The sound of the piano had ceased entirely, and before I knew it, it was August. All the roses had withered, the ones that during the rainy season I had feared might overtake the house with millions of blossoms. With their flowers gone, leaves were all that remained of the rosebushes. Yet, there were still some small white petals scattered beneath the deep green leaves. I put the petals in my palm, one by one. With no particular celebration or ceremony in mind, I placed the petals next to one another on the sunny windowsill.

隣に住んでいても、そういうものだ。ときどき車庫のシャッターの音がして、二階のキッチンの窓から車が出てゆくのが見えたけど、誰が乗っているのかまではわからなかった。わたしもこれまでとおなじようにポーチのまわりのアイビーやらチョコレートコスモスやらすみれやらに水をやり、いらなくなった葉をじゃきじゃきと切り、虫除けのスプレーをしたり栄養剤を土に埋めたりなんかして、ほかには何もすることのない毎日を過ごした。ピアノの音はあれからぴたりと聴こえなくなって、気がつくと八月になっていた。梅雨のころには恥ずかしいほどにつぼみをつけて、これからどうなってしまうのだろう、家のまわりがばらきちみたいになるんじゃないのと心配までしたばらの花はほとんど枯れて、すこしまえに花をすべて落としてしまうとあとは葉っぱだけになってしまった。それでも深いみどりの葉っぱのかげには小さく散った白い花びらが残っていて、わたしはそれを一枚二枚と手にうけて、何を記念するわけでもなかったけれど、何となく、日のあたる窓辺にならべてみた。

ŌTA YŌKO

Hiroshima, City of Doom

Translated by Richard H. Minear

People who never saw Hiroshima before the bomb must wonder what the city used to be like.

In the distant past it was called not Hiroshima, 'broad island', but Ashihara, 'reed plain'. It was a broad, reed-covered delta. In the Warring States Era, some four hundred years ago, the powerful Mōri Motonari built a castle here. Driven out by the Tokugawa shōgun, Motonari moved west to Hagi in present-day Yamaguchi Prefecture. He was succeeded in Hiroshima by Fukushima Masanori, who expanded the castle and made it his seat.

But the house of Fukushima, too, lasted only one generation. Its successor, the Asano, flourished for thirteen generations before its long rule came to an end in the Meiji Restoration; Lord Asano Nagakoto of the Loyalist faction was the last of the line. In that era of revolution, neighbouring Chōshū rose to a position of great power, but Hiroshima was unable to display similar brilliance. Although Lord Nagakoto was granted the new aristocratic title of marquis and was himself a fine and noble individual, those who served him were said to be wanting in ardour. This fact can be useful in understanding the psychology of Hiroshima people in modern times.

The Hiroshima personality can be as bright as the scenery, but it can also be irresponsible and unsociable. In the local dialect, words are spoken lightly at the tip of the tongue, in stark contrast to the heaviness of the Tōhoku accent of north-eastern Japan. Still, as long as you didn't take things too seriously or become too deeply involved,

大田洋子

運命の街・広島

一度も広島を訪れたことのないひとは、原子爆弾を浴びた前の広島を、いったいどんな街だったろうと思うにちがいない。

遠い昔は広島とよばないで蘆原と云った。一面、葦におおわれた、広い三角洲であった。今から約四百年の昔、戦国時代に、そこへ毛利元就が城を築いた。元就は徳川に追われて、山口の萩に去った。そのあとへ福島正則が来てさらに城を築き添え、そこに入った。

けれども福島も一代で没落した。次の浅野家は、十三代栄えてつづき、勤王派の浅野長勲を最後に明治維新の革命の中にその永かった姿を消した。明治維新のときの広島は、ちかくの山口のように、華々しく大きな力で浮きあがることはできなかった。

長勲侯爵は偉くて立派だったが、麾下のひとびとの情熱が、希薄だったためといわれている。このことは近世の広島人の人柄のうえで、思い知らされないこともない。

人柄はどこか、風光と同じように明るいけれども、東北弁の重厚さに比べて対蹠的である。軽く舌のさきでものを云っているような地方弁のひびきは、投げやりで、非社交的である。

けれども、こちらがとくべつなにか考えたり、深入りをしさえしなければ、気候風土のい

Hiroshima remained a bright and cheerful town with a good climate and material riches: a good place to live.

In terms of its topography, Hiroshima fanned out between the mountain range to the north and the Inland Sea to the south. Seven branches of the Ōta River flowed gently among the delta's various neighbourhoods, spanned by countless bridges, all of them modern, clean, broad, white and long.

White-sailed fishing boats and small passenger boats would navigate well up into the river branches from Ujina Bay. Upstream, the river offered vivid reflections of the mountains.

The rivers of Hiroshima were beautiful – beautiful in a way that made you feel sleepy. The blue rivers themselves could have been asleep as they spread across the broad, even landscape. You couldn't see that they were flowing or hear the pleasant sound of rapids or spend time gazing at gentle shallows. Even on freezing winter days, when snow blanketed the area, the sight of the rivers could induce that sleepy mood.

I liked Hiroshima's rivers best on days when a heavy snow fell. The snow sealed off the various parts of town from each other and turned the city into a silent and uniformly silver world. Yet the seven rivers still flowed, unhurried, the water so clear that the white sand and greenish pebbles on the bottom gleamed through as always. The fine sand of the dry river banks was white, the pebbles white and brown and dark green. On occasion, there would be one that looked as if it had been dyed a pale red.

The surface of the water was a quiet pale blue, like that of a lake deep in the mountains. In winter it appeared to be covered with a thin, blue sheet of smoky glass or overspread with a delicate layer of waxed silken gauze. Each flake of snow pouring down on to it

い、明るい街で、物質も豊かで暮らしいいところだった。

広島の地形は、山岳地帯の北から、南の瀬戸内海へ扇の形にひろがっていて、そのデルタの街々を七つの河川がやわらかに流れている。

町から町を流れている大きな河には、数知れぬ橋がかかっていた。どの橋も近代風で、さっぱりし、幅はひろく、白くて、長かった。どの河にも白々と帆をかけた漁船や、小さい客船などが、宇品湾の方から、かなり上流まで入って来た。上流の河には、山の影がはっきりうつっていた。

広島の川は美しい。眠くなるような美しさである。高低のない広い土地に、眠ったように青く横たわっていて、はっきりした流れも見えないし、気持のいい急湍の音もきこえず、やさしいせせらぎを眺めることもできなかった。雪がふって凍るような冬の日にも、その川を見ていると眠くなりそうだった。

大雪のふる広島の川を、私は好きであった。街々が雪に閉され、ひっそりした銀一色の世界に変っている間に、七つの川は相変らず底の方に白い砂や、みどりがかった小石などを透きとおらせたまま、ゆっくりと横たわっていた。河原のこまかい砂は白く、石ころも白や茶色や、くすんだみどり色や、たまにはうす赤く染めたような石までがあった。

河の面は深い山の湖にそっくりの、あの薄紺の静かな色をしていた。冬の川は、どうかすると青くうすい硝子か蠟をぬった紗をはったように見え、そのうえに降りそそぐ雪は、一ひ

was gently absorbed and disappeared.

The map shows Hiroshima lying towards the west, but the city had a southern warmth, a languid and carefree air, due no doubt to the rivers and to the way its neighbourhoods spread towards the south like an open fan. With the exception of that southern side facing the water, the city was surrounded by mountains. Low and gently rolling, the mountains ran from one into another like the humps of a sleeping camel. Wherever you looked, the mountains were right there, visible even from the middle of the bustling city centre. I had not always lived in Hiroshima, and the nearness of the mountains surprised me.

Hiroshima Castle, too, seemed very near viewed from all parts of the city, rising up on its crumbling stone foundations in bold relief against the mountains. In its quiet tones of white, black and grey, the tall old castle provided the flat city with one sort of variation.

The young women of Hiroshima do not have the white skin and bold faces of mountain women; their colouring is generally dark. Some say the rivers tan their skin. The tide comes straight into the rivers from nearby Ujina Bay, ebbing and flowing several times a day, so it may make sense to speak of 'river burn'.

Most of the young women are stocky. With their black hair and white teeth, they brim with youth, but they have an odd way of swaying when they walk, they run when they don't need to, they avert their vacant eyes as if making fun of people, and on the bus they let their mouths hang open.

らずつ、やさしく吸いこまれては消えて行った。

地図のうえでは西に寄った広島に、なんとはなく、南国のように生あたたかな、そして暢気で悠長な気配がただようのは、このような河川の姿と、南に向って扇のようにひらいている街のためであろう。街の周囲は、南の海の側だけをのこして、三方を山にかこまれていた。

駱駝の寝たような山から山のつらなりは、低くやわらかく波うっていた。繁華街の町のなからさえ、どちらへ向いても山脈はすぐそこに見え、いつもは広島に住んでいない私をびっくりさせた。

そして山と山との間に、くっきりした対照をもって、そびえたっている広島城が、朽ちた石崖とともに、これもまた町々のどこからでも近々と見えていた。白と黒と灰との静かな色調からなり立った高い古城は、平坦な街に一種の変化を与えていた。

広島の娘たちは、山の地方の娘のような、白い皮膚や剽悍な顔はしていないで、たいてい浅黒い皮膚をしている。──ある人はそれを河に焼けるのだと云っていた。河には近くの宇品湾から直接潮が入って来て、一日に幾度か満ちたり引いたりしているのだったから、河焼けの話はあたっているかも知れない。──

娘たちはたいていずんぐりしていて、黒い髪や白い歯は若々しいけれど、妙にゆらゆらと体をうごかして歩いたり、駈けなくていいときに駈けたり、人をばかにしたようにぼんやりした眼をそらしたり、乗物のなかなんぞで唇をひきしめないでいたりする。

Occasionally you do see a tall girl with a bold and beautiful face, but the sound of her soft chatter – using only the tip of the tongue, as I mentioned earlier – can put people off.

Including such easy-to-be-with young women as these, the population of Hiroshima was said to be 400,000. One also used to hear 300,000 and 500,000. The wartime evacuation to the countryside appears to have reduced the figure greatly. Meanwhile, large numbers of military men had poured into the city from all parts of the nation. On 6 August there were, I think, about 400,000 people here.

Using a conservative estimate of one house for every four people, Hiroshima had about 100,000 houses. Before the 6 August attack, houses in every quarter – even historic buildings – had been torn down ruthlessly to create firebreaks. Yet as I looked at the city from the roof of the four-storey Red Cross Hospital just before 6 August, the houses were crammed together so haphazardly I had to wonder where the firebreaks could be.

This was the city above which, one morning at the height of summer, without warning, an eerie blue flash came from the sky.

I was staying in the house where my mother and younger sister lived in Hakushima Kukenchō. Situated on the north-eastern edge of the city, Hakushima was an old, established residential area. Many military men and office workers lived in this very middle-class neighbourhood, which meant that during the day it was full of housewives keeping to themselves behind closed doors.

Ours was an all-female household: my mother, my sister, her baby daughter and myself. My sister's husband had been called up for

たまに背の高い、剽悍な、美しい顔の娘を見かけるが、まえに書いたあの舌のさきだけで軽く喋る調子の低い言葉のひびきは、人の心をはねのけてしまう。

このような気のおけない娘たちをもふくめて、広島の人口は、四十万と云われていた。

三十万とも云われ、五十万とも云われていた。人の疎開で、よほど減っていたようでもあった。そのかわり、軍隊の連中が方々から、ひっきりなしにかたまって入って来ていた。私は、八月六日の日四十万前後の人がいたと思う。

家の数は、一軒に四人いると少く考えて、十万軒くらいと思われた。八月六日の空襲の前、町々の家は、由緒ある建物まで、建物疎開のためにどこもかしこも無惨にこわされていたが、あの少し前、日赤病院の四階の屋上から私の眺めた市街は、どこを疎開したのかと思うほど、ごたごた家並がいっぱいかたまり合って、市には詰まっていた。

このような街に、真夏のある朝、思いがけなく無気味な光が、空からさっと青光ったのだった。

私は、母や妹たちの住んでいる、白島九軒町の家にいた。白島は北東の町はずれにあたっていて、昔から古めかしい住宅地である。いかにも中流社会らしく、軍人や勤人がたくさん住んでいたから、昼間は玄関を閉じて、婦人ばかりひっそりとしているような町であった。

私たちも、母と妹と、妹の女の赤ん坊と、女ばかり四人住んでいた。妹の良人は六月末に

the second time at the end of June, and we had no idea where he was.

I had come back from Tokyo at New Year's, intending to wait until March and then take someone with me to dispose of my Tokyo house. Until the weather warmed up a bit, it was impossible to accomplish anything in Tokyo, where day and night you had to hide underground from the constant air raids.

The very first bombing of Tokyo had taken place on the rainy night of 30 October. Hit repeatedly by bombs and firebombs, Nishi-Kanda and the Nihonbashi area burned from eleven at night until after five in the morning. In the next raid, on 2 November, seventy planes appeared suddenly in the sky over Nerima, where I was living, and scattered bombs and firebombs here and there over the Musashi Plain stretching off to the west, where the houses were spaced more sparsely. People said two hundred bombs were dropped, one per one and a half city blocks. All around me, houses I knew well went up in smoke or were demolished.

I often used to joke with a female friend who lived nearby, another writer, about Admiral Tōgō Heihachirō's dictum, 'The enemy will come when you least expect him.' Exhausted by the round-the-clock bombing of Tokyo and the shortage of food, I had come back to Hiroshima.

I never thought of Hiroshima as a safe place to live during the war, but I couldn't very well move to a house in the country, either, without possessions, so I was planning to retrieve the belongings I had left in Tokyo. March came and went, April came, and the danger of travelling to Tokyo only increased. From Tokyo to the west as far as Osaka and Kobe, eastern Japan was being subjected to ferocious bombing without a day's let-up.

In May I suddenly took sick and was admitted to the Red Cross Hospital. I was there until 26 July. While in the hospital, I rented a

二度目の応召をして、それきりどこにいるともわからないままであった。東京から正月に帰って来た私は、三月をまってから誰かをつれて、東京の家を始末するつもりでいた。

けれどもならぬ東京で、どうすることもできないからだった。

東京では、最初の空襲、十月三十日の雨の夜、日本橋あたりと西神田が、夜の十一時から朝の五時すぎまで爆弾と焼夷弾の連続爆撃で燃えつづけた。そしてその次の十一月二日には、いきなり七十機が、私の住んでいた練馬の空へきて、家のまばらな武蔵野のあちこちへ、爆弾と焼夷弾とを落した。二百の爆弾が、一丁半おきに一つの割で落ちたと云われ、私の住居のまわりでも、よく知っている家々が焼けたり、壊れたりした。

東郷平八郎の、「敵はよもやと思うところへやってくる」という言葉を、近くにいた友達の婦人作家と私とは、くりかえして云い、おもしろがったのだった。私は東京の昼夜の爆撃と食物の足りなさに疲れはて、故郷の広島へかえって来た。

広島が戦争中、安心して住んでいられるところとは思っていなかった。けれども手ぶらで田舎へ入ることもできなかったから、そのままにして来た東京の荷物をとりにいく考えだった。三月が来ても、四月になっても、東京へ出かけることはむつかしくなった。日本の東は

もう大阪や神戸まで、一日の隙もなくすさまじい空襲にさらされていた。

五月になると私は急性の病気で、赤十字病院へ入院した。病院に七月二十六日までいた。

house in the country, but factors like these delayed my departure.

On the morning of 6 August, I was sound asleep. On the night of the fifth, virtually all night long, repeated waves of bombers had hit Ube in Yamaguchi Prefecture. As I listened to the radio reports, the flames seemed to rise up before my eyes.

To the west of us in Yamaguchi Prefecture, one city after another had burnt: Hikari, Kudamatsu, Ube. That very night, Hiroshima too might be turned into a sea of flames. The radio also reported that Fukuyama, on the other side of Hiroshima from Ube, was undergoing its own firebomb attack, although the announcer later retracted the report as erroneous.

The air-raid alarm sounded in Hiroshima, too, and the neighbourhood group sent around a warning to be ready to flee at any moment. So, on the night of the fifth, sleep was out of the question.

At daybreak the red alert was lifted, and shortly after seven o'clock the yellow alert was lifted too. I went back to sleep. I usually slept late anyway, and since I had just been discharged from the hospital, I often slept till close to noon, which is why the others left me alone until that bright blue light flashed.

I was sound asleep inside the mosquito net. Some say the bomb fell at 8.10; some say 8.30. In any case, I dreamed that I was enveloped by a blue flash, like lightning at the bottom of the sea. Immediately afterwards came a terrible sound, loud enough to shake the earth. It was like an indescribably huge roll of thunder, and at the same moment the roof came crashing down with such force it was as if a gigantic boulder had broken from the mountaintop and fallen on the house. When I came to, I was standing in a cloud of plaster dust

このようなことのために、私は病院にいる間に約束しておいた田舎の家へ行くことがおくれていたのだった。

私は八月六日の朝よく眠っていた。前夜の五日の夜は山口県の宇部市がほとんど一晩中、波状攻撃をうけて、ラジオの情報をきいていると、眼のまえに火の山が見えそうな気がした。

山口県は、光、下松、宇部と、つづけざまに焼けたのだから、広島も今夜にも炎の海になるかも知れなかった。あとでアナウンサーがまちがいだと取消していたけれども、五日の夜中には宇部とはべつに、広島をとばして福山市が焼夷弾の攻撃をうけていると放送した。

広島にも空襲警報が出ていたし、隣組からはいつでも避難できるように用意をしておくように伝えて来ていた。だから五日の夜はまるで眠ることができなかった。

夜あけに空襲警報がとけ、七時すぎには警戒警報も解かれた。それから私はあらためて眠ったのだった。寝坊はいつものことだし、病院から出たばかりで、昼ちかくまでねていることも多かったから、家の者たちもまたあの光線が青々と光るまで、私を放っていた。

私は蚊帳のなかでぐっすりねむっていた。八時十分だったとも云われ、八時三十分だったともいうけれど、そのとき私は、海の底で稲妻に似た青い光につつまれたような夢を見たのだった。するとすぐ、大地を震わせるような恐ろしい音が鳴り響いた。雷鳴がとどろきわたるかと思うような、云いようのない音響につれて、山上から巨大な岩でも崩れかかってきたように、家の屋根が烈しい勢いで落ちかかって来た。気がついたとき、私は微塵に砕けた壁

from the smashed walls around me, utterly dazed, struck dumb. I felt neither pain nor fear but only a strange, almost light-headed sort of calm. The bright early morning sunlight had been replaced by a gloom like that of a rainy-season evening.

The air raid on Kure came to mind, where the firebombs were said to have fallen like large, fluffy snowflakes. Wide-eyed, I searched in vain for firebombs amid the bare skeleton of the dark upper floor, where the window glass, the walls, the sliding paper doors separating my room from the next, and the roof had all been blasted away.

I imagined that forty or fifty firebombs had dropped next to me where I lay. Yet there was no flame, no smoke. And I was alive. How could I still be alive? It was too strange. I looked all around me, half expecting to see my dead body stretched out somewhere.

But in this upstairs room there was nothing to be seen, just a little pile of dirt with dust rising from it, shattered glass fragments and a small mound of roof-tile chunks, but no sign of my mosquito net or bedding or my bedside possessions – my air-raid jacket and hat, my watch, my books. There was no trace of the twelve pieces of luggage we had packed for the countryside and stored in the next room, as if someone had made off with them. The several large glass-doored bookcases holding the 3,000 volumes of the library of my sister's husband: I had no idea where they had flown off to.

Inside the house, there was nothing to be seen, but outside, as far as the eye could see – which was much further than usual – there stretched one ruined house after another. The same was true of far-off parts of town. The headquarters of the *Chūgoku Shimbun* newspaper in Hatchōbori and the radio station in Nagarekawa looked to me like silhouettes, deserted and empty.

土の煙の中にぼんやり佇んでいた。ひどくぼんやりして、ばかのように立っていた。苦痛もなく恐駭もなく、なんとなく平気な、漠とした泡のような思いであった。朝はやくあんなに輝いていた陽の光は消えて、梅雨時の夕ぐれか何かのようにあたりはうす暗かった。牡丹雪がふるようだったときについていた呉の焼夷弾のことが頭に浮び、窓硝子も壁も次の間との隣の襖も屋根も、なにもかも崩れ飛んで、骨ばかりになった暗い二階で、私はきょろきょろと焼夷弾を眼で探した。

四十も五十もの焼夷弾が頭の傍にふり落ちたと思ったからである。それにしては焔も煙もあがっていない。それに私は生きている。なぜ生きているのだろう。ふしぎであり、どこかに死んだ私が倒れていないかと、ぼんやりした気持であたりを見たりした。

二階にはなんにも見えなかった。ただ土煙のもうもうと立つ土の小山や、微塵に砕けた硝子や、瓦のかけらの小山があるだけで、蚊帳や寝床さえもあと形もなかった。枕元にあった防空服も防空帽も時計も本もないのだ。次の間に積んであった十二個の田舎行の荷物もさらわれたように、なんの形もなかった。妹の良人の、三千冊の蔵書の入っていたいくつかの大戸棚も、どこへとんで行ったのかわからなかった。

家の中にはなんにも見えはしなかったけれども、外は平素見えなかったところまで、見渡す限り壊れ砕けた家々が見えた。それは遠くの町々まで同じであった。八丁堀の中国新聞社や、流川町の放送局などが、がらんとした空しい様子で影絵のように私の眼にうつった。

All that was left of the house across the street was its stone gate. The house itself had been ruthlessly flattened. A young girl stood in the gate, looking dazed and drained of energy. She stared up at me, in full view on the upper floor, and exclaimed, 'Oh!' Then, in a subdued voice, she said, 'You should come down from there right away!'

But there was no way I could get down. The front and back staircases were still intact, but both were blocked partway down by piles of debris taller than I was: boards, tiles, bamboo.

I asked the girl to summon the other members of my family, but even as I pinned my hopes on them, I felt certain that no one would ever come up to get me.

Smeared with blood, her face monstrously transformed, my sister came climbing partway up the stairs. Her white dress had turned bright red as if she had dyed it. Her jaw was held up by a white cloth wrapping, and her face was as purple and swollen as a pumpkin.

'Is Mother alive?' I asked at once.

'Yes, she's fine. She's looking at you from the cemetery out back. The baby's alive, too. Quick, come down.'

'How am I supposed to do that? It looks impossible.'

道をへだてた前の家には、石の門だけがぽつんと残り、家は無惨に倒れ伏していた。石門のまん中に若い娘が一人、腑ぬけのようにぼおっと立っていた。娘はまる見えの二階の私を見あげると、

「あっ。」

と云った。それから、

「早く下へお降りにならなくては。」

と沈んだ声で云った。私は降りることができなかった。表と裏と、二つついている階段は、折れもせずに残っているが、その中途は私の身丈より高く、板や瓦や竹でふさがっている。

私は前の家の娘さんにたのんで家の者をよんでもらった。それを頼みながら、誰も永遠にあがって来ないという気もした。

血まみれの妹が化物のような顔に変りはてて、階段の途中まであがって来た。白い洋服は染めたように真赤になり、白い布で顎を釣った顔は紫の南瓜のように腫れていた。

「お母さんは生きてるの。」

私ははじめにそう訊いた。

「ええ大丈夫。墓地からお姉さんを見てなさるわ。早くお降りなさい。」

「どうして降りるの？　とても降りられそうにないわよ。」

Hearing that my mother was alive was such a relief, I felt the strength go out of me. My sister tried pushing at the stuff blocking the staircase, but she closed her eyes and seemed about to collapse against it.

'Never mind,' I called to her. 'Go ahead, I'll be right down.'

'You're probably not injured as badly as I am,' she said. 'Get yourself out of there if you can.'

As she said this, I noticed for the first time that the collar of my kimono was drenched in blood. The blood was dripping from my shoulder to my chest. As I left the room, this room I would never enter again, this ten-mat room that had been home to me for several months, I took one last look around. There was not even a single handkerchief to be seen. Where the bed might have been, I finally made out our Singer sewing machine, lying on its side in pieces.

On the stairs, I made an opening in the pile of debris that was just big enough for me to crawl through. The ground floor was not as much of a mess as the upper storey. The chests and trunks and boxes that my sister had packed only two days ago to take with her when she left for the countryside were piled impossibly on top of each other. In the garden behind the house, my large trunk and my mother's wicker trunk lay half buried, as if they had been hurled down with great force. The night before, we had set them out on the edge of the upper-floor concrete balcony, planning to throw them down to the cemetery at the back in case there was a firebomb attack.

The cemetery lay beyond the board fence that enclosed the back yard. A wattle gate led from our property to the large cemetery, on the edge of which we had dug an air-raid shelter and made a small vegetable garden. Now that the fence had been blown away, I could see the whole cemetery. My mother was going back and forth between the cemetery and the house.

母が生きているときとき、私は安心して力がぬけた。妹は階段の障害物を両手でかきわけた。それから眼をとじてそのうえに倒れそうになった。

「お降りなさいよ。すぐ私降りるから。」

「お姉さんの方が傷が浅いから、どうかしてぬけ出てらっしゃい。」

妹に云われてはじめて私は着物の衿が血でびっしょり濡れているのを見た。血は肩から胸のあたりへしたたり落ちていた。部屋を出るとき、再びあがってくることのない、何ヵ月か寝床があったと思われるところに、ばらばらになったシンガー・ミシンのころがっているのがやっとわかった。

私を暮させてくれた十畳の間に、私は別れの眼をそそいだ。ハンカチ一枚そこには見えず、

這い出るだけの穴を私は障害物の中にあけて、階下に降りた。階下は二階ほどめちゃめちゃではなく、二日前に荷造したばかりの妹の疎開荷物の、簞笥やトランクや箱類が、嘘のように積み重なっていた。裏庭には私の大きなトランクと母の行李とが、投げつけられたように土にうずもれ込んでいた。前の夜、二階のコンクリートの露台の端にだしておいたものであった。そのふたつを私どもは焼夷弾を浴びはじめたら、裏の墓地へ放り出すつもりでいた。

庭の板囲いの外は墓地であった。板囲いには枝折戸がついていて、私どものところではその広い墓地の端に防空壕をつくっていたし、少しばかり菜園にもしていた。板囲いは吹きとんでいたから、墓地はまる見えで、母は墓地と家とを行ったり来たりしていた。

The cemetery led to a raised stone embankment, and around the stone embankment stretched a board fence. That fence, too, was gone. Normally I could not see the stone steps of the embankment, but now they were clearly visible, and I could also see that my stepbrother's shrine had been flattened, leaving only its torii gate standing.

I joined my mother and sister in the cemetery.

'Could they have been aiming at the shrine?' my mother whispered to me as if sharing a secret. But despite the fact that so many houses had been destroyed, there were no fires, so it couldn't have been firebombs. Ordinary bombs were unthinkable as well. I had experienced both in Tokyo, and this was different. For one thing, no air-raid alarm had sounded, and we had not heard any planes.

How could everything in our vicinity have been so utterly transformed in an instant? I toyed vaguely with the idea that it might not have been an air raid but something quite different, something unconnected with the war, something that occurs at the end of the world when the globe disintegrates, as we read about in children's books.

A hush had fallen over everything. (The newspaper later said there was 'instant pandemonium', but that was the writer's preconceived notion. In fact, an eerie stillness descended as if people, trees and plants had all died at once.)

墓地のつづきは石崖になっていて、石崖にも板囲いがめぐらしてあったが、その板塀もな
くなっていた。いつもは見えなかった石段がよく見え、義弟の神社が鳥居だけをのこしてぺっ
たりと倒れているのが見渡せた。

私は母や妹と広い墓地で顔を合せた。

「お宮をねらったんじゃろうね。」

母は内緒のことをいうように、小声で私に囁いた。けれどもこれだけの家がこわれてし
まったのに、火事にならないから、焼夷弾とは思えなかった。爆弾とも思えなかった。東京
で見たそのどちらとも違っているし、だいいち空襲警報も何も出なければ、敵機の音もきか
なかった。

なんのために自分たちの身のまわりが一瞬の間にこんなに変ってしまったのか、少しもわ
からなかった。空襲ではないかも知れない。もっとちがうこと、戦争に関わりのない、たと
えば世界の終るとき起るという、あの、子供のときに読んだ読物の、地球の崩壊なのかも知
れない。私はぼんやりとそんな風に思ったりした。

あたりは静かにしんとしていた。（新聞では「一瞬の間に阿鼻叫喚の巷と化した」と書い
ていたけれども、それは書いた人の既成観念であって、じっさいは人も草木も一度に皆死ん
だのかと思うほど、気味悪い静寂さがおそったのだった。）

'We kept calling to you from down here,' my mother said. 'Didn't you hear us? We heard a scream, and then nothing. We called to you over and over, but when you didn't answer, we thought you must be done for.'

I had no recollection of having cried out.

'I was so happy when I looked up from the cemetery and saw you standing there looking around!'

'Really?' I replied. 'We were lucky, weren't we? All of us survived.'

Sitting on a gravestone, her face in her hands, my sister was barely staving off collapse. My mother handed me the sleeping baby. She went back into the house, which looked as if it might fall over at any moment, to get water. She walked through our house, through the house across the street, and kept going, receding into the distance.

The people from next door and other nearby houses gathered in the cemetery. Most were barefoot, and every single one of them was drenched in blood. Heavily wooded, the cemetery was a large and pleasant space. Curiously, not a single gravestone had been knocked over. Everyone was strangely calm. Their faces were still and expressionless, and they talked among themselves as they always did – 'Did you all get out?', 'You were lucky you weren't hurt badly' and so forth. Everyone kept silent about bombs or firebombs, which were not permissible topics of conversation for loyal subjects of the empire.

Soon the large girl from next door started shouting, 'Mother! Mother! Let's get out of here now! The fires are coming. We'll die if we start looking for stuff in the house. It's no time to be greedy.

「下から随分よんだのに、きこえなかった？　きゃっと叫んだような声がしたきり、いくら

よんでも声がしないから、だめかと思いましたよ。」

母が云った。私は叫んだりした覚えはなかった。

「墓場から見たら、きょろきょろして立っているから、うれしいでしたよ。」

「そう？　よかったわね。みんな助かってね。」

妹は墓石に腰かけて、両手で顔をおおい、やっと倒れないでいた。母は眠っている赤ん坊

を私に渡した。母は水を汲むために、今にも倒れそうになっている家の中へ入って行った。

母が自分の家を通りぬけ、前の家をも通りぬけ、ずっと向うまで歩いて行く姿は小さかった。

隣りや近くの家の人たちが、たいていの人ははだしのまま、そしてたれもかれも血でびしょ

びしょにぬれて、墓場へ集って来た。こんもりした森のこの墓地は、感じのいい広々とした

ところで、ふしぎに墓石は一つも倒れていなかった。どの人も妙に落ちついていた。静かな

無表情な顔をし、いつもとちっとも変りのない云い方で、「どなたもみんなお出になりまし

たか」とか、「ひどいお怪我でなくてようございましたね」などと云い合った。誰も爆弾と

も焼夷弾とも云わないし、そんなことは国民はとやかく云ってはいけないのだという風に、

押しだまっていた。

そのうちに隣りの大きなからだの娘さんが叫びはじめた。

「お母さん、お母さん！　早く逃げましょう。火事ですよ。欲ばって家の中を探している

That's what's been happening in all the other towns. Let's get out of here now!'

She was right, we realized. It was too dangerous to just stay there hoping for the best. If we took our time, our mother would be like this girl's, she'd keep going back inside to search for things. We should leave soon, if only to stop Mother from doing that.

Thin smoke started to issue from the eastern end of the flattened neighbourhood, creeping along the ground. I wanted to store the partially buried trunk and wicker suitcase in the air-raid shelter, but I didn't have the strength to move them. And if I gave the baby to my sister to hold, the little thing would be smeared with blood. I gave up on the luggage.

My mother, who had no bloody wounds, brought out some cotton trousers for me and I pulled them on. Then I put on some old straw sandals we used for going out into the fields and shouldered my pack. Each evening we set all our packs in the entryway. Only the things in the entryway were undamaged. Each of us carried a bucket. I used a dark green umbrella for a cane, like an old woman. The shaft of the umbrella was bent in the middle, like the house. My mother had thrown several items out into the cemetery for me – a few pairs of shoes I valued, a summer overcoat and the like. I saw them as I fled, but I did not reach for them, as if I were beyond such desires.

It would be more accurate to say that I had lost interest in anything at all, rather than that I had given up on the luggage. For the same reason, even people who were normally attached to their possessions abandoned things they might well have carried. This numb emptiness lasted a long time, remaining almost unchanged thirty or

と、焼け死ぬんですよ。どこでも死ぬ人はそうなんですからね。逃げましょうよ。早く、早く！」

私どももその叫び声で、いつまでものんきにここにいてはあぶないのだと思った。ゆっくりしていると、私の母も幾度でも家の中へ探し物をしに入って行く。母にそうさせないためにも早くどこかへ行こうと思った。

ぺしゃんこになった町の、東のあたりから、地を這うように薄い煙があがりはじめた。私は土の中へのめり込んでいるトランクと行李とを、防空壕へ入れておくつもりで手をかけて見た。けれども手にはつよい力がなかった。そのうえ妹に赤ん坊を抱かせておくと、赤ん坊は血まみれになってしまう。私は荷物をあきらめた。

私は、血の出る怪我をしなかった母のだしてくれた、もんぺをはき、畑へ出るときに履く古ぼけの草履をはいて、背負袋を背負った。みんなの背負袋はろうそく関の物だけが無事であった。私どもはバケツを一つ持った。私は老婆のように、濃いみどり色の雨傘を杖にした。その雨傘の柄は家と同じように、くの字形に曲っていた。墓地まで母の投げ出してくれた、二、三足の大事がっていた靴や、夏のオーバアなど、逃げ出すとき見るには見たけれど、ちっとも欲のない人のように、手にしなかった。

荷物をあきらめたというよりも、心をうしなっているのだ。だから平素は欲の深い人たちまで持てる物も見捨てて行ったのだった。このしびれたようなうつろさは、その後もながく、

forty days afterwards.

In the shrine compound, we caught sight of my stepbrother's wife. She was wandering back and forth between the flattened shrine and her demolished house. Her husband had been called up for the third time in June and was now serving with the Hiroshima First Detachment, leaving his young wife alone.

By the time we got out on to the road in front of the shrine, fire was already crawling towards us from across the road on the right. Nearby on the left, where the embankment was visible, we saw five or six people walking along the railway tracks on top. They seemed in no rush. Seeing this, we figured the fire couldn't be all that fierce yet.

We were walking through a neighbourhood that had been demolished, but it still aroused no feeling in us. As if this were an ordinary occurrence on an ordinary day, we felt no surprise, we did not cry, we were in no particular hurry as we followed people on to the nearby embankment. On one side of the embankment was a block of government-owned homes for officials. It, too, was part of the Hakushima district in which we lived, but the houses here were of far higher quality, far more grand and beautiful, than the ones in our Kukenchō neighbourhood. Every single one of these houses had been levelled as if flattened by a powerful force. My old friend Saeki Ayako lived here, but her house was one of those destroyed without a trace. What had become of Saeki Ayako herself? The question flashed through my mind and I looked around, but here, too, it was hushed, without any sign of people.

Each of the beautiful homes on the embankment had stone steps leading down from the back garden to the riverbed. There were vegetable gardens on the parts of the riverbed above the water line,

三十日も四十日も経ってからも、ほとんど変りはなかった。

神社の境内で義弟の妻を見かけた。崩れてしまった住居と神社との間を、かの女はうろつきまわっていた。義弟は六月に三度目の出征をし、広島市にある第一部隊にいたので、若い妻は独りであった。

神社の前の通りへ出て見ると、通りの右の方の向うから、もうそろそろと火が土の上を這って来ていた。私どもは左手ちかく見える土手の上の線路を歩いている五、六人の人を見た。その人たちがあわてた様子をしていないのを見ると、火事はまだあまりひどくはないと思った。

私どもは壊滅した町を歩いても、なんの感じもまだ起きなかった。あたりまえのときあたりまえのことが起きたように、びっくりもせず、泣きもせず、だから別に急ぎもしないで、人々のうしろから、近くの土手へあがった。その土手の片側は官有地の住宅町で、同じ白島でも九軒町よりもずっと高級な、美しくて立派な家が並んでいた。そのどの家も大きな力で押しつぶされたように、倒れ崩れていた。古い友達の佐伯綾子の住んでいた家も、見る影もなく倒壊していた。私は佐伯綾子はどうしたかと、ちらと心に浮べあたりを見たが、ここもひっそりと静かで、人の姿はどこにも見えなかった。

土手の美しい住宅はどこの家も裏庭から河原へ降りる石段がついて、そこから河原へ降りるようになっていた。河原の水の流れのない処は耕されて菜園になっていた。菜園の境に

with hedges separating one plot from the next. We walked between demolished houses and down the stone steps to the riverbed. It was about three blocks from our house to the riverbed. Perhaps forty minutes had gone by since we had experienced the blue flash, during which time we milled around, disoriented, in the cemetery before walking there. Only long afterwards did I manage to estimate the time it had taken.

The tide had ebbed. A band of blue water was flowing gently on the other side of the white sand. Here and there on the broad stretch of white grew clumps of weeds, while bundles of straw and such lay where they had come floating up the river at high tide.

We had managed to flee more quickly than those who had been pinned under their houses, and there were still a few flames rising from the ruins, so the river banks did not appear to be very crowded. People wandered about, searching for places to sit, like spectators at an open-air theatre. Individuals made seats for themselves as they wished – beneath the hedges' lush foliage or beside trees that stood between the garden patches, or on the bank very close to the river itself. We chose a spot beneath a fig tree on the edge of Saeki Ayako's garden. It was quite far from the water.

More and more refugees crowded into the area. Soon there were no more good places left, such as beneath a tree, where you could avoid the sun. Everyone who flocked to the riverbed bore wounds, as if only the injured were permitted to come here. Judging from the faces, hands and legs protruding from their clothing,

どうにか思い出した。

間の時間は、四十分くらいのものだった。——しかしこの時間もずっとあとになってから、

の家から河原まで三丁くらい、そして青い閃光を浴びてから墓地でまごまごし、河原へ来た

は生垣があった。そのような河原へ私どもはこわれた家の間から降りて行った。——私たち

河は潮の引いたあとで、白い砂原の向うの方に、青い水が帯のようにゆるやかに流れてい

た。白い砂原はひろびろとしていて、ところどころに雑草がかたまって生えていたり、満

潮のとき、どこからか流れて来た藁の束などがあった。

私たちは下敷になって抜け出すことの出来なかった人にくらべれば、逃げて来かたが早く、

まだどこにも火の手はあがっていないうちだったから、河原にはそれほど大勢の人も見えな

かった。人々は野外劇でも見に来た人のように、うろうろして自分の座席になる場所を探し

た。思い思いに生垣の繁りの下や、菜園の間に立っている木の傍や、または水の流れのすぐ

ほとりなどに、居場所をつくった。私どもは無花果の木の下に場所をとった。そこは佐伯綾

子の住居の庭園のはずれにあたっていた。河の水まではかなり遠かった。もう陽をさける木

避難者はあとからあとからと詰めかけて来るようになった。集まって来る人達はたれもかれ

い場所はなくなっていた。河原は負傷者だけの来るところかとも思われた。負傷者は顔とか手足とか、着物から出

た。河原は負傷者だけの来るところかとも思われた。負傷者は顔とか手足とか、着物から出

it was impossible to tell what had given them their lacerations. But each person had a half dozen or more cuts, and they were covered in blood.

Some people had streaks of dried blood on their faces and limbs, while others still had fresh blood dripping everywhere on their bodies. All their faces had been hideously transformed. The number of people on the riverbed increased minute by minute, many of them now with severe burns. At first we didn't realize that their injuries were burns. There were no fires, so where and how could they have been burnt so badly? Strange, grotesque, they were more pathetic than frightening. They had all been burnt in the same way, as if the men who bake rice crackers had roasted them all in those iron ovens. Normal burns are part red and part white, but these were ash-coloured, as if the skin had been grilled rather than burnt. Ash-coloured skin hung from their flesh, peeling off in strips like the skins of roast potatoes.

Virtually everyone was naked to the waist. Their trousers were tattered, and some people wore only underpants. Their bodies were puffy and swollen, like those of drowning victims. Their faces were ponderously swollen. Their eyes were swollen shut, the skin around the edges pink and split. They held their puffy, swollen arms out, bent at the elbows, like crabs holding up their two claws. Grey skin hung down from both arms like rags. On their heads some appeared to be wearing bowls; the black hair on top was still there, having been protected by their field caps, but from the ears down the hair had

ているところを、なんで切ったのかよくわからないが、五カ所も六カ所もの裂傷を受けて血だらけになっていた。

血ももう乾いて、顔や手足に血のかたまりの筋を幾つもつけている人や、まだ生々しく流れる血で、顔も手も足もびっしょり血でぬれている人もあった。もうどの人の形相も変り果てたものになっている。河原の人は刻々にふえ、重い火傷の人々が眼立つようになった。はじめのうちはそれが火傷とはわからなかった。火事になっていないのに、どこであんなに焼いたのだろう。ふしぎな、異様なその姿は、怖ろしいのでなく、悲しく浅間しかった。せんべいを焼く職人が、あの鉄の蒸焼器で一様にせんべいを焼いたように、どの人もまったく同じな焼け方だった。普通の火傷のように赤味がかったところや白いところがあるのでなくて、灰色だった。焼いたというより焙ったようで、焙った馬鈴薯の皮をくるりとむいたように、その灰色の皮膚は、肉からぶら下っているのだ。

ほとんどの人が上半身はだかであった。どの人のズボンもぼろぼろになっていたし、パンツ一つしかつけていない人もあった。その人々は水死人のようにふくれていた。顔はぽってりと重々しくふくれ、眼は腫れつぶれて、眼のふちは淡紅色にはぜていた。どの人もみな、蟹がハサミのついた両手を前に曲げているあの形に、ぶくぶくにふくれた両手を前に曲げ空に浮かせている。そしてその両腕から襤褸切れのように灰色の皮膚が垂れさがっているのだ。

頭の毛は椀をかぶった恰好に、戦闘帽から出ていた黒い髪がのこり、耳の傍から後頭部へか

disappeared, leaving a dividing line as sharp as if the hair had been shaved off. Those who looked like this, we knew, were members of a unit of young soldiers, well built, with broad chests and shoulders.

With their strange injuries, these victims were soon lying down on the hot, sunbaked sand of the riverbed. Most of them had been blinded. Even though they were in such frightful shape, nowhere did pandemonium arise. Nor did the term 'ghastly' apply. This had partly to do with the fact that no one said a word. The soldiers, too, were silent. No one called out in pain or complained of the heat or spoke of their fear. As we watched, the broad riverbed filled up with wounded people.

Here and there on the hot white sand, people were sitting or standing or lying stretched out as if dead. The burnt ones vomited continually, a nerve-wracking sound. Saeki Ayako's German shepherd prowled the riverbed. With people arriving all the while, the human mass on the riverbed grew still larger.

Each new arrival would quickly find a little spot and settle in.

In any situation, human beings are always impatient to find a place to call their own, it seemed. Even when the sky is their only roof, they prefer not to be jumbled together but instead want to take possession of a seat that is unambiguously theirs. Soon fires began to break out all over the city. Even then, people still did not dream that the whole city of Hiroshima had been set ablaze all at once. Each thought that only his or her own part of town – for me, it was Hakushima – had been hit by a major disaster.

けての毛は、剃りとったようにくっきりと境目をつけて、なくなっていた。私どもはこの同じような姿をしたたくさんの人が、厚い胸や広い肩をした、いい体格の年若い兵隊の集団であることを知った。この不思議な負傷を負った犠牲者たちは、いつか太陽に焼かれている河原の熱砂の上にころがっていた。眼が見えないのだ。このようであっても、阿鼻叫喚はどこからも起らなかった。酸鼻という言葉もあてはまらなかった。それは誰もがだまっているからでもあった。兵隊たちもだんまりで、痛いとも熱いとも云わないし、怖ろしかったとも云わないのだった。見る間に広い河原は負傷者で充満した。

熱い白砂の上には、点々と人が坐り、佇み、死んだように横たわっていた。火傷の人たちの吐きつづける音に神経をたまらなくした。佐伯綾子の家のシェパードが河原をうろついていた。河原の群衆は一層ふえ、ひっきりなしにやって来た。

そして自分々々の小さな住居を早速見つけだしてそこに落ちついた。人間はどんな場合にも自己の腰を下す場所を、性急にとり決めるものと思えた。野天であっても人とごっちゃにならないで、はっきりと座席を独占したいのである。やがて全市に火災の火群がくるめき出した。人々はそのころになってもまだ、広島中へいちどきに火がついたなどとは思わなかった。互に自分の町、私なら白島だけに大変な事件が起きたのだと思っていた。

One after another, pillars of fire rose up in our Kukenchō neighbourhood. Then the grand homes on the embankment, the residences of officials, began to burn. The houses on the opposite bank of the river burst into flames, and beyond a white fence over there, in Nigitsu Park, tall pillars of flame suddenly shot up. From out of the flames came terrible, loud reports of things exploding. Always short-tempered, I was now starting to get really angry and said to my mother and sister, 'Why are they letting these fires start everywhere? Don't they know it's the end when that happens? Didn't we go through all that training to put out fires? This is not from firebombs, so it must be carelessness. If only people had put out their stove and charcoal fires before they fled!'

My mother and sister kept silent as if to say that nothing could be done.

Resignation was an attitude I detested. As if blaming the two of them for not getting angry, I went on: 'These fires are a disgrace for the people of Hiroshima. Now everyone will be making fun of us. We should never have let this happen.'

The sky was still as dark as at dusk. The roar of aeroplane engines had been audible up there for some time now, and word spread through the crowd to watch out for strafing. People rushed to conceal everything white or red. Some stuck their heads into the hedges while those who planned to jump into the river moved closer to the edge of the riverbed. The sparks and flames from the row of houses burning on the embankment were so hot we couldn't stay by our fig tree and went out on to the sandy bank.

私たちの家のある九軒町の方角に炎々と燃え立つ火柱が立ち並んだ。それから土手の官有地の豪奢な住宅が燃えはじめた。河向うの岸の上の家が燃え出し、その向うの白い塀をへだてて饒津公園に高い火柱が突っ立った。火の中で何か爆発する音が、どどんどどんと、ひどい音を立てた。怒りっぽい私はそろそろ腹を立てはじめて母や妹に云った。

「なんだってあんなに方々で火事を出したんでしょうね。火を出してはおしまいだわ。火を消す稽古をあんなにしたんじゃありませんか。焼夷弾じゃないのだから、火の不始末よ。火くらい消して出ればいいのに。」

母と妹は仕方がないというようにだまっていた。

「こんな火事にしたのは市民の恥ね。あとでよその人に笑われてしまう。こんな火事ってないことよ。」

すべてのことに仕方がないという態度のきらいな私は、母や妹が怒らないのを責めるように云いつづけた。空は夕暮のように暗いままだった。暗い空にはさっきから飛行機の爆音がきこえ、誰いうとなく機銃掃射があるかも知れないから注意するようにと、口から口に伝えられた。白いものや赤いものをあわててかくしたり、垣根の中に頭を突っ込んだり、水にとび込むつもりの者は河原の端へ出て行った。私たちのいる無花果の木のあるあたりは、土手の家並の火の熱さと火の粉とで、もうじっとして居ることは出来なくなった。私たちは砂原へ出た。

What with the heat of both the sun and the flames, we soon found ourselves at the water's edge. The area was full of soldiers with burns, lying face up. Time and again they asked us to soak towels in the water for them. We made the towels sopping wet and spread them as asked on their chests, but soon the towels were bone dry once more.

'What happened to you?' my mother asked a soldier.

'We were on a labour detail at the primary school. I don't know what it was, but we heard this enormous noise, and the next thing we knew we were burnt like this.'

His whole face was swollen and torn as if with some kind of grey leprosy. The contrast with his broad, rugged chest and with the youthfulness of his well-built, handsome body was all too pathetic.

The fires spread fiercely, with irresistible force. Flames even began to spurt from the engine of the freight train stopped in the middle of the railway bridge close by on the right. One after another, the train's black carriages burst into flame, and when the fire reached the end carriage, it showered sparks and belched powerful flames as if it had been crammed full of gunpowder. With each explosion, it spat fire, as if molten iron were gushing out of a tunnel. Below the bridge, we could see the shore of the elegant park, the Asano Izumi Villa, where demonic deep red flames were crawling on the other side of the river. Soon the surface of the river itself started to burn, and we could see groups of people crossing to the other side. Now the river was burning fiercely. The people around us on the bank tried to flee upriver. Overhead, the familiar incessant

太陽の暑さと火事の焔の熱さとで、いつの間にか流れの水の傍へ行っていた。そのあたりには火傷の兵隊たちがいっぱい、仰向けに倒れていた。その人たちは幾度でも私たちにタオルを水にぬらして来ることを頼んだ。びっしょりぬらして、云われるように胸をひろげてかけておくタオルは、すぐからからに乾いた。

「どうなさったのですか。」

母が兵隊に訊いた。

「国民学校でみんな作業をしていたんですよ。なんだか知らないが、物すごい音のしたときは、こんなに焼けていたんです。」

その顔はまったく腫れつぶれた灰色の癩のようで、そのいかつく見えるほどの幅ひろい胸や、がっちりした恰好のいい全身の青春にくらべて、あまりにみじめすぎた。火災はとり返しのつかない勢いで猛々しく燃えひろがった。右手にほど近い鉄橋の真中に停っていた貨物列車の機関車からも、火を吐きはじめた。黒い貨物列車は一箱ずつ次々に燃え移って行き、うしろの方まで来ると、爆発薬でもつまっていたように、火花を散らして強い焔を吹いた。

だだん、だだん、しゅっ、しゅっと火を吹き、トンネルの入口から焼けただれた鉄が流れ出るように見えた。鉄橋の下から向うの浅野泉邸の瀟洒な公園の岸が見えるが、その岸にも悪魔のような深紅の焔が這い、やがて河の面が焼けはじめ、人の群が河を渡って向う岸へ行くのが見えた。河は炎々と燃えていた。私どものいる河原の人は上流に向って逃げようとした。

roar of circling B-29s told us that at any moment strafing, firebombs or conventional bombs might pour down on our dark gathering.

People felt certain that a second wave of attacks would be coming. But surely there was no need to drop any more of those things on us, a part of me was thinking.

While we hid in the grass or squatted beside the river in fear of a strafing, up in the sky they were taking photographs. Out in the open as we were, we were having our pictures taken from overhead, as was the entire devastated city.

Some sort of typhoon seemed to be blowing nearby, and we were getting the less direct gusts followed by large raindrops. I had heard that the burning of Osaka had also caused wind and rain and that people had emerged from their shelters carrying umbrellas even though the sun was shining. So I opened my green umbrella. The rain was a watery black colour, and along with it countless sparks poured out of the sky.

These 'sparks' that I assumed to be small grains of fire were actually bits of rag and scraps of wood glowing bright red as they were swept along by the high wind. The sky became darker still, as if night had come, and the red ball of the sun appeared to be plunging down out of a mass of black clouds.

My sister leaned against me, whispering, 'Look, way up there in the sky, a firebomb! A firebomb!'

'What are you talking about? Can't you see it's the sun?' We

　B29の爆音は頭の上で、ひっきりなしにあのきき馴れた旋回のうなりを立てている。機銃掃射や焼夷弾や爆弾はいつ私どもの暗い集りの上に降り注いでくるかも知れなかった。

　人々は第二波の攻撃が必ずあるものと思った。私は心のどこかでもうこの上に、そのようなものをわざわざ落し添える必要はないだろうと思うのだった。

　私どもが機銃掃射をされると云って草の小蔭にかくれたり、水の傍にしゃがんだりしていたとき、空では写真を撮っていたのである。私どもは野ざらしのまま、空々寂々とした全市とともに頭のうえから写真にされていたのだ。

　どこかに颱風のような風が起っている。その風は余波だけがこちらへ流れて来て、やがて大粒の雨が降った。大阪でも火災のとき風が起って雨がふり、それから待避のとき、太陽が照っていても雨傘を持って出たときいていたので、私は青い傘をひらいた。雨はうす黒かった。その中をおびただしい火の粉がふりかかって来るのだった。

　火の粉と云えば、小さい火の粒かと思っていたが、強風にふきまくられて来るその火の粉は、真赤に燃えている襤褸切や板の端であった。空はいっそう暗く夜のようになり、黒い雲のかたまりの中から、太陽の赤い球がどんどん下の方へさがってくるように見えた。

　「お姉さん、あの高い空から焼夷弾、焼夷弾！」

　妹が小声で云い私によりかかって来た。

　「なに云っているの。太陽じゃありませんか。」

tittered nervously, our first bit of laughter in all this. But by then neither she nor I could open our mouths easily.

'We may not be able to eat anything for another day or more,' I said to her. 'Let's drink some river water now and scoop some up for later.' I filled the bucket, thinking that any time now dead bodies might come floating down the river. Still, there was a pale rainbow hanging in the distant sky. The rain had just let up. There was something eerie about that faintly coloured rainbow.

'Water! Water! Let me have a drink!' the burnt soldiers pleaded incessantly.

'Burn victims die if you give them water. Don't do it!'

The faint shadow of death could already be seen between those warning against giving water to the soldiers and the soldiers themselves, who went on pleading for it.

The fires swelled into hills of flame, beat back everything before them, and proceeded to destroy the city block by block. The heat was unbearable. We could see the fires spreading through distant neighbourhoods and hear endless violent explosions from all directions. Not one Japanese plane showed itself in the sky.

We could not conceive of the day's events as being related in any way to the war. We were being crushed by a sheer force – an intense and one-sided force – that had nothing to do with war. Neither did

私たちははじめてかすかな笑い声を立てた。けれどもそのときはもう妹も私も口が自由に

あかなくなっていた。

「明日になってもごはんを食べられるかどうかわからない。今のうち川の水をのんだり汲んでおこうよ。」

私は妹に云ってバケツへ水をくんだ。河にはいまに死骸が浮きはじめると思えた。それで

いて向うの空にはうすい虹がかかっていた。雨はふり止んだばかりだった。向うの空にか

かっている淡々とした虹の色は無気味に見えた。

「水をくれ、水をくれ、水をのましてください。」

火傷の兵隊達はしきりに水をほしがった。

「火傷に水をのませると死ぬ。のましてはいけない。」

そう云ってとめる人たちと、水をくれと云いつづける人たちとの間に、死の影がすでに仄

見えた。

火災は丘のようにふくらみ、いっさいを撥ね返し、市街の一画ずつが亡びて行った。たま

らない暑さであった。遠くの町の燃えひろがるのが見え、はげしい爆発音はどこからともな

くひきつづいて聞こえる。日本の飛行機は一機も空に姿を見せはしなかった。

私どもはこの日の出来ごとを戦争と思うことは出来なかった。戦争の形態ではなく、一方

的に、強烈な力で押しつぶされているのだった。そのうえ日本人同士はべつに互いを力づ

we as fellow Japanese encourage one another or console one another. We behaved submissively and said nothing. No one came to tend the injured, no one came to tell us where or how to pass the night. We were simply on our own.

Saeki Ayako's German shepherd was still wandering among the crowds of wounded on the riverbed, never making a sound. It was widely known in Hiroshima as one of the fiercer dogs of the city, but the way it came and went with its tail hanging down, it was like a human being in misery, having lost all powers of resistance. Saeki Ayako was nowhere to be seen. Since coming to the riverbed, I had been half-consciously looking for her or for the mother-in-law or the sixteen-year-old daughter, Yuriko, who shared her home, but even after dusk, I saw no sign of them.

Night fell, but I was not sure when. The day itself had been so dark there was no clear break between day and night. When night did come, however, both city and riverbed were red from the reflection of the fires. We ate nothing during the day or the night, but we did not feel hungry. Each of us had taken pains to fashion a place for ourselves during the day, but we were unable to stay put for long. The sparks, the rain and the sound of enemy planes chased us away. People said that the tide would rise after dark, so we gathered in the vegetable gardens and by the clumps of trees below the gardens on the way down to the sandy riverbed. We fashioned a place to lie down in front of the hedge facing the riverbed.

け合うわけでもなぐさめ合うわけでもなく、なんにも云わないでおとなしくしているのだった。どこからも負傷者の手当に来てもなく、夜はどこでどのようにすごせと云ってくる人も
なく、放っておかれた。

　佐伯綾子の家のシェパードは、まだ河原の負傷者の群像の間を、一度も吠えないでうろうろしている。その犬は広島でも有名な猛犬と云われていたけれども、尾を垂れ、侘びしい時の人間とそっくりな、抵抗力を失った様子で行ったり来たりしているのだった。佐伯綾子はどこにもいなかった。いっしょにいる義理のお母さんや、十六になる一人娘の百合子さんを、私は河原に来た時からそれとなく眼で探した。三人の姿はとうとう夕方になっても見かけることは出来なかった。

　夜が来た。夜はいつ訪れて来たのかわからなかった。昼も暗かったのだから、夜との境目ははっきりしないのだった。ただ夜が来ると、火事の照り返しのために町も河原も真赤であった。昼も夜も食事をしないけれど、お腹の減っていることは感じなかった。昼間は折角てんでの居場所を作ってからも、火の粉や雨や、敵機の音に追われてひとつところに長くじっとしていることは出来なかった。けれども、日暮から潮がくるというので、人々は菜園の中やそのはずれの砂原へ降りる途中の、樹立のあたりなどへ集った。私たちも砂原に向った垣根の前に身を横たえる場所をつくった。

Pulling up lots of weeds and spreading them out, we covered them with straw that the river had carried to the sandy bank and on top of that laid the coat that my mother had worn over the baby on her back. The four of us took our places on this makeshift theatre box. A chubby eight months old, the baby had slept all day and did not wake at night. My sister and I removed the kerchiefs that had protected our necks and faces through the day. This was the first good look we had had of each other's angry faces, but smiling was an impossibility.

We couldn't see our own faces, but looking at each other gave us the idea. My sister's face was puffed up like a round loaf of bread, and her eyes, normally large, black and uncannily clear, had become mere slits, their edges dark as blue-black ink. A cross-shaped cut extended from the right edge of her lip into her cheek, twisting her whole mouth into a sideways inverted letter L, a sight so ugly I could not look at it for long. Her hair was caked with blood and the red clay of our house's walls, as if she had been on the streets, begging, for years. Both of us had bound our wounds with odd bits of fabric. I can't recall where we found it, but three or four days earlier, in preparation for autumn and winter, my mother had dyed a piece of crêpe – the broad collar of an old kimono. We had each wrapped the cloth under our chins and knotted it on top of our heads. I had a deep cut from the middle of my left ear, opening like a valley to a spot below the ear.

Our injuries were covered over with strands of hair caked with blood. Our mouths were swollen shut and difficult to open, not so much because of the pain as the feeling that they had been glued in place and locked.

雑草をたくさんぬいて敷き、その上に砂原に流れ残っていた藁を敷いて、母が赤ん坊を背負って来たねんねこ半纏をひろげて敷いた。その小さな平土間のような桟敷に四人が坐った。くりくりした生後八ヵ月の赤ん坊は昼間も眠り通しに眠っていて、夜も眼をさまさなかった。

妹と私は昼間じゅう頭から顔をつつんでいた風呂敷をとった。私たちは怒ったような顔をはじめて互いにしみじみ眺めたけれど、微笑し合うことは出来なかった。

自分の顔がどんなになっているのか、互に自分ではわからないけれど、相手の顔を眺めて見当がついた。妹の顔は丸いパンのように腫れて、大きくて黒く、無気味なほど澄んでいた平生の眼は糸のように細くなり、そのふちは青黒いインクを流したようであった。唇の右の端から頬へ向けて十文字に切った傷のために口ぜんたいがねじれ曲ったへの字になり、醜くて長く見てはいられなかった。髪は血と壁の赤土で、もう長い間乞食でもして来た女のようであった。妹も私も妙なもので傷を繃帯していた。どこにあったのか思い出すことができないが、三、四日まえ母が秋や冬にかける用意に濃い紫に染めておいてくれた古い縮緬の半衿で、二人とも頤をつり、頭のうえでくくっていた。私は左の耳の中から耳の下へかけて谷のように切られていた。

傷の上には血がかたまった髪の毛がかぶさっていた。妹も私も傷のために腫れふさがった口を、思うように開くことが出来なかった。痛いというよりも膠附のようで、口に錠を下ろされている感じであった。

'What were you two doing yesterday morning?' I asked, barely able to move my lips.

'Yesterday? It was *this* morning!' my sister said with a smile, her lips puckered as if she were trying to whistle.

My mother remembered what she was doing at the time and said with regret, 'This morning I got out the salted bamboo shoots I had been saving for a special occasion. I boiled them in soy sauce with carrots and potatoes I had grown out back. It was delicious! I had just eaten a mouthful with rice when there was that blue flash.'

'What did you think it was?' I asked. 'A bomb? A firebomb?'

'That huge bang happened before I even had time to think what it was, and the cupboard fell over. I threw myself down when the flash hit, and the cupboard fell on top of me, but fortunately the closet behind me kept the cupboard from falling all the way. I was bent over in a kind of cave like being curled up under a desk or something, so nothing happened to me. Then I heard you give a shriek.'

My sister had been sitting across from my mother in the family room. She, too, had just eaten a mouthful of breakfast. When she saw the flash, she rushed to the baby in the next room. Because there were mosquitoes about even in the morning, she had put the baby to sleep under a mosquito net. She threw herself down on top of the baby, who was sound asleep but, thinking that a lot of fire-bombs must have fallen on the family room, she turned to look in that direction. At that moment there was a sudden gust of wind, and

「きのうの朝、あなた達はどうしていたんですの。」

私はやっと口さきでものを云った。

「きのう？　今朝のことよ。」

妹は口笛を吹く口元で笑った。

「今朝は私が前からたしなんでおいた塩漬けの筍を探し出して、私が裏へ作った人参やじゃがいもといっしょにおいしいお煮〆を煮たのよ。それをそえて一口ごはんを食べたと思ったら、ぴかッと青いものが光ったん。」

妹は思い出して残念そうに云った。母は思い出して残念そうに云った。

「なんだと思いました？　爆弾と思いました？　焼夷弾と思った？」

「なんだろうとも考える暇もないうちに、ぱさァと大きな音がして戸棚が倒れかかって来たからね。私は光った時に伏せていましたよ。そのうえへ戸棚が倒れたけれど、いいあんばいにうしろの押入れで戸棚が支えられてね、机の下へでもかがんだように私は穴のようなところへかがんでいて、なんともありませんでしたよ。そのときに洋子さんがきゃァと云ったのをきいたのよ。」

妹の方も茶の間で母と向い合ってやはり食事を一口たべたところであった。かの女は光を見たとき、次の座敷の赤ん坊のところへ飛びこんで行った。朝のうちも蚊がいるので赤ん坊は蚊帳の中にねせてあった。よく眠っている赤ん坊のうえに妹は自分の体を伏せたけれど、よほどたくさんの焼夷弾が茶の間へ落ちたものと思い、その方をふり返った。するとぱっと

she immediately started bleeding.

'The blue flash lasted only an instant, but I must have flown to the baby in the first instant of that instant. Still, I have no memory of ducking under the mosquito net.'

My mother spoke again: 'That breakfast this morning – what a waste!'

I said, 'So, what do you think happened this morning? I have no idea what that was. My umbrella shaft had no bend in it before.'

My sister seemed to think she had to say something. 'Maybe it was *iperitto.*'

'*Iperitto*? What's that?'

'Mustard gas. Poison gas.'

'That's it, for sure. But poison gas couldn't have knocked the houses down.'

'They combined it – with conventional bombs.'

Having no clear idea what had happened, we talked nonsense. The fires continued to burn fiercely in the distance, soaring up into the sky. In the space of one night, all of Hakushima had burnt itself out: Kukenchō, nearby Higashimachi, Nakamachi, Kitamachi, the houses on the embankment, everything there had dimmed to an ashen grey. Two or three houses on the opposite river bank continued to burn out of control. Their wild flames writhed like giant

風が来て、すぐ血が流れはじめた。

「青い光も瞬間だったけれど、その瞬間のまたはじめの瞬間にあたし赤のところへとんで行ったらしいね。でも蚊帳をくぐった記憶がちっともないのよ。」

「今朝のおかずは惜しいねえ。」

母がまた云った。

「ねえ、なんだろう？　今朝のあれは。どうしたのだかちっともわかんないのね。こうもり傘の柄だって昨日まではあんなに曲っていなかったのよ。」

私が云った。妹は何か云わなくてはという風に答えた。

「イペリットかしら。」

「イペリットってなに？」

「糜爛性毒ガス。」

「それね、きっと。だけど家がこわれたのは毒ガスじゃないわね。」

「交ぜたのよ。爆弾といっしょに。」

はっきりした考えもなく私どもはうつけたように話した。火事はまだ遠くの方に、天をついてもの凄く燃えつづけている。白島は、九軒町もその附近の東町も中町も北町も、土手の家々もすっかり燃え落ちて夜の中に漠として灰色にかすんでいた。川向うの岸では二、三軒の家がしつっこくまだ火をしずめなかった。猛火は大きな蛇のようにくねくねと身もだえし

snakes. The Ushita area had been on fire during the day, and when night came, the flames moved from peak to peak along the low, wavy range of hills, looking like lights in a far-off town. Chunks of flame flew continually across the space between one peak and the next like shooting stars, and then the second peak would start a new fire.

After night fell, we started hearing dull groans from the distance. The low, monotonous groans echoed all around us.

At around that time, someone brought word that food was going to be distributed. We hadn't given the slightest thought to supper, so we responded with happy cries.

The energetic voice of someone passing among us, probably a soldier, called to those of us lined up along the hedges: 'All those who can walk, please go to the East Parade Ground to pick up food.' Everyone began to chatter, and for the first time you could tell that the silhouettes moving along the riverbed were in fact flesh-and-blood human beings. Of our little group, both my sister and I ached all over and were unable to stand or walk. My mother went, helped by the young woman next to her. It was a mile or more to the East Parade Ground. She came back with four white, triangular rice balls that were still warm, wrapped up in a square of cloth. She also received four bags of hardtack.

'A feast!'

We gladly took hold of the rice balls and found them heavy to the touch. But neither my sister nor I could open our mouths wide enough to eat. Like a dentist, I forced my paralysed mouth open with the thumb and index finger of my left hand while, with my right hand, I pressed the rice through my lips a few grains at a time.

て燃えた。牛田の方は昼間から燃えていて、夜になると低く波うつ山脈の峯から峯に火がと
もり、遠い街の灯のように見えた。焔のかたまりが峯から峯の間を流星めいてしきりにとび、
そこが新しく火の丘になるのが見えた。夜になってからは遠くの方から間の伸びた呻き声が
きこえて来るようになった。単調な呻き声は低く沈んで、あちこちから聞こえる。

そのころ、配給の食事のあることをつたえて来た人があった。私たちは今夜の食べものの
ことなどは考えていなかったので、よろこびの声をあげた。

「歩けない人以外は東練兵場までとりに行って下さい。」

兵隊らしい人の元気のいい声が垣根に並んでいる人々によびかけて通った。みんながやが
や云いはじめ、影絵のように河原を歩いて行くのが、人間の生活のあたたかな一片に眺めら
れた。私どものところでは、私も妹ももう体中の痛みで立つことも歩くことも出来なくなっ
ていたので、母が隣りにいた若い女の人につれられて行った。東練兵場まで十五丁はあった。
母はまだぬくもりのある大きな白い三角のむすびを四つもらって、風呂敷にじかに包んで来
た。乾パンも四袋あった。

「豊富ね。」

私たちがうれしがって、むすびをつまむと重いくらいであった。けれども妹と私はどうし
てもものを食べるほど、口をあくことができなかった。左手の拇指と人さし指で歯医者のよ
うに、無理にしびれている口を上下にひらき、右手で少しずつ、白いごはんの粒を押し入れ
た。

'Is Tokiwa Bridge still there?'

'Both railings were burnt away, but the road itself is still there, all bulged out. Things are really pretty bad everywhere. There's nothing left unburnt.'

Listening to the conversations of people sitting lined up in front of the hedge facing the river, it became clear to us that today's conflagration had consumed the entire city of Hiroshima, leaving no part of town untouched. This was no minor fire caused by some individuals' carelessness; enemy planes had scattered sparks over the whole city.

'They scattered sparks? No wonder the whole place burned! With bombs, it would have taken a hundred or two, even five hundred or a thousand. They didn't just "drop" bombs – they sprayed the place.'

In the local dialect, 'spraying' meant they had rained bombs down in clusters, like a waterfall. There was not a single crater anywhere, though. People still didn't realize it meant there had been no bombs. They had so little idea what had happened, they didn't have a lot to say.

We stretched out on the ground. Owing to the surrounding forest fires and the conflagration on the other shore of the river, it was bright and warm. We heard groans from far and near like mournful musical instruments, and these were joined by the cries of insects. It was all so very sad.

My entire body numb with the sadness and pain, my tangled thoughts gave way to a somewhat clear idea: this numb feeling, this intensely odd numb feeling from an external shock, was my body's direct physical response to the moment when the morning's strange blue flash and powerful noise became one with the total destruction

「常盤橋はまだありました？」

「両方の欄干がみな焼けてしもうてね、中がふくれたようにのこってますよ。ほんとにまあ、ひどいことで、どこもかしこも焼けんところはないのよ。」

垣根の前に、河原に向ってずらりと並んで坐っている人々の話をきいても、今日の火災は広島全市で、のこった町はひとつとしてないことがわかった。火は市民達の火の不始末といううそんなささやかなものでなく、敵の飛行機が全市に向って火の粉をふりまいたというのであった。

「火の粉をふりまいたのか。道理でいちめんに焼けたんだな。爆弾でも百や二百や、五百や千とは云わんね。それも落したんじゃないのよ、さぜ落したんじゃね。」

さぜ落すというのは爆弾のかたまりを滝のようにふりかけるという方言である。人々はたった一つの穴さえどこにもないのに、それが爆弾でないことには気づかないのだ。だから人々は今日のことをかれこれと語らないのだった。もの憂い楽器の音色をきくように、遠くや近くにきこえる呻き声をきいていると、虫の音もいっしょに耳にはいって来た。ひどく悲しかった。

悲しみと痛みとでからだ中がしびれたように感じたとき、私の頭にいくらかはっきりした理念がほぐれて来た。しびれた感じ。外からの衝動ではげしく異様にしびれた感じ。これが今朝の青いふしぎな光と強烈な物音と、市街の崩壊が一つになって起った瞬間にうけた、肉

of the city. It crossed my mind that some kind of colourless, odourless intangible substance might have burnt up the air in a process involving physics or physical chemistry, not something that would stink or be visible or have a smell such as a poison gas. Out of a desire to pin something down, I tried to find it based on that physical sense of mine.

I fell easily, naturally, into a primitive mode of thought. Like a child, I recalled the nitrogen, oxygen and carbon dioxide gases in the air. Perhaps the enemy planes had sent electrons, via very high-frequency radio waves, into these things invisible to the human eye. Without giving off any sound or smell or exhibiting any colour, these airborne radio waves must have turned into huge, white flames. Unless I drew a mental picture of a new mystery world like that, I couldn't conceive of how there could have been so many victims with such strange burns. I thought it fairly remarkable that I was able to formulate such thoughts – or perhaps I should say such instinctive feelings – before descending into an unbearably painful sense of defeat.

'The war's over,' I whispered to my sister on the ground beside me.

'What are you saying?' she demanded.

'There's nothing more we can do,' I muttered. 'Japan's got two months at the most.'

The fires in the mountains continued to burn spectacularly,

体への端的なひびきであった。物理的な作用、あくまでも物理科学的な、毒瓦斯と云っても、

それはくさかったり、眼に見えたり、匂いのあるものではなく、色もなく匂いもな

い、しかもなにかの物体が、空気を焼いたのではないかと私は思った。私はなにかをつきと

めたい欲望で、私のからだに受けた感覚からどうにかしてそれをさがし出そうとした。

私は自然にすらすらと原始的な考え方にひきこまれた。子供のように、私は空気中の窒素

や酸素や、炭酸瓦斯などを思い出した。そういう人間の眼にふれぬものに敵機は超短波のよ

うな電子を送ったのかも知れない。空気中の電波が音も匂いも立てず、色彩も見せないで、

白色の大きな焔になったのにちがいない。そのような新しい神秘世界を心に描くよりほかに、

あまりにおびただしい、ふしぎな火傷の負傷者を考えることは出来なかった。私は私の考え

方、考え方というよりも、官能にうけた感じから、こんな風に考えることをなんとなく素晴

らしいと思い、そして耐えがたい敗北感に落ちて苦しくなった。

「戦争はすむわよ。」

私は小さい声で、並んでいる妹の耳に囁いた。

「なぜなの?」

妹はとがめるように訊いた。

「だってもう出来ないもの。もう長くて二ヵ月ね。」

私はぼそぼそと云った。山火事は峯から峯を伝って華やかな色に燃えつづけていた。夜ふ

spreading from peak to peak. The night deepened, but no one came to tend to the injured. We heard the cries of the insects among the low, heavy human groans that welled up all around us.

けても負傷者の手当にはどこからも来なかった。方々から湧き起る低く重い人間の呻き声を
縫って、虫の音が聞こえた。

ŌBA MINAKO

The Smile of a Mountain Witch

Translated by Mizuta Noriko

Let me tell you about a legendary witch who lives in the mountains.

Her scraggly grey hair bound with a length of cord, she waits in her house for a man from the village to lose his way so she can devour him. When an unknowing young man wanders up to her lair and asks for a night's lodging, the owner of the house grins, a comb with missing teeth clamped between her own yellowed teeth that shine in the flickering lamplight. The eerie hag terrifies him and she says to him, 'You just thought, "What a creepy old woman! Like an old monster cat!" didn't you?'

Startled, the young man steals a glimpse at her from under his brows as he gulps down his millet porridge and thinks to himself, 'Don't tell me she's planning to devour me in the middle of the night!'

Without a moment's hesitation, the mountain witch tells him, 'You just thought, "Don't tell me she's planning to devour me in the middle of the night!" didn't you?'

Turning pale, the man replies, 'I was just thinking that with this warming bowl of porridge I finally feel relaxed and that my fatigue is catching up with me,' but his body goes as hard as ice and he thinks to himself, 'The reason she's boiling such a big pot of water must be that she's preparing to cook me in the middle of the night!'

大庭みな子
山姥の微笑

山姥の話をしよう。

昔語りの山姥は、山の中の一軒家で、白髪のざんばら髪を縄で結い、里から迷いこむ者をとって食おうと待ちかまえている。それと知らずに山姥の棲家に迷いこんで一夜の宿を乞うた若い男が、まばらに歯のぬけ落ちた櫛をくわえてにっと笑う宿の主の奇怪な形相におびえると、ゆらぐ灯にその歯を黄色く光らせてこう言う。「お前さんは、今こう思ったね、〈薄気味の悪い、まるで老いさらばえた化け猫みたいな女だな〉と」

男はぎくりとして、更に思う。〈まさか、夜半におれをとって食うつもりではあるまいな〉

すると山姥はすかさず、彼女を上眼遣いに盗み見ながら粟粥をかきこんでいる男にこう言う。「お前さんは今、心の中で、〈まさか、夜半におれをとって食うつもりではあるまいな〉と思ったね」

男は蒼ざめ、「わたしはただ、この暖かな粥でやっと人心地ついて、急に疲れがでたなと思っていただけですよ」と言うが、心の中では〈さっきから、あんな大きな鍋に湯を煮立てているのは、やっぱりこのおれを、夜半に煮て食うための準備に違いない〉とからだを氷の

With a sly grin, the old witch says, 'You just thought to your-self, "The reason she's boiling such a big pot of water must be that she's preparing to cook me in the middle of the night!" didn't you?'

The man becomes even more terrified. 'You accuse me wrongly. I was only thinking that I'm really tired from walking all day and that I ought to excuse myself and retire for the night while I'm still warm from the porridge, so that I may start out early tomorrow morning.'

But he thinks to himself, 'What a spooky old hag! This monster cat of a woman must be one of those old mountain witches I've heard so much about. That's how she can read my mind so well!'

Without a moment's hesitation, the mountain witch says, 'You just thought, "What a spooky old hag! This monster cat of a woman must be one of those old mountain witches I've heard people talk about. That's how she can read my mind so well!" '

The man becomes so frightened he can hardly keep his teeth from chattering, but he manages to shuffle along on shaky knees, saying, 'Well, I must excuse myself and retire for now –'

Practically crawling into the next room, he lies down on a straw mat without undoing his travelling attire. The witch follows him with a sidelong glance and says, 'Now you're thinking that you'll wait for a chance to escape.'

ように硬ばらせて思うのである。

山姥はにやりと笑い、「お前さんは今心の中で、〈さっきから、あんな大きな鍋に湯を煮立てているのは、やっぱりこのおれを、夜半に煮て食うための準備に違いない〉と思っただろう」と言うのである。

男はますます怯え、「何を、あなたはへんな言いがかりを。——わたしはただ、一日歩いてすっかりくたびれたので、この暖かな粥であたたまったからだが冷えないうちに、横にならせていただき、あすは朝早く出立したいものだと考えていたのです」と言う。

だが、心の中では〈全く気味の悪い女だ。やっぱりこの化け猫のような女は、あの噂にきく山姥に違いない。他人の心の中の言葉をこんなにはっきり読むんだからな〉と思う。

すかさず山姥は「お前さんは今こう思ったのさ。〈全く気味の悪い女だ。やっぱりこの化け猫のような女は、あの噂にきく山姥に違いない。他人の心の中の言葉をこんなにはっきり読むんだからな〉」

男はもう歯の根が合わないほどだったが、がくがくした膝頭で辛うじてからだをいざらせながらこう答える。「では、ひとまずお先に失礼して——」

そして這うようにして次の間にひっこみ、旅装をとかずに筵の上にからだを横たえると、山姥は男を流し眼に追って、「お前さんは今、すきを見て逃げ出せるとでも思っているのさ」と言うのである。

Indeed, the man had stretched out in order to take her off her guard, hoping for a chance to escape.

These old mountain witches are able to read every thought that crosses a person's mind, and in the end the victim runs for his life away from the witch's abode. She pursues him relentlessly and the man keeps running. At least this is the form the classic mountain-witch tales assume.

They call them *yamauba* – 'mountain hags' or 'mountain crones' – but surely these witches cannot have been wrinkled old hags from birth? At one time they must have been babies with skin like freshly pounded rice cakes and the faint sweet-sour odour of the newborn. They must have been maidens seducing men with their moist, glossy complexions of polished silk. Like tiny pink shells, their shining fingernails must have dug into the shoulders of the men they suffocated in ecstasy between their swelling breasts.

For some reason, though, no tales have been handed down of tender, young mountain witches. The young ones can't remain shut up in the mountain fastnesses and instead they take up residence inside beasts or birds – cranes or foxes or snowy herons – which then become beautiful wives that live in human settlements, or so their stories have been transformed, it seems.

These metamorphosed animals who turn into human wives are always very intelligent and sensitive, but their fates are invariably tragic. After years of devoted service to their husbands, they revert to emaciated animals at the end, their fur or feathers dropping out as they flee back into the mountains. Perhaps these poor creatures, with all their bitterness and resentment, are the ones who become old mountain witches. After all, devouring may be the ultimate expression of affection. Does not a mother, full of emotion, often squeeze

全く、男は山姥の言う通り、すきを見て逃げ出せるように、山姥を油断させようとして横になったのだった。

ともかく、山姥というのは次から次に相手の心の中を読み、遂に相手は命からがら山姥の棲家から逃げ出す。山姥はどこまでもそのあとを追ってきて、男はただ一目散に逃げるというのが、昔から語り伝えられた山姥の物語である。

しかし、山姥といえど、生まれたときから皺くちゃの婆さんであったわけではなく、つきたての餅のような肌の、甘酸っぱい匂いのする赤児であったことも、ねり絹のように輝く肌をぬめらせて男を誘う乙女の時代もあったであろう。桜貝のように光る爪を男の肩の肉に喰いこませて、むっちりとした乳房の間で恋人を窒息させたこともあっただろう。

だが、どういうわけか、うら若い山姥の物語は伝わっていない。どうやらうら若い山姥は山に籠っていることはできず、いろんな動物に、たとえば鶴とか狐とか鷺などに宿って、美しい女房になり、人里に棲むといった話につくり変えられるらしい。そして、そういう動物の化身の女は、みんな頭がよくて、情にこまやかなのに、なぜか末路は哀れで、さんざん男に尽くしたあげく、物語の終末では無残に毛の脱け落ちた痩せ細った動物のからだに戻り、山に逃げ帰ると相場がきまっている。もしかしたらその哀れな動物たちが、恨みつらみをこめて山姥になるのではなかろうか。それにまあ、食うというのは極度の愛情の表現でもある。よく感極まった母親は赤ん坊をぎゅっと抱きしめて、

her child and exclaim, 'I love you so much I could eat you up!'?

Now, the woman I'm going to tell you about was an absolutely genuine mountain witch.

She died at the age of sixty-two.

At sixty-two, when her soulless naked body was cleansed with surgical spirit, her skin was glossy and youthful like the wax figure of a goddess. Her hair was half white, and on the mound beneath her gently sloping belly were a few strands of silver. And yet, around her calmly closed eyelids and her faintly smiling lips, there lingered the strange innocence and bashfulness of a little girl who is forcing a smile when she is ready to burst out crying.

She was a mountain witch among mountain witches, and though she longed for a dwelling in the mountains, she never lived in one. Instead, she spent her entire life in a temporary abode as a human woman in a human settlement.

She had been an old mountain witch ever since she could remember.

When still a tiny thing, she would be so engrossed in play she would often wet her pants. And when her mother came running, the little mountain witch would say to her, 'Oh, you naughty girl. You've got to tell Mummy in time before it's too late. We don't have any fresh undies for you today.'

At that, her mother would burst out laughing, so the little mountain witch would continue, 'I'm no match for this child! What can I say?'

When her father was late coming home at night and her mother glanced at the clock on the wall, the child would say, 'What in the

「食べちゃいたいくらい可愛いわ」と言うではないか。

さて、彼女は、正真正銘の山姥だった。

彼女は六十二歳で死んだ。

六十二歳の、魂が飛んで行ったあとの彼女の裸体は、アルコールで拭き清めると、つややかで若々しく、蝋でつくった女神の像のようであった。髪は半白で、なだらかな腹部の終りの丘には銀色の薄の幾筋かがなびいていたが、そのおだやかに閉じた瞼と、いくらかほころばせた口元のあたりには、不思議な、あどけなさと、泣き出しそうなのをこらえて笑っている少女のようなはにかみがあった。

彼女は全く山姥の中の山姥だったが、山の棲家を想いながら、ついぞ一度もそこに棲むこともなく、里の仮住いで人間の女としての一生を終えたのである。

彼女は物心ついたときに、すでに山姥だった。

まだときどきおしっこの失敗をする幼い頃、彼女は遊びに夢中になってついおもらしをしてしまったとき、とんできた母親に向ってこう言うのである。「マタ、チッパイ、チチャッタノ。マニアウヨウニ、イウンデチュヨ。モウ、キョウハ、カワリノパンツガナイノ二、ホントニコマッタコネ」

母親がつい笑い出すと、「アーアー、コノコ二ハ、カナワナイワ、ホントニイヤニナッチャウ」

夜、父親の帰りが遅くて、母親が時計を見上げると、「ホント二、マイバン、マイバン、イッ

world is he up to, coming home late night after night! He says it's work, but I know he's really staying out as late as possible because it's so boring at home. As if he's the only one who feels that way!'

At that, her mother would cast a wry grin and scowl at her, but before she could say anything, the little girl would exclaim, 'You foolish girl! Come on now, go to bed. Little children who stay up late never grow. They stay little forever and ever.'

Appalled at her daughter's ability to read her mind time after time, the mother would give in, saying, 'This child is very bright, but she really tires me out!'

When she was a little older and her mother brought her a new toy, the girl would say, 'This will keep her quiet for a while.' Annoyed, her mother would give her a look, whereupon the daughter would say, 'Why in the world does this child read people's minds all the time? She's like a mountain witch. People will probably come to dislike her as they would a mountain witch.'

Of course, her mother would blurt out such thoughts all the time, so the girl was merely parroting her mother's words.

When she started going to school, her mother was relieved to have time away from her daughter, but soon she noticed that the little girl had ended her habit of echoing people's thoughts and was

タイ、ナニチテルノカチラネエ。チゴトチゴトダッテ、ホントハ、ウチニカエッタッテオモ
チロクナイカラ、ナルベクソトニイタインダワ、ミンナ、ダレダッテ、ソウチタイノハ、ヤ
マヤマナノニネエ、アーアー」

母親が苦笑して睨みつけると、「オバカサン、コドモハ、モウネナチャイ。イツマデモオ
キテルコハ、イツマデタッテモ、オオキクナラズニ、イツマデモコビトサンデイルシカアリ
マチェンヨ」

次から次に他人の心を読む子供に母親はあきれ果てて、「この子は頭がいいけれど、全く
ひとを疲れさせちゃうわね」と辟易した。

少し大きくなって、母親が新しい玩具を買い与えると、「サア、コレデ、シバラクハシズ
カデ、ホットスルワ」と言い、母親がいくらかむっとして彼女を見つめると、「ナンダッテ、
コノコハ、ナニカラナニマデヒトノキヲ、ヨムノカシラ。ヤマウバミタイ。ヤマウバミタイ
ニ、ヒトニキラワレルンジャナイカシラ」

もちろん、そういうことを、母親が常日頃述懐していたので、彼女は単に復誦しただけの
ことなのである。

やっと彼女が学校に行くようになると、母親は子供から離れた時間を持ってほっとした
が、いつの間にか娘が人の心を復誦する癖をやめ、だんだん無口になったことに気づいて、
ある日こう訊ねた。

growing quieter day by day. 'You're so quiet all of a sudden now that you're at school,' she said one day.

Her daughter replied, 'When I say what's on my mind, people give me nasty looks, so I'm just going to shut up. Grown-ups like it when kids pretend to be stupid and unaware of things, so I've decided to keep grown-ups happy from now on.'

Conscious of her unique accomplishment in having given birth to a mountain witch, the mother responded firmly, 'Go ahead and say whatever is on your mind. You don't have to pretend anything. You're a child, after all.'

But the girl merely regarded her mother with a disdainful smile.

The child received good grades at school for the most part. Whenever she did poorly on a test, she would tear it up and not show it to her mother. Her mother would complain when she did not finish the lunch she brought to school, so on days when she had little appetite, she threw her leftovers into a rubbish bin on her way home. To ward off suspicion, she would leave a little food in her lunchbox now and then and tell her mother, 'The teacher talked longer today, so I didn't have time to finish it.'

The child bloomed into maidenhood, but the family could not afford to buy her expensive dresses. When she and her mother went shopping, the girl would pick the dress she knew her mother found most appropriate and pretend that she really liked it. Putting herself in her mother's place, she would say, 'I think this is really sweet. If I wore something fancy at my age, people would think some rich old man was keeping me.'

「学校に行くようになったら、あんたは急におとなしくなっちゃったのね」

すると、娘はこう答えた。「思っていることをそのまま言うと、みんながいやな顔をするから、黙っていることにしたの。これからは大人たちを喜ばせることにしたの」

母親もまた山姥を生んだ母親だけのことはあって、きっとこう言い返した。「思っていることをなんでも言いなさい。フリなんかしなくてもいいのよ。子供の癖に」

しかし、子供は母親の顔をじっと見て、軽蔑した笑いを浮かべた。ときどきあまりよい点をとらなかったときは、答案用紙を破って母親に見せなかった。お弁当を食べ残すと母親が文句を言うので、食欲がなくて食べられなかったときは、家へ帰る前にごみ箱に捨てて帰った。しかし疑われないように、ときどきはほんの少し残し、「今日は先生のお話が長くなって、時間が足りなかったの」

と言いわけした。

やがて娘は年頃になったが、彼女の家はそれほど豊かではなかったから、娘に高価な衣裳を買い与えることはできなかった。母娘で一緒に買物に行くと、娘は母親がこれぐらいが相応だと思ってみつくろっているものを、自分が殊更に気に入っているふりをして選んだ。

「これが可愛らしくていいわ。若い癖にあんまり豪華なものを着たりするのは、お金持のおじいさんに囲われている女の人みたいだもの」娘は母親の代りに言ってやった。

On such occasions, her mother would look at her a little sadly, and on the way home, for no apparent reason, she would buy her daughter something way beyond her means. The girl would pretend not to notice her mother's impulse and act genuinely pleased.

The girl would assume whatever manner was expected of her as though it was what she herself wanted to do, not only with her family but with anyone she wanted to please. When they wanted her to laugh, she would laugh. When they wanted her to remain silent, she remained silent. When talkativeness was desired, she chatted merrily. With a person who considered himself intelligent, she would act a little stupid – though not *too* stupid, because that type of person usually thought it a waste of time dealing with very stupid people. And with stupid people, she would make a show of appreciating their simplicity.

Probably because she wanted so desperately to be liked by far too many people, she had to squander a frightening amount of mental energy every day. Before she realized it, she had become antisocial, reading books in her room all day, avoiding contact with others.

'Why don't you go out with your friends?' her mother would ask, to which she would answer simply: 'I get so tired . . .'

Her mother, too, found it tiring to be with her. It was a relief when her daughter was not around. She began to long for the day

そういうとき、母親はいくらか哀しげな顔をして娘の顔をみつめ、その帰りに、突然、分不相応なものを理由もなく娘に買い与えたりした。すると娘はそうした母親の衝動に気づかないふりをして、すなおに喜んでみせた。

娘は身内の者に対してばかりでなく、気に入られたい相手に対しては、相手が自分に欲していることを、自分が欲しているようにしかふるまわなかった。相手が笑って欲しいと思っているときは笑い、黙っていて欲しいと思っているときは沈黙し、おしゃべりをのぞんでいるときは、ぺちゃくちゃとしゃべった。自分を頭がよいと思っている人間には、それよりもほんのいくらかバカなふりをし、――あまりひどくバカではいけない。そういう人間はあまりバカを相手にするのは時間の無駄遣いだと思うものである。――バカな人間に対してはその素朴さを尊んだ。

多分彼女はあまりに強慾で、あまりに多くの人間に気に入られたいため、おそろしい精力の浪費をしなければならなかったのである。そして、気がついたとき、娘はだんだん人嫌いになり、一日中部屋に閉じこもって本を読み、他人と一緒にいることを避けるようになった。

「どうして外でみんなと遊ばないの」と母親が訊ねると、娘はただ「疲れるから――」と言葉少なに答えた。

母親もまた、娘と一緒にいると、疲労を感ずるようになり、娘がそばにいないとほっとし、

when her daughter would find a suitable young man and leave her. In other words, mother and daughter had arrived at that natural phase of life when they were ready to part.

The daughter knew that she was a burden to her mother – had known it all too well as far back as she could remember. She wanted to free her mother – and herself – as soon as possible. At the same time, somewhere in her heart she held a grudge against her mother, a grudge that was sometimes so strong she would feel surges of inexplicable rage. That is to say, she was going through the short, rebellious phase of puberty, but she realized that her hatred and anger were directed at the cunning ways of her mother as a same-sex competitor: her mother's despicable techniques of taking advantage of her motherly authority and of avoiding direct confrontation. With this realization came a sudden awareness of how much her mother had aged and how much she herself had matured.

As a mature girl, she naturally found a man

He was an ordinary, run-of-the-mill sort of man. Like all men, he had been doted on by his mother, and so he firmly believed that because his mother was of the opposite sex, he was allowed to express himself as freely as he pleased with other women beyond all reason. When such a man matures physically, the woman with whom he shares his bed must be a substitute for his mother. She must be as magnanimous as a mother, as dignified as a goddess. She must love him as limitlessly and blindly as an idiot. And moreover, like a sinister beast, she must have a spirit possessed by evil. Fortunately, however, the daughter's man at least had the male characteristic of

いっそのこと一日も早く娘が適当なよい相手を選んで、自分のもとから離れて行ってくれることを夢みるようになった。つまり、母と娘は自然に別離する時期に達したのである。

娘のほうもまた、自分が母親にとって重荷であることを知り——実のところ、彼女はもの心ついて以来、自分が母親にとって重荷であることをいやというほど知っていた——母親を一日も早く解放してやりたいと思うと同時に、自分も解放されたかった。しかし、そう思うかたわら、そんな母親を心のどこかで憎み、その憎しみはときに跳躍するはげしさでもんどり打ち、娘はわけのわからない怒りにかられた。つまり短い思春期の反抗である。だが、その憎しみと怒りが、今や同性の競争者となった母親のずるがしこいやり方、つまり母親の権威をふりかざして、実力を競うことを避ける卑劣さに向けられているものだとわかると、突然娘は母親の老いに気づいて、自分が成熟したのを知った。

成熟した娘は当然のことながら、男を得た。

その男はごく普通の、ありふれた男であった。母親に溺愛されて育ち、母親が異性であるということで、あらゆる理屈を越えて、息子の自分は自由な表現を赦されているという自信を持っている典型的な男である。そういう男は肉体的に成熟すると、同衾する女は母親の代用であり、女というものは母親のように寛容で、女神のように威厳があり、阿呆のように際限もなく溺愛してくれ、なおかつ邪悪な動物のように悪に憑かれた魂をも兼ねそなえているものでなくてはならなかったのである。しかし、まあ、幸いなことに、男は女が好きである

liking women.

The woman was gratified by the man and came to believe that she should reward him for this by exerting herself in every way to please him. This proved to be a monumental effort for her because, after all, every corner of his mind was transparent to her. Seeing into his heart was exhausting and stood in the way of her happiness.

First of all, the man wanted the woman to be constantly jealous, so she had to exert herself to appear that way. When another woman's shadow approached the man, she would have to act as though she thought of the other woman as a competitor, and the man would be satisfied.

'Don't ever leave me. I can't live without you. I'm helpless. I can't do anything when you're gone,' she would cry and cling to him. And as she spoke these words, she would have the illusion that she really was a weak, incompetent creature.

The man wanted the woman to evaluate other men as beneath their true worth. She had to close her eyes to other men's virtues and observe only their vices. He was not a total fool, however, and would not allow her to overstate the men's flaws. To please him, she had to render equitable judgements demonstrating an awareness of the others' shortcomings while concluding that, although the others might have certain virtues, they were finally not to her liking. Thus every little opinion she expressed had to be well thought out.

という男性の特質だけは備えていた。

女は男によって歓びを得たので、その代償にあらゆることをして男の機嫌をとってやってもよいと思うようになった。何しろ、男の心のすみずみまで、女には手にとるように透けて見えるのだから、女にとって、それは大層な重労働だった。相手の心が見えさえしなければ、人は疲れもしなければ、幸せなのだが。

まず第一に、男は女に常に嫉妬されたがっていたので、女は努力して嫉妬してやらなければならなかった。男のそばに、だれか他の女の影が近づいたときは、その女を意識して競争的に振るまうと男はよい気分なのである。

「どこへも行っちゃいや。あなたがいなければ、あたしは生きられないのよ。あたしは無能で、独りじゃなにひとつできないんだもの」女は男にすがりついてすすり泣きながら、呟いているうちに、自分が芯から無能な、弱い生きものになったような錯覚を起した。

また男は、女が他の男たちを真実以下に評価することを常にのぞんでいたので、女は他の男の美点に眼をつぶって、欠点だけを拾いあげてみせなければならなかった。もっとも男は極端にバカではなかったから、女が他人に対して見当はずれな評価を下すのも赦さず、正当な評価の上に立って、なお他の男の欠点をよく認識し、かりに多少の美点はあったにしてもそれは結局自分の好みではないと女が判断を下すのを一番快く思っていたので、女はすべての表現にいろいろと気を遣わなければならなかった。

Strangely enough, the man tended to feel pleasure in his exclusive possession of a woman who was constantly being pursued by other men. Far from merely tolerating her pretended flirtations with other men, he tended to encourage them. Deep down, it seems, all men long to join the species we call 'pimps'.

There would be no end to a list of such examples, but at times the woman would forget to act jealous or to flirt with other men, or she would carelessly state her true womanly impressions of attractive men. At such times the man would become bored or think the woman lazy or thick-skinned or lacking in sensitivity. Even if the woman did succeed in behaving as he wished in everything, he would assert with the arrogant air of an all-knowing sage, 'Women are stupid, cowardly, unmanageable creatures, full of jealousy, capable only of formulating shallow ideas and telling small-scale lies. The word "man" can stand for all human beings, but a "woman" can only be fully human by clinging to her man.'

Thanks to this illogical treaty of inequality, the two managed to live somewhat happily, but eventually both the man and the woman grew old and the man reached the age when he would grumble all year long about one or another part of his body that had gone bad. He demanded that the woman worry about him all the time and said that, if it looked as though he was going to precede her in death, he would be so concerned about leaving her behind that he could not

　その上、奇妙なことに男は女を他の男たちが常に欲しがっていて、それを自分だけが独り占めにしていることに快感を持つ性向を持っていた。だから、女が真実性のない媚を他の男に売ることは許容するどころかむしろすすめる向きさえある。男というものはどうやら、ヒモと呼ばれる種族に心の底では憧れているらしい。

　あれやこれや、例をあげればきりがないが、ときには女も嫉妬することを忘れたり、男に媚を売ることを忘れたり、ついうっかり、他の魅力的な男に対する女としての正直で真実味のある感想を述べてしまうこともあった。すると男は退屈し、女を怠け者だと思い、神経が太くて、繊細さに欠けていると思うのである。その上、かりに女が何から何まで男の気に入るように振舞ったとすると、男は何もかもわかっている賢者のような尊大な口調で、「全く女というものは、嫉妬深くて、浅知恵しか働かず、小さな嘘はつくが遠大な嘘はつけず、結局はバカで小心で、手に負えない代物だ。英語でマンというのは男であると同時に人間だが、女というのはまあその男にくっつくことによってしか人間たり得ないね」と述懐するのである。

　この理屈に合わない不平等条約のお陰で、二人はどうやら幸福な半生を送り、やがて、男も女も年をとり、男は年中からだのどこかしらが悪いとぶつぶつ言う年齢になった。そして、男それを女が案じてくれることを強要し、もしものことがあって自分が先に死んでしまうようなことがあったら、後に残す女のことが気になってとても死にきれないだろうと言った。女

die in peace. In the course of demonstrating to him how agitated this made her, the woman became truly agitated and convinced herself that he might be seriously ill. Unless she truly believed this, she could not set his mind at ease, and if her man were not at peace, she herself could not attain peace. Thus, even though she hated the nursing profession so much that she would rather die than commit herself to it, she became a nurse the way a woman in desperate circumstances might sell her chastity. Seeing her in her new line of work, the man commended her, saying that nursing was the one profession most truly in keeping with a woman's instincts, that at least where nursing was concerned, women were blessed with an innate talent against which no man could compete.

Around that time, the woman became grotesquely fat. A few short steps were all it took to make her shoulders heave with every breath, like a pregnant woman. The obvious main reason for this was that she possessed exceptionally healthy digestive organs that gave her an enormous appetite. In addition, she had the pitiful trait of wanting to make others feel good. Even if she did not desire a particular dish, she would eat whatever people offered her in order not to disappoint them. Everyone thought that she just loved to eat; they would be deeply offended if she refused their food. On the other hand, her husband often boasted that he was a man of iron will. When he saw her eating and exclaiming, 'Here I go again!' he would ridicule her: 'You're such a weak-willed woman.' Even if someone put her heart and soul into cooking something to please

はおろおろして見せているうちに、だんだんほんとうにおろおろとし、しまいには男が大変な重病人であるかもしれないと思いこむようになった。なぜなら、そう思いこむ以外に男に平安を与えることはできなかったし、男が平安でなければ、結局は自分もまた平安が得られなかったからである。そして、女は看護婦にだけは死んでもなるまいと思うほどそれが嫌いな職業であったにもかかわらず、女は看護婦こそは全く女の本能に向いた職業であり、女という男は看護婦に転職した女をみて、切羽詰ったものが操を売るような気分で看護婦になった。ものは少なくとも看護に関してだけは天賦の才に恵まれていて、到底男には及びもつかないと賛えた。

その頃、女は異様に肥り始め、少し歩くとはあはあと妊婦のように肩で息をするようになっていた。もちろんそのもっとも大きな原因は、彼女がすぐれた消化器官を持っていて、常に旺盛な食欲にかられていることだったが、それにつけ加えて、彼女が他人の気分をよくしたいという哀れな性格を持っているためであった。彼女は他人がすすめる食べものを、それほど好まなくても、相手をがっかりさせないために食べてしまうのである。彼らはみんな彼女が食べるのが大好きな喰いしん坊だと思っていたので、その彼女が自分の供した食べものを拒絶したりしようものなら、ひどく侮辱されたように感ずるのである。一方、強固な意志を持っていると誇っている彼女の夫は、「ああ、また食べちゃうわ」と言いながら食べる彼女を見て、「全くお前は意志の弱い女だ」と嘲笑した。彼はその料理が彼を饗応するために

him, he had the will power to refuse it outright if it was not good
for his health, which is to say that his strong nerves allowed him to
ignore another's feelings without shame.

His use of expressions such as 'strength of will', 'insensitivity'
and 'laziness' so differed from hers that she would at times be over-
whelmed by an acute sense of loneliness. She came to fear not only
her husband but many of the others around her, as though she were
surrounded by foreigners who spoke another language. Sometimes
she dreamed of living alone in the depths of the mountains the way
she had locked herself up in her room all day when she was a little
girl, not playing with anyone.

In the mountains, there would be nobody to trouble her, and
she would be free to immerse herself in her fantasies. The thought
of getting even with all those who had tormented her in the human
settlement made her heart race – all those who could keep wearing
the expressions of happy heroes just because they were dull-headed,
slow-witted and incapable of reading other people's minds. What
relief it would give her to be able to say aloud to them like the legendary mountain witches, 'You just thought . . . didn't you?'! How
good it would feel to slit the skin of her temples and let her horns
grow out – horns that were itching to sprout but could not do so
on their own!

When she imagined herself living alone in the mountains,
she saw herself as a beautiful fairy, sprawled in the fields, naked in
the drenching sunlight, surrounded by trees and grasses and animals.
But once a familiar human being appeared from the settlement, her
face would change into that of a demon crone. He would stare at

精魂を傾けてしつらえられたものでも、それが自分の健康によくないものであれば、断固と
して拒絶するだけの強い意志力、つまり相手の心を無視しても恥じない強靭な神経の持主で
あった。

彼女は、意志力、無神経、怠慢などの言葉遣いに対して、夫と自分の使用法があまりにも
違うので、ときにはひどい孤独に追いこまれた。夫に限らず、世間の多くのひとびとに対し
て、彼女は言葉の通じない外国人にとり囲まれているような恐怖を感じ、かつて少女の頃誰
とも遊ばず、部屋に閉じこもってしまったように、いっそのこと山にでも入って、独りでひっ
そりと暮したいと夢みることもあった。

山では誰も彼女を悩ます者はなく、彼女は好き勝手な妄想ができる。里でさんざん彼女を
苦しめた者を、頭の足りない、勘の鈍い、他人の心を読めないばっかりに、いつものほほん
と幸福な英雄の顔附きをしていられる者たちを、いたぶってみる空想は彼女をわくわくさせ
た。あの昔語りの山姥のように、「〈お前は今、──と思っていたな〉」と口に出して言ったら、
何と頭がすっきりすることだろう。こめかみの脇でうずいている、生えようとして生えられ
ない角を、頭の皮を切って、にょきにょきと生えさせてやる快感だろう。

彼女は独りきりの、その山の暮しを想像するとき、木や草や動物たちに囲まれ、太陽のふ
りそそぐ草原に裸で寝そべっている美しい妖精に自分をなぞらえてみた。だが、ひとたび里
で見覚えのある人間の誰かが目の前にあらわれると、彼女の形相は鬼婆になる。人間は阿呆

her, his mouth hanging open like an idiot, uttering coarse, incoherent, self-righteous words that made her fly into a rage.

On such occasions, her husband would be sure to appear, dressed in shabby beggar's clothing, wandering aimlessly around the den of the transformed woman, and like a brat who has lost a fight, he would shriek, 'Without her to hide my unreasonable desires for me, I'm lost.'

Hearing his voice, she would look at her reflection in a mountain spring. Half her face wore the smile of a loving mother, while the other half seethed with demonic rage. Half her mouth dripped blood as it tore and devoured the man's flesh, while the lips of the other half caressed the man where he lay curled up like a baby, sucking at the breast that hid his face.

Her obesity put increasing pressure on her blood vessels, causing hardening of the arteries. Parts of her body grew numb and she developed headaches and ringing in the ears. The doctor ascribed these symptoms to menopause. She received this diagnosis in her early forties and was forced to live with it for a full twenty years.

The man cited statistics proving that women, as a rule, were more durably constructed than men, their minds and bodies more robust, their lifespans longer, which was why he was sure to die before she would. The woman thought the reason men's lives were statistically shorter than women's might have something to do with the fact that men end their own lives in youth by participating in wars and other

のように口をあけて、とんちんかんなひとりよがりの下品な言葉を喋り、彼女をかっとさせた。

そういうとき、夫は必ずみすぼらしい乞食のなりで、姿を変えた女の棲家のまわりをうろついた。そして喧嘩に敗けた悪童のように喚いていた。「理屈に合わないおれの欲望を何とかごまかしてくれるあいつがいなければ、もうダメだ」

彼女はその声を聞き、自分の顔を泉にうつしてみる。すると、顔半面は慈母の微笑を浮かべ、半面は悪鬼の忿怒をたぎらせている。口半分は血をしたたらせて、男の肉をひき裂いて食い、唇の半分は片側の乳房の陰に、赤児のようにからだを丸めて乳首をしゃぶる男を愛撫していた。

さて、彼女は肥満のため、だんだん血管が圧迫され、動脈硬化を起し始めた。からだの方々がしびれ始め、頭痛がして耳鳴りがするようになり、医者にかかると、医者は更年期障害だと診断した。彼女は四十過ぎて間もなく更年期障害だと言われ、それ以後、実に二十年間に亘って同じ病名を着せられた。

男は、女というものは概して男に比べると耐久力があり、心身共に強健で、人生を長く生き伸びることになっていると、統計をもって示し、二人のうち先に死ぬのは自分のほうであるのは間違いないと断言した。女は、男の寿命が統計的に女より短いのは、もしかしたら、男が若い頃戦争その他のさまざまな暴力的な行為によって勝手に自分の命を断つのが原因か

violent acts, but demonstrating this with statistics would have been too much trouble, so she kept quiet.

'It's true,' she said. 'Men have larger builds, but at heart they're more frail and sensitive. That's why all women love men.' She knew she was lying, but she also knew that the world would be a place of darkness without men. And so she spent several hours every day massaging the man where he said it hurt and making and feeding to the man the kind of delicate ground food that people give to little birds.

She knew full well that her own fat body with its hardened arteries would not last much longer, but she could think of no other way to live than to continue providing food for the little bird of a man who believed in his own frailty.

One morning, the woman studied herself closely in the mirror. Her face was covered with the deep wrinkles of a mountain witch, and her yellowed teeth were gapped and ugly as an aged cat's. White frost had fallen on her hair, and she felt chilling pain as though needle ice was ready to pop out all over her body.

She felt a faint numbness as if her body might belong to someone else. The stiffness tied in with the distant memory of her mother, who had died so long ago. The flow of her blood seemed to stagnate in places, and she felt herself growing dizzy. She drifted off momentarily, and when she regained consciousness she found her limbs paralysed, her mind dimming and parts of her body gradually growing colder.

もしれないとも思ったが、そういうことを統計的に証明するのが面倒なので黙っていた。

「そうよ、男のひとはからだばかり大きくても、心は繊細で、優しく弱いものなのね。だから女はみんな男が好きなのよ」女はそう言い、たとえ、それが嘘にしたって、男がいなければ世の中は闇になってしまうだろうと思い、やれあそこが痛い、ここが痛いという男のからだをさすったり、繊細な小鳥に与えるすり餌のような食事を男のためにつくって食べさせるために、一日数時間も費やした。

肥満して動脈硬化を起した彼女は、自分のからだがいつまでつづくかわからないのを、自分でも悟っていたが、繊細だと信じている男という小鳥に餌を与えつづける以外に、やはり自分の生きつづける道はないと思うのであった。

女は或る朝、鏡の中にしげしげと自分の顔をみつめた。その顔は山姥のように深い皺で覆われ、黄ばんだ歯が老いた猫のようにまばらに醜かった。髪には白く霜が降り、からだのすみずみから音を立てて霜柱が起きあがってくるような冷たい痛みを彼女は覚えた。

彼女は自分のからだが他人のものでもあるようなかすかな麻痺を感じた。それは遠いはるかな、ずっと昔に死んだ母親の記憶につながる硬ばりであった。流れる血がどこかで停滞し、彼女はもうろうとした。突然ほんのわずかなまどろみが彼女を襲い、ふとわれにかえると、彼女は手足がきつくしびれ、意識が薄れ、からだのそこここがじょじょに冷えていくのを感じたのである。

On any other morning, she would have been up long ago preparing his breakfast, but when her husband awoke to find that she was still in bed (they had slept side by side for forty years), lying face down like a frog in rigor mortis, he sprang into action with a suddenness that belied his many physical complaints and carried her to the hospital. Surprisingly, the doctor who until the day before had written her off as a case of menopause now declared as if he were a different person that she had the symptoms of cerebral thrombosis and if luck were against her she would survive no more than a day or two. The man reacted with total confusion, but he managed to pull himself together and decide that the first thing he should do was send for their son and daughter, both of whom lived far away. The two children came immediately and with their father they knelt around their stricken mother, who had lost the power of speech.

The next two days and nights might well have been the best two days of her life. The three of them took turns rubbing her arms, rubbing her legs and even taking care of her down below without relying on the nurse.

Those two days went by without any sudden changes in her condition, either positive or negative, but her consciousness gradually dimmed until she could no longer recognize the people around her. Puzzled, the doctor said, 'Considering her weight, her heart is surprisingly strong. She may last longer than I expected.' When he told them about a case of cerebral thrombosis in which the unconscious patient lived for two years on nothing but intravenous feeding,

いつもの朝なら、とっくに起きて食事の支度をしている筈の女が、いつまでも起きず、自分のかたわらで（――彼らは四十年間よりそって寝ていた）硬直した蛙のようにうつ伏せになって動かなくなっているのを見つけた男は、さすがにあわて、いままでどこが悪い、ここが悪いと言っていたからだを急にしゃんとさせ、女房を病院にかつぎこんだが、驚いたことについ昨日までは彼女を更年期障害だと診断を下していた医者は別人のような顔つきで、これは脳血栓の症状で、運が悪ければもう今日か明日の運命ということも考えられると宣言したのである。男はすっかり頭が混乱してしまったが、とにかく気をとり直して、遠くにいる息子と娘を呼び寄せることこそ急務であると判断した。二人の子供たちはすぐにとんで来て、もはや言語障害を起して舌のまわらなくなっている母親のまわりに父親と三人でうずくまった。

それからの二晩がおそらく彼女にとって生涯で最良の日だったかもしれない。彼らはかわるがわる母親の足をさすったり、腕をさすったりして、下の始末さえ看護婦には任せなかった。

だが、二晩たっても母親の状態が急変もせず、決して芳しい方向にも向わず、ただ意識がだんだんと混濁して周囲の者たちを認めることさえできなくなると、医者は首をかしげ、「この方は肥っているにもかかわらず、非常に確かな心臓を持っておられるから、あるいはもっと長く持つかもしれない」と言い、ある同じ症状の脳血栓の患者は意識不明のまま二年間も

the three members of the woman's family fell silent and gathered around her.

Soon the son said there was a limit to how long he could stay away from work. Since it looked as though there would be no changes in the immediate future, he would return home for the time being. The daughter's expression darkened, and she began to worry about her husband and children.

The poor man became anxious; he would not know what to do if his daughter left. He pleaded with her to stay on, sounding so helpless that the daughter, as worried as she was about her own family, reluctantly agreed to remain.

The daughter recalled the time when she had been critically ill as a child and her mother had stayed up for days watching over her. If it had not been for this woman who lay before her, unconscious, straying between life and death, she would not be alive today. She waited beside the bed, thinking this could be the last time she would ever see her, but when another two days had passed, she began to wonder how long her mother would remain in her present condition, unable to respond when spoken to, just a living, breathing corpse. At sixty-two, her mother was still too young in terms of the average lifespan to be departing this world, but everyone had to die sooner or later. Even if she were to pass on here and now, they should perhaps be grateful that she could go while being watched over by her husband and daughter.

点滴だけで生きのびたという例をあげると、三人の家族は病人を囲んですっかり黙りこんでしまったのである。

やがて、息子は勤務を休むのは限度があるからと言いわけし、今すぐどうこうということもないからひとまず帰ることにすると言い、娘は憂鬱な顔つきで夫や子供たちのことを心配し始めた。

哀れな男は娘に帰られてしまったのではどうしようもないと不安で、「どうか、お前だけでももうしばらく様子を見てくれないか」と心細げに懇願するので、娘は主婦が留守の家族のことを案じながらも、しぶしぶと居残った。

娘はそのむかし、自分が大病をして、母親の幾晩もの寝ずの看護でやっと命をとりとめたことなど思い起し、自分が今あるのは、今ここにこうして意識不明のまま生と死の谷間をさまよっている母親のお陰だとあらためて思い直し、もしかしたらこれが最後になるかもしれない母親の床のそばに待っていた。しかし二日もすると、話しかけても返事があるわけでもない母親の、ただ呼吸をしているにすぎない生きた屍を眺めながら、いったいこの状態がいつまで続くのであろうと思い、母親の六十二歳という年齢を考え、それが現代の平均寿命から言っても、此の世に別れを告げるにしてはまだ早すぎるとは言え、人間というものは遅かれ早かれ死ぬのだから、ここで母親がこのまま逝ってしまったとしても、こうして夫と娘に看とられながら昇天できるのなら、感謝すべきことかもしれないとも考えた。

The daughter felt strangely uneasy to think of the doctor's patient who had survived for two years on intravenous feeding. If her mother did that, was her father prepared to pay the medical expenses? And medical expenses aside, neither she nor her brother could possibly abandon their families in order to stay by their mother's bed.

Just then she thought of her own five-year-old daughter, whom she had left in the care of her mother-in-law. She herself had fallen ill and run a high fever at that exact age, nearly contracting meningitis. She recalled with strange clarity how her half-mad mother crouched, unmoving, by her pillow in their miserably untidy house. The memory led her, of all things, away from her mother, who lay moaning between life and death before her very eyes, and instead towards the imagined – unlikely but terrifying – possibility of her own daughter falling ill in her absence.

Unaware of her daughter's anxieties, the mother survived another two days, often fixing her empty eyes on points in space and emitting incomprehensible, animalistic moans. On the morning of the third day, the daughter woke feeling too weary to climb out of bed after a week of intensive nursing. It was a dull, gloomy morning, typical of the hazy weather of the cherry blossom season. She stared vacantly at the profile of her unconscious mother, whose quiet breathing continued as before, and whose sunken cheeks made her look, if anything, younger and more beautiful.

When the morning round had ended, the daughter thought of how soiled her mother must be, and she asked the doctor if she

娘は点滴だけで意識不明のまま二年も生き長らえたという医者の話を妙な不安の中で思い浮かべ、もし母親がそんなことになったとしたら、いったい父親にはそれだけの医療費をまかなうだけの用意があるのであろうかと心配になった。そして、費用のことはともかくとしても、そんなに長い間、兄にしても自分にしても、それぞれの家族を放り出して、母親のそばにつききりでいるわけにはいかないと思うのであった。

彼女はふと、姑に任せてきた五つになる幼い娘のことを考え、自分が丁度その年頃、ひどい高熱が続いて脳膜炎を起しかけたとき、半狂乱になった母親が無残に荒れ果てた家の中で、自分の枕元にうずくまって動かなかったさまを、妙にはっきり思い出した。そして、こともあろうに、その記憶は、目の前で瀕死の呻きをあげている母親をさておいて、幼い娘がもし自分の留守中に病気になったりしたら、というありもしない想像につながり、おそろしい不安にかられた。

そうした娘の不安をよそに、母親はときどきうつろな眼を宙に据えて、わけのわからない獣のような呻きを発するだけで、更に二日を生きのびた。三日目の朝は花曇りの鬱陶しい日で、娘は母の病床に馳けつけて以来、おおかた一週間の疲れがでて、朝起きるのもけだるく、同じように平穏な呼吸を続けながら、意識を失っている母親の、いくらか頬の肉がそげ落ちて、かえってすっきりと美しく若返った横顔をぼんやりとみつめた。

午前中の医師の回診があったあとで、娘は汚れている母のからだを思い出し、病人のから

could wipe the patient down. He said he would instruct the nurse to do it and left the room. Soon the nurse came in and performed her duties as instructed in a businesslike manner, rolling the unconscious patient over as though she were a log.

Nervously, the daughter lent a hand. The patient was rolled over and stripped of her nightclothes soiled with perspiration and excrement. At that very moment, the mother opened her eyes wide and stared straight at her daughter, who stood facing her, helping to support her weight. She produced a faint smile as the light returned to her eyes. The radiance had the sad, momentary brilliance of a child's sparkler, and when it faded, the mother's eyes lost their light again. Saliva dribbled from the corner of her mouth, a spasm shook her throat, and the movement of her eyes came to a dead stop. It all happened in an instant.

Rattled, the nurse ran off to tell the doctor of this sudden change. He rushed in and started to perform artificial respiration. He also injected cardiac medication directly into her heart with a thick needle. He seemed more to be shaking a laboratory animal that had failed during an experiment than treating a living human being. In any case, the people around her were doing their best to restart her heart.

The woman died.

Or perhaps it would be more accurate to say that she summoned up her last ounce of strength to drown herself by washing her accumulated saliva down her windpipe.

だを拭いてやりたいと言うと、医師は看護婦にその旨を指示して立ち去った。間もなく指示を受けた看護婦がやってきて、非常に事務的に、意識のない病人のからだをまるで丸太のようにひっくり返し始めた。

娘はこわごわとそれを手伝ったが、病人は汗と排泄物で汚れた寝巻をひきはがれてころがされた拍子に、かっと眼を見開き、丁度その真向いで自分のからだを支えている娘の顔を真っ直ぐにじっと見つめ、甦った光のあふれる眼で微かに笑った。やがて、花火は消え、病人の眼は再び光を失い、途端に唇の脇から口の中に溜っていた唾液をしたたらせ、咽喉をぎくりと痙攣させ、線香花火にも似た華やかで寂しい輝きであった。それは、ほんのわずかな、瞳の動きをはたと停止し、硬直したのである。それは、ほんの一瞬のことであった。

この異変に、看護婦は慌てふためき、大急ぎで病人の急変を医師に通報すると、担当の医師が馳けつけて人工呼吸をほどこし、更に太い針を心臓に突き立てて強心剤を打った。それは生きている人間をとり扱うというよりは、実験に成功しなかった実験中の動物をゆり動かすという感じに似ていたが、ともかく、周囲の者たちはあらゆることをして、その停止した心臓の鼓動を再びとり戻そうと努力したことだけは確かである。

女は死んだ。

というよりも、咽喉にたまった唾液を気管に流しこみ、われとわが身を窒息させる行為を、彼女は最後の渾身の力をふりしぼって遂行したのである。

In the last smile she exchanged with her daughter, she clearly read her daughter's mind. Her daughter's eyes were saying that she did not want to be tied down by her any longer. 'Mother, I don't need you to protect me any more. You've outlived your usefulness. If you have to be dependent on me, if you can't take care of yourself without being a burden to others, please, Mother, please disappear quietly. Please don't torment me any longer. I, too, am preparing myself so that I won't trouble my daughter as I am being troubled by you. I'm willing to go easily. That's right. It's what we ought to do. I never want to be the kind of parent who, for lack of resolve, continues to press her unwanted kindnesses upon her offspring.' This daughter of hers, this product of her husband and herself, possessed a twofold strength of will. Either she would overcome all temptation, exercise moderation and live robustly until the moment of her death at one hundred, or live arrogantly and selfishly to the end, retaining the energy to kill herself at eighty. In either case, the woman was satisfied with the daughter she had borne and raised.

Through her daughter's face, she saw the son who was not there, walking among the crowds of the metropolis. He was talking to her with a crooked smile on his face. 'Mother, I have incessantly chirping chicks at home. I myself don't know why I have to keep putting food in their mouths. But when I catch myself, I'm always flying towards

娘とかわした最後の微笑の中で、女ははっきりと娘の心の中を読みとったのである。娘の眼は、母親にこれ以上縛りつけられていたくないと語っていた。「あたしはもう、お母さんに保護される必要はないのよ。あなたはもう御用済みよ。あなたが誰の迷惑にもならず、自分だけで自分のことをやっていけるならともかく、あたしの世話にならなければならないなら、どうかすうっと消えて頂戴。もし、これ以上あたしを苦しめたくないのなら。あたしだって、いずれ、自分の娘に今あたしがあなたのそばで味わっているような苦しみを味わわせないために、どうにかあっさりと身の始末をつけることを、今から覚悟して、いろいろと心の準備をしているわよ。そうよ、そうすべきなんだわ。そういう覚悟をするのがいやなばっかりに、親切の押売りをする親には絶対なりたくないと思っているの」女と夫との合作である娘はどうやら二重の意味で強い意志を持っていた。どんな誘惑にも負けず、節度のある生活をして、百歳で死ぬ瞬間まで頑健に生きるか、あるいは八十歳でも自殺するほどのエネルギイを持って、傲慢に、自己中心的に最後の最後まで生きのびるか、どちらかだろう。──

女は自分が生み、自分が育てた娘に満足した。

彼女は更に、娘の顔に重ねて、そこには姿の見えない息子の顔を遠い都会の雑踏の中に浮かべた。彼はゆがんだ笑いを浮かべてこう言った。「お母さん、ぼくにはひっきりなしにぴいぴいと鳴きたてる、雛がいるんだよ。どうして、ぼくが、そいつらに餌を運ばなければならないのか、ぼく自身にだってわからないよ。気がつくと、いつだって、餌をくわえて巣を

the nest with food in my beak. I do it before I even think about it. If it were all right for me to stop carrying food to them and stick close by your side, the human race would have perished long ago. In other words, for me to do what I do for them is the only way I can prolong and preserve the warm blood you gave me.'

Next she saw her aged husband, who was standing nearby with his head drooping and a stunned look on his face. This happy mad old man was moved by the beauty of his wife's naked body and carried away by his own fidelity in having tended her to the very end. The greatest happiness for a human being is to make another happy. She was satisfied to see this man who had the ability to change any given circumstance into happiness, and she blessed the start of his life's second chapter. At the same time, she thought she heard the pealing of her funeral bells.

With her own hands, she drew her white shroud closed around her, right side over left. The wind rushed across the dry riverbed and she glanced back to see someone running with dishevelled hair. She asked the reason for this, speaking to another deceased traveller, a stranger who had joined her out of nowhere. 'A mountain witch is chasing him,' came the answer.

She felt the warm heart of a mountain witch suddenly beating again beneath her drawn-together shroud, and she smiled. The heart of the mountain witch kept up its healthy beating, but the blood vessels meant to transmit its powerful pulsing were completely closed, cruelly and solidly blocked.

The time had come for the spirit of the witch to return to the quiet mountains. The day had come for her to stand on a rocky ledge, letting her white hair stream in the raging wind, her eyes wrenched

めがけて飛んでいるのさ。考える前にそうしているのを
やめて、お母さんのそばにべったりくっついているような
さ。つまりあいつらにそうしてやることこそ、お母さんに貰った血を少しでも先まで暖かく
ひきのばして保っておく唯一の方法なんだからね」

次に彼女は傍らに放心したような表情で突っ立っている老
老人は妻の裸体の美しさに感動し、最後までその妻をみとった自分の誠実さにうっとりして
うなだれていた。人間の最も大きな幸福は他人を幸福にすることである。同時に彼女は自分の野辺送りの鉦の音を聞いたように
思った。

彼女は白い経帷子を自分の手で左前に合わせた。風がさあっと渡る河原で、彼女がふとふ
り向くと、髪をふり乱して逃げていく者がある。いつの間にか道連れになった見知らぬ亡者
にわけを訊くと、「山姥に追われているのさ」と答えた。

彼女は自分の合わせた経帷子の下で不意に暖かな山姥の心臓の鼓動が甦ってくるのを感じ
て、微笑んだ。山姥の心臓は健全に脈搏っていた。ただその、力強い鼓動を伝える血管はすっ
かり閉じていたのである。固く、冷酷に塞がれていた。

山姥の霊は今や静かな山に帰るときが来た。風の吹きすさぶ山の岩角に、白髪をなびかせ、

open like golden flames, her wild laughter echoing forever among the hills. Her transient dream of living down in the human settlement disguised as an animal had ended.

She shook her head, recalling the days she had spent dreaming of living alone in the mountains, and the old sorrow came back from girlhood when she had first begun to dislike human beings. Had she lived in the mountains all that time, she would have been a witch who captures and devours humans from the settlement below.

Which would have made her happier, she wondered: to live in the mountains and become a man-eating witch; or to live in the settlement with the heart of a mountain witch? It seemed to her now that it would have made no difference. If she had lived in the mountains, she would have been called a mountain witch. Living in the settlement, she could have been called either a fox spirit incarnate or an ordinary woman with a healthy mind and body who lived out her natural life. That was the only difference. It would have been the same either way.

Just before she took her last breath, it crossed her mind that her own mother must have been an absolutely genuine mountain witch as well.

Strangely enough, she died with the sweet, innocent smile of a baby on her lips, passing from this world in complete peace. Her daughter clung to her, sobbing, her tear-swollen eyes revealing an indescribable sense of liberation as she whispered, 'Mother, how beautiful you are in death! You must have been a truly happy woman.' The wide-open fish eyes of the woman's husband overflowed with tears as he mourned in silence.

金色の炎のような眼をかっと見開き、その永遠の哄笑を山間に響かせる日が来た。動物の姿を借りて山を下って里に棲んだ、つかの間の夢はすぎ去ったのである。

山の中に棲むことを夢みた過ぎ去った日々の暮しや、ずっと昔、初めて、人が嫌いになった少女の頃の哀しみが甦ってきて、彼女は首を振った。もし、あのとき、山に棲んでいたら、自分は里から迷いこんだ人間を追いかけて、とって食う山姥になっていたのであろう。

山に棲んで人を食う山姥になるのと、山姥の心を持ちながら里に棲むのと、どちらが幸せであっただろうかと、思ったりもしたが、今となってはどちらでも同じだったように思う。

山に棲めば山姥と名附けられ、里に棲めば狐の化身と言われるか、心身共に壮健な天寿を全うした平凡な女と言われるかの違いだが、中身は結局同じなのである。

多分、死んだ母親も、正真正銘の山姥であったのだろうと、息をひきとる前に女はちらと思った。

不思議なことに、彼女は死んだとき、妙にあどけない顔に、赤児のような無邪気な笑いを浮かべていた。この大往生を遂げた女にとりすがってむせびながら、娘は泣き腫らした眼にも言われぬ解放感を浮かべて「——きれいな死顔、お母さんはほんとうに幸せだったのね」

と呟き、夫は泪のあふれた魚のような眼を見開いたまま、声を立てずに慟哭した。

AKUTAGAWA RYŪNOSUKE
The Great Earthquake

Translated by Jay Rubin

The Great Earthquake (1923)

The odour was something like that of overripe apricots. Catching a
hint of it as he walked through the charred ruins, he found himself
thinking such thoughts as these: *The smell of corpses rotting in the sun
is not as bad as I would have expected*. When he stood before a pond
where bodies were piled upon bodies, however, he discovered that
the old Chinese expression 'burning the nose' was no mere sensory
exaggeration of grief and horror. What especially moved him was
the corpse of a child of twelve or thirteen. He felt something like
envy as he looked at it, recalling such expressions as 'Those whom
the gods love die young'. Both his sister and his half-brother had lost
their houses to fire. His sister's husband, though, was on a suspended
sentence for perjury.

Too bad we didn't all die.

Standing in the charred ruins, he could hardly keep from feeling this way.

芥川龍之介
大地震

それはどこか熟し切った杏の匂に近いものだった。彼は焼けあとを歩きながら、かすかにこの匂を感じ、炎天に腐った死骸の匂も存外悪くないと思ったりした。が、死骸の重なり重った池の前に立って見ると、「酸鼻」と云う言葉も感覚的に決して誇張でないことを発見した。殊に彼を動かしたのは十二三歳の子供の死骸だった。彼はこの死骸を眺め、何か羨ましさに近いものを感じた。「神々に愛せらるるものは夭折す」——こう云う言葉なども思い出した。彼の姉や異母弟はいずれも家を焼かれていた。しかし彼の姉の夫は偽証罪を犯した為に執行猶予中の体だった。……

「誰も彼も死んでしまえば善いのだよ」

彼は焼け跡に佇んだまま、しみじみこう思わずにはいられなかった。

UCHIDA HYAKKEN

Kudan

Translated by Rachel DiNitto

A large yellow moon hung in the distance, all colour, no light. Was this night time? Probably not. Was the pale blue streak of light in the sky behind me from a setting or a rising sun? A dragonfly floated across the moon's yellow surface, but when its silhouette left the moon, I lost sight of it. The field around me extended as far as the eye could see. I stood soaking wet, water dripping from the end of my tail. As a child, I'd heard stories about the *kudan*, never thinking I would turn into such a pathetic monster myself. But now here I was, a cow with a human face. What should I do in this vast, empty field? Why had I been put here? Where was the cow that had spawned me?

At some point, the moon turned blue. The sky darkened, leaving only a thin band of light on the horizon. The band grew even thinner, and just when it seemed about to disappear, small black dots began to show up in it. They increased in number, and by the time they formed a line on the horizon, the band of light was gone and the

内田百閒

件

黄色い大きな月が向うに懸かっている。色計りで光がない。夜かと思うとそうでもないらしい。後の空には蒼白い光が流れている。日がくれたのか、夜が明けるのか解らない。黄色い月の面を、蜻蛉が一匹浮く様に飛んだ。黒い影が月の面から消えたら、蜻蛉はどこへ行ったのか見えなくなってしまった。私は見果てもない広い原の真中に立っている。軀がびっしよりぬれて、尻尾の先からぽたぽたと雫が垂れている。件の話は子供の折に聞いた事はあるけれども、自分がその件になろうとは思いもよらなかった。からだが牛で顔丈人間の浅間しい化物に生まれて、こんな所にぼんやり立っている。何の影もない広野の中で、どうしていいか解らない。何故こんなところに置かれたのだか、私を生んだ牛はどこへ行ったのだか、そんな事は丸でわからない。

そのうちに月が青くなって来た。後の空の光りが消えて、地平線にただ一筋の、帯程の光りが残った。その細い光りの筋も、次第次第に幅が狭まって行って、到頭消えてなくなろうとする時、何だか黒い小さな点が、いくつもいくつもその光りの中に現われた。見る見る内に、その数がふえて、明かりの流れた地平線一帯にその点が並んだ時、光りの幅がなくなっ

sky was dark. Then the moon began to glow. This was when I knew that it was nightfall and that the fading light had been coming from the west. My body dried off, and each time the wind blew across my back, my short fur stirred in the breeze. As the moon grew smaller, its blue light flowed in all directions. Here in the middle of this field, which seemed as if it were under water, I recalled things about my human past with regret. But the sequence was a blur: try as I might, I couldn't tell at which point my life as a human being had ceased. Folding my front legs, I tried lying down. But I didn't like the sand sticking to my hairless chin and got up again. As the night deepened, I wandered aimlessly or stood still in a daze. The moon descended into the western sky. As dawn approached, a gust of wind rose from the west like a giant wave, carrying the smell of sand, and I understood that my first day as a *kudan* was beginning. Then the terrifying thought I'd let slip from my memory suddenly returned. The *kudan* lives only three days, and before it dies it reveals a prophecy in human language. Having been reborn in this form, I didn't care how long I might live, so it didn't bother me that I'd be dead in three days, but the part about the prophecy was troubling. I had no idea what prophecy to make. For the moment I didn't need to worry. Here in the middle of the field with nobody around, I could keep my mouth shut and wait for death. Just then the wind picked up and I could hear the clamour of human voices. Frightened, I gazed into the distance, and as the wind blew, I heard the voices again: 'Over there!

て、空が暗くなった。そうして月が光り出した。そうして月が光り出した。その時始めて私はこれから夜になるのだなと思った。今光りの消えた空が西だと云う事もわかった。からだが次第に乾いて来て、背中を風が渡る度に、短かい毛の戦ぐのがわかる様になった。月が小さくなるにつれて、青い光りは遠くまで流れた。水の底の様な原の真中で、私は人間でいた折の事を色色と思い出して後悔した。けれども、その仕舞の方はぼんやりしていて、どこで私の人間の一生が切れるのだかわからない。けれども、考えて見ようとしても、丸で摑まえ所のない様な気がした。私は前足を折って寝て見た。すると、毛の生えていない顎に原の砂がついて、ぼんやり立ったりしている内に夜が更けた。そうして、ただそこいらを無闇に歩き廻ったり、夜明けが近くなると、西の方から大浪の様な風が吹いて来た。

月が西の空に傾いて、これから件に生まれて初めての日が来るのだなと思った。すると、今迄うっかりして思い出さなかった恐ろしい事を、ふと考えついた。私は風の運んで来る砂のにおいを嗅ぎながら、件は生まれて三日にして死し、その間に人間の言葉で、未来の凶福を予言するものだと云う話を聞いている。こんなものに生まれて、何時迄生きていても仕方がないから、三日で死ぬのは構わないけれども、予言するのは困ると思った。第一何を予言するんだか見当もつかない。幸いこんな野原の真中にいて、辺りに誰も人間がいないから、まあ黙っていて、この儘死んで仕舞おうと思う途端に西風が吹いて、遠くの方に何だか騒騒しい人声が聞こえた。驚いてその方を見ようとすると、又風が吹いて、今度は「彼所だ、彼所だ」と云う

Over there!' The voices seemed vaguely familiar.

That was when I realized that the black dots on the horizon the evening before had been people, that they'd crossed the field in the night to hear my prophecy. I had to escape – as soon as possible. I fled eastwards. A pale blue light filtered into the eastern sky, turning white as the sky lightened. Across the field I could see a terrifying crowd approaching like the ominous shadow of a cloud. A wind rose up from the east, carrying their shouts of 'Over there! Over there!' Their voices were now definitely familiar, and they sounded nearby. In a panic I fled north, but the north wind blew and their shouts rode back to me on the breeze. The same thing happened when I ran south. The wind changed direction and the mass of people closed in on me. I was trapped. The huge crowd was coming to hear the prophecy from my mouth. If they knew I had nothing to say even though I was a *kudan*, they'd be furious. I didn't mind dying on the third day, but the torment before that would be unbearable. I stamped on the ground in vexation, ready to flee. The yellow moon hung hazily in the western sky, growing larger. The scenery was the same as last night's. I gazed at the moon, bewildered.

The day had fully dawned.

The crowd encircled me in the middle of the vast field. The frightening mass of people must have numbered in the thousands,

人の声が聞こえた。しかもその声が聞き覚えのある何人かの声に似ている。

それで昨日の日暮れに地平線に現われた黒いものは人間で、私の予言を聞きに夜通しこの広野を渡って来たのだと云う事がわかった。これは大変だと思った。今のうち捕まらない間に逃げるに限ると思って、私は東の方へ一生懸命に走り出した。すると間もなく東の空に蒼白い光が流れて、その光が見る見る内に白けて来た。そうして恐ろしい人の群が、黒雲の影の動く様に、此方へ近づいているのがありありと見えた。その時、風が東に変って、騒騒しい人声が風を伝って聞こえて来た。「彼所だ、彼所だ」と云うのが手に取る様に聞こえて、又北風が吹いて、大勢の人の群が「彼所だ、彼所だ」と叫びながら、風に乗って私の方へ近づいて来た。南の方へ逃げようとすると南風に変って、矢っ張り見果てもない程の人の群が私の方に迫っていた。もう逃げられない。あの大勢の人の群は、皆私の口から一言の予言を聞く為に、ああして私に近づいて来るのだ。もし私が件でありながら、何も予言しないと知ったら、彼等はどんなに怒り出すだろう。三日目に死ぬのは構わないけれども、その前にいじめられるのは困る、逃げ度い、逃げ度いと思って地団太をふんだ。西の空に黄色い月がぼんやり懸かって、ふくれている。昨夜の通りの景色だ。私はその月を眺めて、途方に暮れていた。

夜が明け離れた。

人人は広い野原の真中に、私を遠巻きに取り巻いた。恐ろしい人の群れで、何千人だか何

perhaps tens of thousands. Several dozens of them stepped forwards and quickly got to work. They brought in timber and constructed a large fenced-in area around me. They erected scaffolding and made a grandstand. Time passed, and before long it was noon. Unable to do anything, I watched them work. Their activity could only mean that they intended to sit and wait three days for my prophecy. They were surrounding me like this, even though I had nothing to say. I needed to escape, but there was no way out. People filled the upper reaches of the gallery, which grew dark with the crowd. The overflow stood below the grandstand or crouched by the fence. After a while, a man in a white kimono appeared from below the western stands holding up a ceremonial vessel and approaching me in silence. The crowd went quiet. The man advanced with great solemnity and stopped when he was very close to me. Then he placed the vessel on the ground and retreated. The vessel was filled with clean water. Sure that he meant it for me, I approached and drank it.

The crowd suddenly came to life. 'He drank it!' someone said.

'Finally. It won't be long now!' another said.

I was caught off guard and looked around. Apparently, they thought I would speak the prophecy after I drank the water. But I had nothing to say. I turned away and took a few steps at random.

万人だかわからない。其中の何十人かが、私の前に出て、忙しそうに働き出した。材木を担ぎ出して来て、私のまわりに広い柵をめぐらした。それから、その後に足代を組んで、桟敷をこしらえた。段段時間が経って、午頃になったらしい。私はどうする事も出来ないから、ただ人人のそんな事をするのを眺めていた。あんな仕構えをして、これから三日の間、じっと私の予言を待つのだろうと思った。なんにも云う事がないのに、みんなからこんなに取り巻かれて、途方に暮れた。どうかして今の内に逃げ出したいと思うけれども、そんな隙もない。人人は出来上がった桟敷の段段に上って行って、桟敷の上が、見る見るうちに、黒くなった。

上り切れない人人は、桟敷の下に立ったり、柵の傍に蹲踞んだりしている。暫らくすると、西の方の桟敷の下から、白い衣物を着た一人の男が、半挿の様なものを両手で捧げて、私の前に静静と近づいて来た。辺りは森閑と静まり返っている。その男は勿体らしく進んで来て、私の直ぐ傍に立ち止まり、その半挿を地面に置いて、そうして帰って行った。中には奇麗な水が一杯はいっている。飲めと云う事だろうと思うから、私はその方に近づいて行って、その水を飲んだ。

すると辺りが俄に騒がしくなった。「そら、飲んだ飲んだ」と云う声が聞こえた。

「愈飲んだ。これからだ」と云う声も聞こえた。

私はびっくりして、辺りを見廻した。水を飲んでから予言するものと、人人が思ったらしい。もけれども、私は何も云う事がないのだから、後を向いて、そこいらをただ歩き廻った。もう

Dusk seemed to be approaching. If only night would come faster!

'Hey, he's turned his back on us,' someone said, as though surprised.

'It may not happen today.'

'Then the prophecy is bound to be important.'

I was sure I had heard all their voices somewhere before. I spun around and saw the familiar face of a man who was crouching by the fence and staring hard at me. At first I couldn't recall with any clarity, but slowly I began to remember, and soon I recognized the faces of my friends, my relatives, my teachers, my students. I hated the way they were elbowing their way forward to get a better look at me.

'Hey,' someone said, 'this *kudan* looks familiar.'

'I don't know. I'm not so sure,' someone else replied.

'He does look like somebody, but I can't remember who.'

This talk threw me further into confusion. I couldn't bear to have my friends know I'd become this hairy beast. I thought I'd better hide my face and tried not to look in their direction.

Before I knew it, the sun had set and a dim yellow moon hung in the sky. As it slowly took on a blue tinge, the stands and fence

日暮れが近くなっているらしい。早く夜になって仕舞えばいいと思う。

「おや、そっぽを向いた」とだれかが驚いた様に云った。

「事によると、今日ではないのかも知れない」

「この様子だと余程重大な予言をするんだ」

そんな事を云ってる声のどれにも、私はみんな何所となく聞き覚えのある様な気がした。そう思ってぐるりを見ていると、柵の下に蹲踞んで一生懸命に私の方を見ている男の顔に見覚えがあった。始めは、はっきりしなかったけれども、見ているうちに、段段解って来る様な気がした。それから、そこいらを見廻すと、私の友達や、親類や、昔学校で教わった先生や、又学校で教えた生徒などの顔が、ずらりと柵のまわりに並んでいる。それ等が、みんな他を押しのける様にして、一生懸命に私の方を見詰めているのを見て、私は厭な気持になった。

「おや」と云ったものがある。「この件は、どうも似てるじゃないか」

「そう、どうもはっきり判らんね」と答えた者がある。

「そら、どうも似ている様だが、思い出せない」

私はその話を聞いて、うろたえた。若し、私のこんな毛物になっている事が、友達に知れたら、恥ずかしくてこうしてはいられない。あんまり顔を見られない方がいいと思って、そんな声のする方に顔を向けない様にした。いつの間にか日暮れになった。黄色い月がぼんやり懸かっている。それが段段青くなるに

dissolved into the gloom, and night fell.

In the darkness, the crowd lit bonfires around the fence. All night long the flames leaped into the moonlit sky. The crowd stayed awake, waiting for a word from me. The deep red smoke of the bonfire drifted up and darkened as it crossed the face of the moon, whose brightness faded, and the wind of dawn began to blow. Day broke once again. Thousands more must have crossed the field over the course of the night. The area around the fence was even more raucous than the day before. Faces in the crowd kept changing. They grew more and more threatening, and I was full of fear.

The man in the white kimono approached once again, reverently offering me the vessel, and then he withdrew. As before, the vessel was filled with water. I wasn't thirsty and knew I'd be expected to speak if I drank, so I didn't even look at it.

'He's not going to drink,' someone said.

'Shut up. You shouldn't be talking at a time like this.'

'It must be one hell of a prophecy. The fact that he's taking so long must mean something.'

The crowd grew noisy again as people came and went. The man in the white kimono kept bringing me water. The crowd fell silent each time he offered me the vessel, but as soon as they saw I wasn't drinking from it, the noise got worse. He brought water more frequently, putting it closer to me each time. I found this annoying and

連れて、まわりの桟敷や柵などが、薄暗くぼんやりして来て、夜になった。

夜になると、人人は柵のまわりで篝火をたいた。その欲が夜通し月明かりの空に流れた。人人は寝もしないで、私の一言を待ち受けている。月の面を赤黒い色に流れていた篝火の煙の色が次第に黒くなって来て、月の光は褪せ、夜明けの風が吹いて来た。そうして、また夜が明け離れた。夜のうちにまた何千人と云う人が、原を渡って来たらしい。柵のまわりが、昨日よりも騒騒しくなった。頻りに人が列の中を行ったり来たりしている。昨日よりは穏や

かならぬ気配なので、私は漸く不安になった。

間もなく、また白い衣物を着た男が、半挿を捧げて、私に近づいて来た。半挿の中には、矢張り水がはいっている。白い衣物の男は、うやうやしく私に水をすすめて帰って行った。私は欲しくもないし、又飲むと何か云うかと思われるから、見向きもしなかった。

「飲まない」と云う声がした。

「黙っていろ。こう云う時に口を利いてはわるい」と云ったものがある。

「大した予言をするに違いない。こんなに暇取るのは余程の事だ」と云ったのもある。

そうして後がまた騒騒しくなって、人が頻りに行ったり来たりした。それから白衣の男が、水を持って来る間丈は、辺りが森閑と静かになるけれども、その半挿の水を私が飲まないのを見ると、周囲の騒ぎは段段にひどくなって来た。そして益幾度も幾度も水を私が持って来た。水を持って来る間丈は、辺りが森閑と静かになるけれども、その半挿の水を私が飲まないのを見ると、周囲の騒ぎは段段にひどくなって来た。そして益頻繁に水を運んで来た。その水を段段私の鼻先につきつける様に近づけてきた。私はうるさ

became angry. Then another man, carrying another vessel, walked up to me and stared at me. He shoved the vessel up under my face. I recognized him. I couldn't say exactly who he was, but the sight of him only increased my anger.

When he saw that I had no intention of drinking the water, he clicked his tongue impatiently. 'Come on, drink it, will you?'

'No, I don't want to,' I replied in anger.

The crowd went crazy. I looked around and saw to my shock that people in the stands were jumping down and those behind the fence were climbing over it. They ran towards me, shouting terrifying curses at one another.

'He spoke.'

'He finally said something.'

'What'd he say?'

'Who cares? It's what he's *going* to say.'

When I looked up, I saw the yellow moon again. The light over the field was growing dim. The sun was setting on my second day. I was still unable to prophesy anything, but I didn't think I would die, either. Perhaps the prophecy itself would cause my death, which meant that if I didn't say anything, I might not die at the end of three

くて、腹が立って来た。その時又一人の男が半挿を持って近づいて来た。私の傍まで来ると暫らく立ち止まって私の顔を見詰めていたが、それから又つかつかと歩いて来て、その半挿を無理矢理に私の顔に押しつけた。私はその男の顔にも見覚えがあった。だれだか解らないけれども、その顔を見ていると、何となく腹が立って来た。

その男は、私が半挿の水を飲みそうにもないのを見て、忌ま忌ましそうに舌打ちをした。

「飲まないか」とその男が云った。

「いらない」と私は怒って云った。

すると辺りに大変な騒ぎが起こった。驚いて見廻すと、桟敷にいたものは桟敷を飛び下り、柵の廻りにいた者は柵を乗り越えて、恐ろしい声をたてて罵り合いながら、私の方に走り寄って来た。

「口を利いた」

「到頭口を利いた」

「何と云ったんだろう」

「いやこれからだ」と云う声が入り交じって聞こえた。

気がついて見ると、又黄色い月が空にかかって、辺りが薄暗くなりかけている。いよいよ二日目の日が暮れるんだ。けれども私は何も予言することが出来ない。だが又格別死にそうな気もしない。事によると、予言するから死ぬので、予言をしなければ、三日で死ぬとも限

days. In that case I'd rather live, I thought. At that moment, the ones at the front of the crowd reached my side. Those behind kept pushing forward, admonishing each other, 'Quiet, quiet.' Who knew what would become of me if I were grabbed by this angry, disappointed mob? I wanted desperately to get out, but I was trapped by the human fence. The crowd grew more unruly; shrieks could be heard over the din. The human fence grew tighter and tighter around me. I was paralysed with fear. Without thinking, I drank the water in the vessel. In that instant the crowd fell silent. I was stunned when I realized what I'd done, but there was no way to undo it. The look of anticipation on their faces was even more frightening. I broke out in a cold sweat. As I remained silent, the crowd slowly came back to life.

'What happened? Something's wrong.'

'No, it's coming, an absolutely amazing prophecy.'

I heard this much, but otherwise the commotion around me was not too bad. There seemed to be a new uneasiness in the crowd. I relaxed a little and looked at the faces of the ones who'd formed the human fence, realizing that I knew every one of those in front. A strange anxiety and fear registered on each of their faces. As I

らないのかも知れない、それではまあ死なない方がいい、と俄に命が惜しくなった。その時、駆け出して来た群衆の中の一番早いのは、私の傍迄近づいて来た。すると、その後から来たのが、前にいるのを押しのけた。その後から来たのが、又前にいる者を押しのけた。そうして騒ぎながらお互に「静かに、静かに」と制し合っていた。私はここで捕まったら、群衆の失望と立腹とで、どんな目に合うか知れないから、どうかして逃げ度いと思ったけれども、人垣に取り巻かれてどこにも逃げ出す隙がない。騒ぎは次第にひどくなって、彼方此方に悲鳴が聞こえた。そうして、段段に人垣が狭くなって、私に迫って来た。私は恐ろしさで立ってもいてもいられない。夢中でそこにある半挿の水をのんだ。その途端に、辺りの騒ぎが一時に静まって、森閑として来た。私は、気がついてはっと思ったけれども、もう取り返しがつかない。耳を澄ましているらしい人人の顔を見て、猶恐ろしくなった。全身に冷汗がにじみ出した。そうして何時迄も私が黙っているから、又少しずつ辺りが騒がしくなり始めた。

「どうしたんだろう、変だね」

「いやこれからだ、驚くべき予言をするに違いない」

そんな声が聞こえた。しかし辺りの騒ぎはそれ丈で余り激しくもならない。気がついて見ると、群衆の間に何となく不安な気配がある。私の心が少し落ちついて、前に人垣を作っている人人の顔を見たら、一番前に食み出しているのは、どれも是れも皆私の知った顔計りであった。そうしてそれ等の顔に皆不思議な不安と恐怖の影がさしている。それを見ているうちに、

watched this happen, my own fear dissipated and I was able to relax. I suddenly felt thirsty and took a sip from the vessel in front of me. This time nobody spoke. The shadow of fear deepened, and everyone seemed to be holding their breath. It was like that for a while, until someone broke the silence: 'I'm scared.' The voice was soft but echoed across the crowd.

The circle around me widened. The crowd was slowly backing off.

'Now I'm afraid to hear the prophecy. By the looks of this *kudan*, who knows what terrible thing he'll say?'

'Good or bad, it's best not to know. Let's kill him quickly before he has a chance to say anything.'

I was shocked at the threat to kill me, but the voice was what took me by surprise. It belonged to my son, my own human son. The other voices had sounded familiar, but I was unable to place them; yet the voice of my son I recognized. In an effort to see him I stood on my hind legs.

'The *kudan* is lifting its front legs.'

'He's going to make his prophecy,' I heard someone say in a

段段と自分の恐ろしさが薄らいで心が落ちついて来た。急に咽喉が乾いて来たので、私は又前にある半挿の水を一口のんだ。すると又辺りが急に水を打った様になった。今度は何も云う者がない。人人の間の不安の影が益濃くなって、皆が呼吸をつまらしているらしい。暫らくそうしているうちに、どこかで不意に、

「ああ、恐ろしい」と云った者がある。低い声だけれども、辺りに響き渡った。

気がついて見ると、何時の間にか、人垣が少し広くなっている。群衆が少しずつ後しさりをしているらしい。

「己はもう予言を聞くのが恐ろしくなった。この様子では、件はどんな予言をするか知れない」と云った者がある。

「いいにつけ、悪いにつけ、予言は聴かない方がいい。何も云わないうちに、早くあの件を殺してしまえ」

その声を聞いて私は吃驚した。殺されては堪らないと思うと同時に、その声はたしかに私の生み遺した倅の声に違いない。今迄聞いた声は、聞き覚えのある様な気がしても、何人の声だとはっきりは判らなかったが、これ計りは思い出した。群衆の中にいる息子を一目見ようと思って、私は思わず伸び上がった。

「そら、件が前足を上げた」と云うあわてた声が聞こえた。その途端に、今迄隙間もなく取巻いてい

panicked voice. The tightly packed human enclosure began to break down, and without another word the crowd scattered in all directions. Jumping the wooden fence and ducking under the stands, they ran as fast as they could. In their wake, night once again approached and the moon began to cast its hazy yellow light. With great relief, I stretched out my front legs and yawned three or four times. Perhaps I wouldn't die after all.

た人垣が俄に崩れて、群衆は無言のまま、恐ろしい勢いで、四方八方に逃げ散って行った。柵を越え、桟敷をくぐって、東西南北に一生懸命に逃げ走った。人の散ってしまった後に又夕暮れが近づき、月が黄色にぼんやり照らし始めた。私はほっとして、前足を伸ばした。そうして三つ四つ続け様に大きな欠伸をした。何だか死にそうもない様な気がして来た。

Acknowledgments

'The 1963/1982 Girl from Ipanema' by Murakami Haruki is reprinted by permission of Harukimurakami Archival Labyrinth, © Harukimurakami Archival Labyrinth, 1982. Translation © Jay Rubin. The song 'The Girl from Ipanema' ('Garôta de Ipanema') is featured in *The Color of Money*: music by Antônio Carlos Jobim, English words by Norman Gimbel, original words by Vinícius de Moraes; © 1963 Antonio Carlos Jobim and Vinicius de Moraes, Brazil. Renewed © 1991 and assigned to Songs of Universal, Inc., and Words West LLC. English words renewed © 1991 by Norman Gimbel for the World and assigned to Words West LLC (PO Box 15187, Beverly Hills, CA 90209 USA). This arrangement © Songs of Universal, Inc., and Words West LLC. All Rights Reserved. Used by Permission. Reprinted by Permission of Hal Leonard Europe Ltd.

'Shoulder-Top Secretary' by Hoshi Shin'ichi first appeared in the magazine *Fujin Gaho* in 1961 under the title 'Kata no Ue no Hisho', © 1961 the Hoshi Library, and was published in 1971 in Bokko-chan by Shinchōsha Publishing Company Ltd. Japanese and English translation rights arranged with the Hoshi Library through Japan Foreign-Rights Centre. Translation © Jay Rubin.

'Peaches' by Abe Akira is © the estate of Abe Akira. Translation © Jay Rubin.